THE NAZI'S BOY

BY

Rob Loveboy

Based on a true story.

COPYRIGHT

The Nazi's Boy

Acknowledgements

This story is dedicated to:

Jan Lewinsky (1925 – 2011)

You are sadly missed as patriarch of our local LGBT community. Your legacy left unfilled, our memories alive and well. Thank you for faith in me to share your incredible childhood story.

James FitzHugh (long suffering editor)

I couldn't have done it without you, Baggie.

Vince Berg (technical support & my writing guru)

Thank you for believing in me and the many patient hours spent getting me on my feet.

Francis Symes (cover graphic artist)

Your hard word and patient modifications greatly are appreciated.

Cole Lesko (my lover)

You never stopped loving me.

TABLE OF CONTENTS

CHAPTER I: LOSS OF INNOCENCE

It was during the Second World War; I was barely fourteen and the city in which I resided was a time bomb; the Nazis could not be far off in their quest to capture all of Poland. Other cities were already under siege and rumors of atrocities were rampant. It was rumored that rape, torture, murder, mass incarceration and even deportation of people that were deemed not to fit the Nazi profile were being carried out in the wake of the invasion of my homeland.

I understood little, at the time, being the only child of a loving, well-off Polish father and Swedish mother. I was sheltered from evil-doings as much as possible. I did however overhear, as children are wont to do, the whispered discussions of adults and the very scary sounding man blaring from the RCA Victor. Not understanding German, I was truly frightened by the very tone of his loud, angry voice.

My parents struggled but, in the end, made the final decision to send me off to live in the country with my maternal aunt and uncle, and my younger female cousin. It was said that life there, some 200 miles to the south, was still serene and safe, as the Nazis had bigger fish to fry. Their strategy seemed to follow the pattern of 'Conquer the major cities and the rest of the population would fall to its knees'. My mom, despite her tears, put on a brave face as she put me on the train that early spring morning saying, "It would be temporary, at least until things settled down and then they would bring me home." My destination was a village of no more than five-hundred residents. My uncle owned a small farm on the rural outskirts. Chickens, a noisy rooster, a few cows and pigs and a vast vegetable garden provided sustenance for his family. Their home was a small, modest structure, actually quite primitive from the city homes I was used to. There was no running water, indoor plumbing and electricity were to be enjoyed as a luxury if one could afford them, but the family seemed content existing on basic necessities, their self-reliance and their staunch Catholic faith.

My make-shift bedroom was a windowless converted storage area off the kitchen that I shared along with shelves and boxes containing the normal paraphernalia for which storage rooms are generally intended. It was rather cramped, with no ventilation and small. It had a curtain strung across the opening where a door may have previously hung. But it did offer some privacy and the old feather bed tucked into the corner was very comfortable indeed. It was certainly a much better alternative than sharing a room with my cousin, Beth, who enjoyed a very spacious room all to

herself. After all, although we were cousins it just wasn't right for a boy and a girl of our age to share sleeping quarters which was fine with me.

Not that I wasn't fond of Beth, because I was. She was very pretty with her blond hair and blue eyes similar to mine, traits inherited from our Swedish mothers and in reality, our resemblance was so alike that we could easily have been taken as brother and sister. I was of the age where boys had a mild, but growing, interest in the fairer sex and a rather compelling interest in my pubertal development and its amazing wonders.

I had discovered masturbation at an earlier age. It was about the same time I learned snippets of information regarding sexual matters. I knew the basics; men get women pregnant, but the actual knowledge of how one went about doing so only came to light when I happened upon a cousin and his friend enjoying the day at a mutually shared favorite fishing hole. My cousin Henry, fifteen, and his friend Joseph, fourteen, had stolen a bottle of red wine from a vendor's cart in the city and were sharing the pilfered contraband when I happened upon them. I was immediately sworn to secrecy, of course, but wasn't offered the opportunity to share in the inspiration of their giddiness.

It was a very hot afternoon and the fishing hole also served as a fine swimming area for the local kids. Before long, both boys had stripped naked and were frolicking and horsing around in the water, dunking and crawling atop one another giggling like a couple of school girls.

When they exited the water, both boys sported erections which they made no attempt to hide from each other or, for that matter, from me. I had never before seen another boy in such a state and, of course, their development was even more intriguing compared to my own small, still hairless genitals.

Henry was far more advanced than his friend. He had a long, thick shaft under which were suspended a hairless sac holding his low hanging testicles and above which there was a mat of wet black hair plastered to his groin area. Joseph was maybe equally as long but lacked the girth and his pubic hair was sparse. His testes were smaller and not unlike my own.

My interest was that of sheer boyhood curiosity and not of a sexual nature by any means. I gawked a little as I took in the remarkable male genital stages, from my own boyhood immature display, to Joseph's mid-range development and, finally, to the manhood proportions that I suspected Henry had reached.

To make a long story short, the previous evening the boys claimed to have witnessed a couple of prostitutes servicing two Polish military men in a dark alley. Henry and Joseph began to mimic the sex acts as they say them performed in the darkened alley, laughing and talking like girls, making the same lewd sexual comments that they had overheard.

From a standing position, Henry turned Joseph around. He immediately bent him over, enabling him to support himself on a fallen tree. Henry then placed his large erection between his friend's legs and, with exaggerated gusto, began pumping; hooting and hollering very foul words. Joseph, for his part in this little reenactment, was begging in a mock female voice for Henry to do "it" harder.

The playful shenanigans lasted only for a few moments before both boys broke into hysterical laughter. But the show being put on for my benefit wasn't quite

finished yet. Henry, placing his strong hands on Joseph's shoulders, told Joseph to get on his knees and suck his "big Polish dick." They were obviously mimicking another sexual act seen in that dark alley.

I was aghast when I quickly figured out what this new scene entailed. Even though Joseph didn't actually take Henry's thick penis into his mouth, he made open mouth gestures with it just grazing the head with his lips while his hand was firmly wrapped around the shaft slowly stroking it as Joseph thrust his hips to and fro.

Although it was a playful reenactment of events, I remember Henry becoming serious and, looking down, asking Joseph to actually perform oral sex on him. I truly believe that Joseph was contemplating doing exactly that after several more prodding attempts by Henry but, after a quick glance my way, he rose to his feet red in the face.

Joseph began asking Henry to masturbate himself so that he could again see an apparent "geyser" shoot out; something that Henry had obviously done and Joseph had seen at some previous point in time. Henry obliged. He lay down on the grass and frantically beat his meat. I was bewildered at the purpose and objective which Joseph was so keen to witness again. Joseph was so anticipating the end result that when Henry's hand grew tired, his hand reached out, took control of the matter and shortly thereafter brought the "geyser" forth much to my amazement and awe.

So that was my basic induction into fornication and oral sex, although both acts had been simulated. But, the act of masturbation was a very real eye opener for me to witness and I did experiment with such regularity that I developed a very painful friction burn. When the actual joy of ejaculation finally took place, it was not nearly as voluminous and ivory-white as my cousin Henry had spewed that hot summer day, but I was very proud of my new accomplishment nonetheless.

The Nazi military infrequently passed through the village of my temporary exile, stopping only briefly to replenish supplies of whatever they needed, procured free of charge of course in the name of the Fuhrer. These 'visits' were always forewarned in advance as mass amount of troops moving north could not go unnoticed and word traveled quickly to the hamlets in their path.

As a precautionary measure, teenage girls and unwed women were sent underground. The intent was to get them out of harm's way lest the Nazis had intentions of overstaying their welcome and deciding to alleviate their pent-up manly desires and take advantage of their arrogant wartime lawlessness.

This was, in fact, the case one day in mid-August when several battalions stationed themselves near the village. It was rumored that they were awaiting orders to occupy my home city. Soldiers outnumbered residents at least four to one as they settled and erected a base camp nearby that disrupted the meek inhabitants' peaceful way of life. Life as the village had known it had finally been met with the ugly face of war.

High ranking officials commandeered private homes to reside in while they awaited orders. It was expected that homeowners would house and feed these VIP's without question and with open arms. People were so fearful of the Nazis that they went out of their way to host such powerful men. It became a fierce competition to attract those most powerful into their dwellings as it was believed that a certain safety factor was gained by accommodating them to ensure their home and family would be safe from pillage or destruction. A swastika hung on a door signified that the home was off limits to rogue infantry marauders.

My aunt and uncle were no different in their plight for self-preservation and opened their home to such a man. I did not know his rank or his name but he was in his mid-thirties and so handsomely blond and blue-eyed he could have been the poster boy for Hitler's "ultimate" race.

The very first night of his arrival he was treated like royalty. Liquor was flowing like water between my uncle and the man.

My aunt prepared a fabulous meal of roast pork, chicken and all the trimmings. She was manicured, primped and dressed in a gorgeous white frock, more beautiful than she ever portrayed herself before. Beth and I could only look at each other and shrug shoulders at the unusual behavior of her otherwise religious, tee-totaling parents who were practically falling over the man to be hospitable.

Lanterns illuminated the surroundings like never before seen in the household. Kerosene was scarce and rationed, but our prestigious boarder saw fit to supply the liquid-gold; most likely for his own convenience and comfort.

Even at my young, naive age it occurred to me as if my aunt was flirting with the Nazi guest at our table. Her willingness to be bedded by the man, with her husband's consent, was only a noble effort to deflect attention from their young daughter, should the man be so inclined. The parents had gone through great effort to disguise Beth's true beauty by making her appear quite unkempt with messy, lard greased hair, soiled skin and baggy clothes.

The two different languages, German and Polish, didn't seem a barrier because each party compromised on a limited repertoire of broken English; a language that I had only just began studying in school and had yet no proficiency in. Throughout dinner and beyond, the man stared at me and would beam a broad smile when I met his gaze, toasting me often which seemed to cause an uneasy tension between my guardians. Their eyes locked upon each other's in some form of unspoken discussion, then upon mine.

I could easily read a certain fear in the sudden change of aura but, as quick as it would happen, a semblance of normality resumed when my aunt or uncle would sway the man's attention away from me and a round of laughter ensued.

The interpretation given to me by my uncle was that the German thought I was too pretty to be a boy. It was a comment I heard so often in my life that I loathed it. I felt there may have been more said but that was all that was relayed to me.

Earlier that evening our guest had selected Beth's room to be his sleeping quarters, obviously because it was spacious and a far nicer accommodation as befitting his status. He certainly had no interest in my tiny, cramped, airless, impromptu bedroom. Beth's parents had decided that Beth would bunk in with me for the duration of his visit despite the moral improprieties. I surmised that some things could be overlooked in a time of crisis.

Beth and I were finally excused from the table to prepare for bed. As I stood to bid a polite good night, the man pulled me into him and ran his hand through my hair and down my face mumbling something that I didn't understand. Whatever he said was not translated for my benefit. It was apparent that my aunt and uncle understood because the forlorn look returned to their faces.

This time they were staring bug-eyed on the German who was chuckling to himself in self-amusement as he groped my bum and held me there a long while as

the adult conversation and revelry waned. His voice took on a serious tone and his eyes peered intently at my uncle, until some kind of agreement had been sealed at which time my uncle lowered his head, as if in dismay, studying his goblet of liquor.

My gut instinct told me that I was the center of all the angst. I didn't believe that I had done anything disrespectful and, had I done so, why was I not being reprimanded? The German dismissed me with a pat on the bum and a jovial laugh that only added to my confusion.

White as a ghost and trembling visibly, my aunt rose from the table and summoned Beth to follow. The sleeping arrangements were abruptly changed and Beth was told she would share her parents' bed. Perhaps the ethical implications, however innocent they seemed to me, became too much of a burden on their religious conscience or so I reasoned.

Whatever had dampened their earlier merriment had been forgotten. The drunken festivities continued long into the night. My uncle and the Nazi officer could be heard talking, singing and laughing to the frequent sound of clinking glasses and the decanting of a bottle replenishing goblets.

Lying on my side facing away from the curtained doorway, I awoke to the hairs standing on the back of my neck. A soft glow from a carried lantern made shadows dance upon the walls and ceiling. The edge of the bed gave concave and the springs squeaked to the unmistakable settling of a person whose heavy breaths were quite audible along with a low throaty cooing.

My relatives had never paid a visit to my room during the night mainly because I was old enough to tuck myself in and I was no longer in need of a goodnight kiss. I was frozen in fear because I knew for certain who had invaded my space but for what reason was beyond me. I felt his fingers play with my hair, gently twisting it like my mother sometimes did when we cuddled.

Over top of the bed sheet another hand was stroking my left hip and wandered to my bum, gently cupping and squeezing one cheek and then the other. The breathing intensified as I lay there mortified, paralyzed and holding my breath.

After he made a slight adjustment in his position, I sensed his face close to mine and the smell of liquor and cigarettes gave way to the tickle of his whiskers against my cheek which he kissed tenderly. I wanted to yell out for help but something deep within me told me that the effort would be futile. I didn't know why that was, just that the man possessed power over all logical thinking that even my young brain could reckon as being truth. My weasel like uncle would be no match for this virile, slightly younger man.

The protective sheet that surrounded me was slowly lowered as he urged me onto my back. I kept my eyes closed as he lifted my nightshirt up to my belly exposing my genitalia under the dim light of the lantern resting on a box close by. He played with them; groped and manhandled me so roughly that his actions caused me to yelp. My feigning sleep was no longer possible and I opened my eyes wide.

After staring into his eyes and friendly enough smile, I couldn't help but look down along his body and notice his lower region.

My fears doubled when I saw him holding what appeared to be his baton between his legs. I thought it was the same baton that adorned his belt which one couldn't help but notice amongst his pistol, bullets and other displayed weaponry. It was only when

he moved forward that I realized he had his trousers down and it was his manhood that he was grasping. It was huge by all standards that I knew. It was much larger in size than my only other comparison, my cousin Henry.

He kissed my lips breathing heavily, followed by his tongue probing entry into my mouth; just as I'd seen others do at social dances. His taste of smoke and liquor was putrid. I was being suffocated. It had been a slow recuperation from a summer cold and my sinuses still clogged. I could scarcely breathe. Merciful, he grew weary of slobbering my mouth.

Aghast, all I could do was lie there and stare when he suddenly rose and stripped himself. As he was standing naked staring down at me for a few moments, I had the distinct impression that he was peacocking himself almost as if seeking my approval of his manliness. The soft glow of the lantern cast enough light to see that he was indeed well-endowed and hairless down to his groin where a nice thick golden bush flourished. His testicles were large and suspended beneath the upright pointed shaft where a bead of liquid glistened at the purplish tip. Taking a long, slow look up the length of his strong, well-defined body to meet his eyes, I couldn't help but admire the beautiful sight and strangely, I smiled.

That subtle and naive sign of admiration seemed to please him. His hands tugged at my night shirt, pulling it from under my bum and over my back. A slight tear was heard as he forced it upward over my head and tossed it atop the pile of his own clothing. Ogling my nakedness laid out before him, it was his turn to give an assuring smile. I had absolutely no comprehension of my sexual fate; however, I somehow knew in my heart that this night would change my life.

The German lay on top of me slowly pushing my arms up to behind me head. He then commenced with the slobbery kisses beginning at my ticklish armpits, slowly making his way across my chest, taking time to nibble my nipples so that each suddenly took on a slightly larger and firmer form of their own. Tender in using his teeth and tongue, I found the strangeness of it not at all unpleasant. I had heard boys talk of suckling titties claiming that girls loved the sensations. Now having the experience I reasoned that the pleasure wasn't gender restricted.

He continued to lick and nibble down my torso, swabbing my navel for a short while before reaching my groin. He toyed with my sac, kneading and rolling the contents in his fingers as his other hand wrapped around the base of my shaft that I hadn't even realized had become hard. Shame overwhelmed me. My inner-self battled with my emotions. Surely what was happening was wrong and yet my erection clearly deceived all logic. How could it be wrong when it felt so right?

He did what Henry wanted Joseph to do so badly that day not all that long ago. His mouth felt nice upon me His warm and moist lips secured tightly over the entire length while the heavy breath from his nostrils fluttered my sparse pubic hair and was warm upon my skin.

Clearly, he wanted to take me to orgasm. He paused his blissful assault on my rampant cock and muttered something in German I just knew was encouragement to allow myself the mental freedom to relax and let nature take its course. I came moments later with my fingers gripping the sheets and my pelvis meeting his piston like mouth with every gratifying spasm of ejaculate. Oddly enough, the fact that I was spunking in his mouth only seemed to increase the eager ravage of my genitalia. I was

not at all offended nor did I lay there in disgust. It shouldn't have come as a surprise that I would be expected to perform the same deed on him.

It was evident that my own experience had been applied by him as a demonstration. My whole body was trembling, not in passion but fear. I was shaking as if the ninety degree temperature of the room had been below zero. The scent of his crotch was strong. It had an odor that I was hard pressed to compare with anything else. Warm and velvety to the touch in my hand, I studied his large sausage-like member for a while, curious about the ooze flowing over the crown that I wiped away with my hand in preparation to take the meat in my mouth. But, just as soon as I would wipe the clear liquid away, another dollop would seep forth.

After a great deal of hesitation and at his insistent urging as he pushed on (upon) my head, I mimicked the pleasurable performance he had bestowed upon me although, I'm sure, not with the same enthusiasm. But I went through the motions ... He didn't complain even though I mostly masturbated him with perhaps only a quarter of his length in my mouth. I didn't fondle or lick his balls (other extremities) as he had done mine. It was simply a case of he didn't ask and I didn't volunteer.

It seemed to go on forever and my jaw was beginning to ache. At one point I thought he had fallen asleep, only to have him hold my head and force it back down the length of his sword. Throughout it all, I found the metallic and salty taste of his meaty manhood not at all unpleasant.

I hoped that the man would give me fair warning because I was sure I wouldn't be expected to take his semen in my mouth as he did mine. The thought made me nauseous, but it really should have been the least of my concerns because, whether I knew it or not, my sexual lesson had only just begun!

After one final lunge into my mouth, he pulled out and rolled me over onto my chest and into a fetal position. I felt his tongue on my rectum but had no idea why he was doing that disgusting act. After the initial shock wore off, the sensation amazed me.

Again, he spoke in a soft, reassuring tone causing me to relax and enjoy the bewilderment of delight that area had to offer but, at the same time, hoping that the act wasn't another lesson to be reciprocated.

He secured me with one arm under my hips; I felt what had to be his cock sliding along my crack before it found its mark.

Oblivious to his intentions, he rose up and slammed his hard cock into me. I screamed out in agonizing pain something never felt before even when I broke my arm at ten years old. That pain was nowhere near as excruciating as the pain associated with his turning my boy pucker into a boy pussy. I began to cry and wail. I begged him to stop and even offered to suck him much better. I somehow felt that his ramming his baton up my ass must have been my punishment for not performing oral sex to his expectations. My pleas, however, accomplished nothing. He was both persistent and relentless in forcing his big, thick cock deeper into my new boy pussy while holding my hips in a vice-like grip.

I expected my uncle and aunt, upon hearing my screams, would come to investigate and rescue me ... But, the man certainly wasn't concerned about that given he never once tried to muffle me into silence. I heard my cousin scream out my name but no rescue attempt ensued. I was mortified when it occurred to me that my

relatives had prior knowledge of what was going to happen or, at the very least, suspected as much. I was the sacrificial lamb being led to the slaughter in order to protect Beth's virginity.

My attempts to wiggle free by using my hands to grasp the mattress and pulling myself ahead were thwarted when he laid his heavy body on top of mine. The pain inside me sharpened with every inch slowly slithering into my bowels. I submitted to defeat and buried my face in a pillow sobbing and letting him take me uncontested.

I don't know where the pain went but I do know that only numbness was felt after a short while. Perhaps I even passed out for a brief time. The iron headboard banged the wall and the bed springs creaked loudly until suddenly he screamed out and collapsed along the length of my body panting in deep breaths. I surmised that it was over when I could actually feel his erection deflating inside me. He was soon asleep and snoring. Fortunately, I managed to slide out from under his crushing weight but was trapped and pressed between the wall and his large frame. I lay there and did not move a muscle, feeling both confused and betrayed by my caregivers. Exhausted, I thankfully fell asleep before too long.

CHAPTER II: SAVING MY COUSIN'S INNOCENCE

I awoke to the smell of bacon frying and dishes clamoring from the kitchen just meters beyond the curtained doorway. My stirring caused him to open his blue eyes and he smiled pulling me back into him. Feeling his hardness pressed against my lower back, I feared he would again wish to penetrate me.

I dared rolling over to face him, my hand took his member and he smiled. Repositioning himself on his back was a great relief. I went down on him despite where it had been a few hours prior. I reasoned that if I excelled at oral sex he would no longer take me anally. It was surprisingly clean upon inspection, only the musky odor was a lot stronger. I exceeded my previous performance, even playing with, and licking his heavy, hairy testicles that shed their fur and stuck in my mouth.

I knew by his demeanor - purring like a kitten - that he was nearing orgasm. I felt the eruption pulsate in his shaft before I could taste it. His hand remained firmly on my head to ensure I understood that I was expected to accept the snot-like texture with the bitter taste.

When he removed his hand from my head I heaved and let it spill from my mouth onto his belly. He became very angry at that and mashed my face into it as he yelled at me. I heard a dish break in the kitchen, perhaps my aunt was frightened by his outburst. He made me lap it up and then had me clean the residual semen from his cock head. Satisfied, he fluffed my hair and smiled.

I pulled on my nightshirt and entered the kitchen and bade a meek good morning to my aunt who was cooking and my uncle who was seated and reading over some papers. Young Beth greeted me in return with a big smile but otherwise the tension in the room was thick. My aunt's eyes were red and puffy, she had been crying. My uncle wouldn't look me in the eye and fidgeted silently, his hands shaking visibly almost spilling his coffee.

To make matters worse, the German came out of my room stark naked with a boisterous greeting and stood, reaching to the ceiling to stretch out the morning stiffness of his muscular physique without a care that a young girl and a lady were present. That shocking entrance did cause my uncle to knock over his cup and my aunt to run and shield Beth's vision. Thankfully, he didn't linger and traipsed off to Beth's commandeered room to dress.

Although I had seen his nude form laid out in my dimly lit room, I saw him in a new perspective. He had a very nicely tanned, agile body. His genitals were impressive

as they swayed with each step. Except for Beth, I sensed that everyone was aware that I had been shamelessly intimate with the man who had just brazenly displayed himself naked. Especially when my aunt produced a washcloth and disdainfully wiped around my mouth, closing her eyes and turning her head. A fleeting look of disgust from my uncle penetrated deep into my soul.

Imagine the confusion I felt at such a young age. In hindsight I should have lashed out against my uncle. I should have blamed him for whoring me out to save his own skin and that of his family. The cowardly sorry excuse for a man, his jowls quivering at the mere sight of me, left me feeling that I had been somehow responsible for my own rape. The same coward who was prepared to offer his own wife, but to his good fortune, the Nazi had other carnal desires and his wife, and perhaps his daughter, were spared. Of course, being young and niave, I hadn't come to those conclusions by then.

Getting the cold shoulder from my uncle, and being doted on by my teary-eyed aunt, I sat there ashamed of myself. For exactly what, I had no clue. I remember thinking in my confusion that perhaps what the German had done to me was common between men and boys, why else had uncle not intervened?

The German soon returned for breakfast fully dressed in his military attire. My uncle had the audacity to rise and pull a chair back for the man to sit as my aunt went about fussing with serving him his meal. No mention of the violation of their nephew or of his exposing himself to their young daughter! Everything was just as it had been the night before. They were the perfect hosts.

After breakfast my uncle told me to dress, that the man wanted me to accompany him somewhere. I don't even think my uncle knew where the stranger was planning to take me, he didn't seem to care, regardless., maybe he was relieved that he wouldn't have to look at me when we would share the morning chores.

Our destination in his jeep was the Nazi military encampment on the outskirts of the village. Reels of barbed wire surrounded the compound of tents and artillery vehicles were parked as far as the eye could see. Before entering the camp, we stopped and he chatted with soldiers who were unloading a group of about twenty boys from personnel carriers all of whom looked frightened and confused as they were herded down an embankment toward a lake. I had no idea what fate awaited them. I felt it was highly unlikely it was for a leisurely day at the beach.

Inside the camp I followed him around like a loyal dog and was quite impressed that he must have been a man of importance judging by the nervous salutes and soldiers scrambling to obey his barked orders. My presence didn't go unnoticed, men smiled at me and tousled my long blond hair making comments and laughter toward my prestigious escort. I believe now that he was showing me off, the beautiful boy that he was bedding who could almost pass as Aryan descent, but whose blood was tainted by Polish genes.

He left me alone briefly with two young soldiers that were entrusted with my care, but who ogled me in a sly way along with smirks and comments to one another. One man grabbed at his crotch and pushed his hips forward, causing both men to laugh heartily, followed by the other young man revealing and waving his penis as if offering it to me. Their lewd behavior abruptly ceased when the man returned, seeing the underling's antics, he began berating and chastising them.

The reality of it all suddenly struck me; he had lead me there to be shared with his comrades. My instinct was to flee, jack-rabbit and gain a head start before anyone came to their senses and could react in certain pursuit. I thought he must have read my mind when I felt his vice-like grip upon my neck. However, it wasn't to hold me in place, but to force me to my knees. I understood his true motive immediately seeing the veined spider web of his under-shaft pointed upward at a forty-five degree angle with a familiar slime forming a translucent string that dangled about a half-inch or so. The lurid scenery had most certainly excited my distinguished captor.

Looking up at his face, he was smiling and intent on talking to the young men who loitered along the pathway nervously smoking cigarettes. Considering he hadn't chosen somewhat more privacy as the others had, opting instead to humiliate me in public, I was sure it was a barefaced demonstration to encourage his young subordinates by setting an example.

Held painfully by my hair, I performed fellatio striving to keep from choking on the massive piston hell-bent on plunging beyond my capacity of endurance. I saw him summon a baby-faced lad clad in tented boxer shorts, a few words were exchanged, and then I felt his presence kneeling behind me, his member seeking its mark.

The boy soldier held my hips and managed small increments of headway. His unseen penis I knew to be much slimmer than the one lodged in my mouth that had previously plunged into my innards. Nonetheless, the pain was insurmountable and I forced myself to resist biting down on the firm, meaty appendage.

The soldier seemed satisfied not to push further and began to hump me. Moments later I heard him gasp, his fluid must have smoothed the trail for deeper penetration, as the last thrust had him buried with his bristly pubic hair discernibly mashed against my tender cheeks.

The man must have enjoyed that event. His semen spewed forth clogging my windpipe. Desperate for air, my sinus erupted mucus laden with jism that burned my nasal passage before running down my upper lip.

I wiped the mess with my forearm and remained on my skinned knees anticipating the next of several more young soldiers who gathered to watch, a few with erections expanding the material of their army issued green underwear or menacingly displayed without shame. I wondered if those individuals weren't trying to earn favor of the powerful man in demonstration of their eagerness to abuse the enemy as was expected of them.

The man noted the fear in my eyes, smiled and chuckled in a satisfied, smug way before helping me to my feet. He gently led me by the neck through the throng of bodies along the path which gave way to the man of significant importance and his charge. My eyes remained focused on the ground. I did not wish to view the events at either side of me that my ears endured. The pungent smell of feces, semen and urine on the return trek through the woods almost caused me to vomit.

I was young but not stupid. It was an intentional lesson for me that he was my protector, my savior from the evil-doings of human beings to fellow human beings and to gain my appreciation of his mercy of what might have been. Clearly, I was his and why he shared me with only that one young man was a mystery.

Exiting from the horror of the woods, we cooled off from the baking afternoon heat and frolicked in the lake. As any man would make horseplay with a youngster, he playfully tossed me high in the air or would dunk me.

Tired from our shenanigans, I hung from his neck draped over his chest with my legs around his waist. His hand fondled my growing boyhood under the water and he masturbated me. Assuming that I would endear myself to him in the interest of my own self-preservation, I brought my face to his to initiate a kiss like he had encouraged the night before. He became distraught and I saw fear in his eyes as he scanned the shore pushing me away. I was bewildered by that response and felt a fool. My over-zealousness was seen for what it was, phony.

Things became very clear to me then. Nowhere in public was intimacy to be shown. Although he had caressed my genitals, it was well-hidden from view. It was obvious that the boys in the woods were not being kissed, fondled or fellated as he had shown me in my bed, contrary to the aggression he displayed toward me in the woods. I was very confused by it all.

He wasn't angry for very long, smiling with reassurance, we headed back to the shore. We were joined by a very fat man dressed in a large nightshirt, breathless and sweating profusely from the trek down the hill. He was so large that when he dropped his weight to the blanket, a tremor was felt. The obese man pulled off his garb and exposed his gross nude body, just a very small pink discoloration within a mound of matted black pubic hair was noticed under a roll of blubber that obscured its view. Hairy breasts the size of melons sagged matching his jowls. I was strangely thankful that my man was fit and handsome.

In his company was a teen boy of about fifteen years. The men became engrossed in German conversation as me and the teen chatted in Polish. What I learned in our private parlay spoke volumes to understanding the mayhem and confusion.

His name was Geoff and he spoke English as did his German man-friend, another high ranker that had sequestered comfortable shelter at Geoff's home in the heart of the village. He informed me that earlier that same morning the Nazis had rounded up boys that the fat man claimed was in retaliation for hiding away the young female folk, a blatant insult to the good morals of the Nazi Regime, and bad for troop morale.

Geoff went on to quote the man as saying that German soldiers had long endured the hardships of war for their cause. Where they had once enjoyed fine foods, such as meat and potatoes, they now survived on watery soup and bread. Where they had once enjoyed the company of women, young boys of their enemy would pay the ultimate price for their elders' foolishness.

Geoff became cautious of his words although neither of the men apparently understood Polish, but it was conceivable that certain words may be detected. I suggested we take a swim and he asked for permission in English that both Nazis granted.

The handsome dirty blond teen removed his clothes without shame; smiley words were exchanged by the two ogling men at the sight. Geoff made us all laugh when he did a funny dance with his long penis and testicles slapping each side of his thighs before he was off and running into the water.

In the privacy of the lake and well out of earshot, he again cautioned that we should be careful and feign laughter and horse around while we talked. I thought him

extremely wise in his precaution. I immediately enlightened him on the plight and whereabouts of the village boys, but he had already drawn that conclusion for himself.

He advised me that many Nazi officers were secret homosexuals. He explained to me that homosexuals were men who favored sex with other men or boys. He maintained that the regular rank and file may not be true homosexuals, that they were merely obeying the orders of their homosexual superiors, therefore indulging themselves indiscriminately for sexual gratification having been deprived of woman-folk.

l learned from him that my man was a Colonel in rank and his, a Major. The lesser status soldiers shared in the gang rape of the boys, whereas men of much higher stature allowed themselves sole proprietorship of a boy of their choosing; blond and blue eyed, or so I surmised, judging by Geoff's and my similarities.

He claimed that the fat Major was in fact a homosexual. He didn't elaborate on his conclusion, he didn't have to, I understood fully. My Colonel was also a homosexual, I concluded. How Geoff gathered all that information, I never knew, only guessing that his relationship with the fat man was much more intimate with a common language to communicate. I never saw Geoff again after that day.

The Colonel and I returned to the farm and of course, to a grand welcoming. No one asked where I had been or what I had done all day except for Beth. I simply told her that we went to the beach and had a picnic and the conversation was dropped. Once again, liquor flowed freely after a meal fit for a king. A meal that I did not get to enjoy because my uncle insisted I do my chores left untended all day. The tone of his voice indicated his displeasure with me for wandering off as if that choice had been my own.

Beth had smuggled out a plate of food secretly prepared by my aunt and told me that she overheard her father and a neighbor man talking that afternoon. Apparently word had gotten around about the Nazis rounding up boys from the village but their fate was not known at the time, but it was mentioned that it was done to punish the village Elders for something. She then asked me what a homosexual pedophile was, because her father called the Nazis exactly that. I told her that I didn't know. She was too young to understand such mature things, nor did I know what a pedophile was.

Chores completed, I bade a good night to the two men drinking at the table, but my retreat was interrupted by my uncle. He advised that I would share Beth's larger bed with the Nazi while Beth would take mine in the interest of every one's comfort.

I was not foolish enough to believe that he had came to that arrangement for the good of all concerned, or that he would possibly be able to convince his esteemed guest to be inconvenienced. No, I was certain that it was the Nazi's uncontested suggestion.

Never for a moment did I think the man would not make a trek into my bed that night, I fully anticipated it. The arrangement simply made it more convenient, and my uncle bloody well knew it!

I didn't bother disturbing Beth to retrieve my night shirt from my room, I knew I wouldn't need it and I climbed naked into the big comfortable bed. I was apprehensive but excited at the same time as I lay there waiting. I didn't have to wait very long until the lantern he carried lit up the darkness and I watched him take off his uniform and hang his garments with care.

The sight of him completely naked exited my own penis that he was rather pleased to see that I was both naked and aroused when he lifted the sheet off me. I enjoyed his suckling even more than that morning. I didn't mind his finger toying at my rectum nor the slight pressure and insertion of it. I didn't understand the filthy concept, but I was in no position to argue the apparent, newly introduced homosexual act.

I was very close to orgasm when he stopped, climbed atop me for a kiss that I exchanged willingly but not eagerly. I didn't like kissing all that much; his whiskers were like sandpaper and thankfully it didn't last long. He rolled off me and onto his back. I took my queue and nestled myself between his spread thighs to study his manly genitals before exploring everything with my hands, tongue and lips, even massaging his rectum but couldn't bring myself to insert my finger up there.

Again, it was a premeditated effort in order to prevent him from bumming me, I would do a knock up job of fellatio on him. I felt that I had a better concept of performing the act to his liking and prepared myself to assuredly ingest his semen as my final resolve. He was rather loud in voicing his praises; on one hand I was grateful that he was pleased, on the other I was quite cognizant that his adoration of my efforts was being overheard by my aunt and uncle in the adjacent bedroom, adding to my uncle's recently acquired distaste of me.

Suddenly he sat up and hauled me by my underarms to lie on my back. He knelt between my legs and lifted them to my chest and held them with one hand gripping my ankles as the other struggled to open a jar of petroleum jelly, a common household product used to soothe diaper rash and dry lips that had mysteriously found itself on Beth's nightstand, conceivably by the hand of my aunt. Its new purpose appealed to me, I was going to be impaled again and there was nothing I could do to stop it.

It was only slightly less painful, however I didn't scream out. Instead, I clenched my eyes and teeth, tears welled in my eyes resisting the temptation to even whimper lest my uncle would be angry at the disturbance. Clearly, I had brought disgrace into his peaceful home and I felt that he didn't need any reminder of it as he lay in his bed across the narrow hall.

The man rolled us onto our sides and straddled one leg over my hip. He was gentle and loving, kissing the top of my head often and ran his hand up and down my torso and over my genitals as he pumped his hips slowly. I found the position the most comfortable insofar as it prevented full penetration.

The bed made no less ruckus than my own. Metal on metal, the bedsprings increased in shrill the faster and harder he drove into me. All hope of noise prevention of the obvious was thwarted by then. I envisioned my uncle tightening a noose around my neck and shoving me from the hayloft in the barn.

Almost painful was the man's grip on my penis while he masturbated me vigorously. I did not understand it at the time, but the pain inside me eased to just a mild hurt, a numb feeling overcame me. Not long afterward, the strangest sensation overtook me and I was meeting his thrusts in time This seemed to please him all the more as he began to wail and thrash about until a final, deeper drive caused him to shudder and gasp for air.

I was very close to my own orgasm and quite disappointed when he released me and rolled onto his back and was soon fast asleep. The lantern was still aglow and I admired his body once again. His large cock was flaccid and leaking his man stuff. I wanted to suckle it, to feel it in my mouth in a flaccid state had it not been slimy from the petroleum jelly and having a foul odor. Nonetheless, I played with it, admiring its softness and virility, as well as his loose hairy testicles heavily ladened in the palm of my hand. Finding myself queerly excited by his masculinity, I masturbated. Later, I rolled to face the wall feeling repulsed, indignant and confused as to my immoral thoughts, not to mention the obscure events that unfolded since meeting the Nazi.

I am not sure how long I dozed when nature called. Without the urine receptacle stored under my own bed that I generally used at night, I took the lantern and made my way outside to the latrine to relieve myself without regard for sense of modesty, being such an early hour well before sunrise when my kin would be nestled asleep in their beds.

Nothing could ever describe the fear pulsing through my veins when there stood my uncle with a look of shock and defiance staring down at me. Shamefully covering myself as best I could, the effort was futile. Our chance meeting was precarious enough, but it occurred to even my morals that despite all else, my nakedness only flaunted the shameful fact that I would sleep the night naked in the man's bed, and that would rile him even more so than had I at least shown some self-respect and decency.

He wore a robe that hung open, his own genitals exposed and dangling from his scrawny, bony body and he was unsteady from the liquor that he had consumed. He scanned me up and down with a scowl. He slurred his words terribly but I understood each derogatory statement. He called me a queer, a Nazi cock sucker and a boy whore as he stumbled forward and took hold of my neck, He told me that it was all my fault, that I could have warded off the Nazis advances had I wanted to. He claimed he heard me beg the man to suck his cock the night before and again that very night, how much I obviously enjoyed the Nazi bumming me.

Reinforced, I felt greater shame of myself, I wanted to die. I couldn't refute what he was saying, nor could I explain the reason for those words I said if only to appease the German, especially after having witnessed the hideous events of the day and how I was spared the wrath. Somehow I wished that I had been taken from uncle's home, loaded onto a troop carrier and gruesomely victimized and returned home to tell the tale. At least there might have been sympathy, caring and love to heal the mental and physical trauma, and a reasonable excuse that he was unawares and would have been powerless to protect me, his nephew, entrusted by my parents to keep me safe.

He pulled me into him by a painful grasp of my upper arm, pulling my hair with his other hand forcing me to my knees as he continued a barrage of insults, advising me that as soon as my homosexual Nazi co-sinner left the household, he was putting me on the next train back home. The lantern slipped from my hand at some point and crashed to the ground.

Crying, I tried to pull away but he pulled my head into his crotch and told me to put it in my mouth and service him the way I did the Nazi. The thought of fellating my own uncle sickened me and even under duress, I refused to open my mouth to

accept his expanding member. The terror of it all caused my bladder to release, pissing between his legs.

If not for the lantern that had started the dry grass afire, I probably would have succumbed to his wishes and degraded myself further in his eyes as well as my own. He released my hair and violently pushed me backwards as he tended to the rapid spreading fire by removing his robe and swatting at the flames with it, cursing me for my clumsiness.

I can laugh now at how foolish and funny he looked drunkenly dancing around naked with his semi erection bobbing to and fro, scorching his feet in the process. I scurried away as quick as I could to the safety of the bedroom; as ironic as that was.

The Nazi woke briefly, hauled me into his side and cuddled me. His warmth felt nice and comforting. I suddenly felt abandoned by my parents and ostracized by my uncle. I cried myself to sleep.

CHAPTER III: NOT ONLY THE COLONEL'S BOY-WHORE

I awoke to his stickiness on my groin and lay there fully enjoying it, purring like a kitten. The Colonel seemed oddly zealous, perhaps even fervent using two fingers inside my rectum while the others kneaded my testicles which lay nested in his palm. The other hand held the base of my saliva slick shaft that his mouth and tongue ravished until I sounded a blasphemy of words that had my aunt heard, would surely have earned me a slap and a mouthful of soap.

It wasn't but a few minutes of eagerly performing my duties in returned favor, when the familiar twitch gave way to several throbs ejecting his half-ounce of warm bitter milk. The hand on my head was again applied but only lightly to tousle my hair after his orgasm. I surmised that he was assured that I knew my place by then, the gesture signified a job well done.

Afterward, we dressed. Sensing my insecurity, he took my hand to walk out into the kitchen to face my uncle, whose feet I saw were wrapped in gauze. Our eyes locked briefly. His expressionless face spoke volumes. There was not a hint of remorse, only hate did I see. I wished that I had kept the German's ejaculate in my mouth and spit it in my uncle's hypocritical face. The difficult part was facing my aunt. If she only knew what her husband had attempted to do to me that led to his having scorched feet.

Again that morning, The Colonel took me with him to the base camp and to what must have been his office. A tall man rose from the desk and saluted, making way for the Colonel to sit. I assumed it was a shift change because whatever rank the tired-looking man held must have been of importance but perhaps a level lower than the Colonel. He had been responsible to oversee the night activities. He was younger and quite tall with handsome features. He had blond hair and his bright blue eyes scanned over me and a friendly smile beamed which I graciously returned. The men conversed and laughed conspiratorially. As they carried on their conversation, and in full view of my Colonel, this other officer ran a hand through my hair and down my cheek. I had picked up several German words and blushed when I understood him to say I was a pretty boy.

Coffee was delivered and the two men became engrossed in a discussion which I assumed was military business. Afterwards, the two men rose and saluted. I thought

the man was reaching to politely shake my hand to say goodbye, but he held it and pulled me out of my chair. I was bewildered and looked to the Colonel who only smiled at me and motioned for me to accompany the man.

The officer led me to the rear of the tented structure and opened a canvas flap exposing another room. I saw immediately that we were in the sleeping quarters and I realized what was expected of me. Two cots and lockers on either side of the small room were the only furnishings. He began to undress and hung each item of his uniform with meticulous care. He motioned to me to take off my clothes as well. I was disheartened by the fact that the Colonel was sharing me.

I stood naked covering myself with my hands and watched him fuss with his uniform. He paid no attention to me until he had stripped naked and then he turned to me with a broad smile. He had a very nice muscular body and was hairless except for his groin area. His penis hung flaccid and, although very fat, was oddly short in proportion to his physical size. His testicles were no larger than my own. He laid flat on the cot and motioned me between his legs. No further instructions were necessary, I knew exactly what my role was to be.

The mass of foreskin amused me. Even after he stiffened to full tumescence in my mouth, the length extended by only a mere few more centimeters but the skin remained remarkably fluid. I could lodge the chubby shaft right down to the base without gagging although his thick pubic hair tickled my nostrils.

The man displayed no emotion. There were no audible murmurs. All he did was lay there with a hand resting lightly atop my head. He occasionally caressed my hair. After I had developed one very stiff jaw and very long time later he finally spilled his semen in my mouth. It had a sweeter taste than that of the Colonel, I noted. It was tolerable. I realized then that all males must taste uniquely different.

I wondered why he wanted me naked if bumming me was not on the agenda. But he did look pleased to see that I was erect and made me stand beside the cot and masturbate myself in front of him. It took me a long time to reach orgasm, self-conscious as I was, but he was insistent that I do so. That strange fetish would become a daily routine thereafter.

When I was done, he dismissed me and I dressed. When I returned to the office side of the tent structure, a young soldier was standing at full attention near the door of the colonel's office. He was blond and blue-eyed like myself. His uniform hung loosely from his slim frame and his utility belt holding various pieces of equipment seemed to weigh him down. The Colonel looked up and smiled at my presence from behind his desk and gave instructions to the boy soldier.

His name was Jon. In addition to German, he spoke perfect Polish and informed me that I was his charge for the day. It was a great relief to finally be able to communicate with someone in my own language. Jon would become a confidante and friend over the coming weeks but not before sheer dread had me trembling when he said he was taking me down to the beach. I fully anticipated being thrown to the wolves above the treeline and despaired that I just another village boy to be used and abused by the Colonel's men by day and be his personal bed boy by night.

My nervous behavior didn't go unnoticed by Jon on the walk down the ravine but he made no comment but he did have a puzzled look on his face indicated his

awareness of it. I tried not to stare at boys huddled in the shade; the Germans apparently were not quite finished punishing the villagers.

I was grateful when we walked on by and I confess that I sighed in relief when Jon told me that I could go swimming and enjoy the water until lunchtime when we would be expected back at camp.

It was sweltering hot, more so than the previous day so I didn't hesitate to undress and frolic in the cool lake. Nothing had changed from the previous day. Men came and went and naked village boys huddled together. Later, I would learn from Jon that the boys of my village were returned after dark, dropped in the town square while a fresh herd of lambs had been abducted from another nearby village early that morning.

I watched Jon sitting upon a log in shade. His focus seldom strayed from the goings-on at the forest's edge. When I joined him, he occasionally surveyed my body squatted naked in front of him then would return his gaze down shore. Several times he slyly adjusted his discomfort within the confines of his ill-fitting trousers. I wondered if he desired me or, because he thought I was exclusive to the Colonel, just wished that he could use one of the other boys, if he hadn't already joined in the previous day's mayhem.

He was sweating profusely and I asked why he didn't come in the water with me for a swim. He replied that he was on duty and would be punished severely since most of the men on the beach were his superiors. Several times we were interrupted by some of those angry-voiced men. Jon explained to me that they questioned our distance away from the common area. He told me that some even wanted to take me for themselves but, when they learned I was the Colonels' boy and under Jon's charge, they sheepishly apologized and retreated. Jon seemed to relish in the fact that he held that little power over his superiors.

I liked him a lot. I learned that he was the son of a German industrialist. His mother, on the other hand, was Polish which accounted for his fluency in the language. He had been conscripted by the army that very Spring but had not joined by choice. Because of his second language, he was placed in military intelligence but this really amounted to his being little more than a gopher and servant to the Colonel, whom he did like because he apparently the man treated him kindly. We talked about his home in Germany and mine here in Poland, our likes and dislikes and, after discovering a mutual love for the sport soccer.

I had so many questions to ask him and, my being of somewhat celebrity status, I didn't hold back. I asked him if homosexuality was part of his homeland culture. He replied with a laugh that, no, it wasn't a common practice but in war-time certain moral standards were overlooked. I knew he went out on a limb when he added that homo-sex within the ranks was not unheard of.

Enlisted men never refused the sexual advances of their superiors. That obedience, he claimed, was taught early in the Nazi Youth Program, a sub-military recruiting and training organization. Jon stressed that it was all justified in the name of war because men had basic needs that couldn't be met simply because they weren't at home in the company of their girlfriends and wives. I didn't realize it at the time, but the Nazi commanders had brainwashed the young male adults. Perhaps sexual activity

remained clandestine but the ultimate pedophile manipulation with military sanction was alive, well and flourishing.

Jon was hesitant when I boldly asked, but eventually admitted that he had indeed slept with many men, including the Colonel, who had been quite fond of him before my arrival. I detected a note of jealousy in his voice, his scan of my body done so with a glimmer of envy before he abruptly stood and told me to dress because it was time to go.

We enjoyed lunch in the officer's mess. Stiff-hatted chefs carved legs of lamb and hams at a table in plain view while others prepared the final plates for the waiter staff that was as efficient as any fine restaurant. Others hovered around and decanted wine. Another dished out chocolate mousse dessert with my first taste of this deliciousness being granted to me when our waiter saw me licking the dish clean like I used to do with the bowl when mother finished icing a cake.

We sat with the obese major from the beach, along with the man with the small fat penis that I suckled that morning. Three other men with whom I was not familiar totally ignored my presence at the table. Their talk was boisterous and sounded angry but was generally followed with laughter. To me, German was a harsh, strange language. I was disappointed that the Major's boy, Geoff, was not present

Under the watchful eye of my young guardian, Jon, the rest of the day was spent climbing on top and inside tanks and aboard rocket launchers that were hauled behind trucks. He let me drive the jeep around the compound, first, with me sitting between his legs learning to master the vehicle and then giving me the thrill of a lifetime, driving solo on the highway under strict instructions not to tell the Colonel.

Travelling down a dirt road simply to see where it led, we soon discovered a secluded beach situated at the lake head. We stripped off our clothes. It was easy for me but Jon took longer to shed his gear and uniform which he carefully hung on a tree branch.

Jon had a beautiful body, despite being so pale that his hands, always in the sunlight, stuck out in contrast to the rest of his sun deprived body. He was hairless except for a dark blond trail leading down from his navel which exploded in a thick blond, curly mass above his thick and long uncut manhood under which rested two flared, fully packed pink testicles.

It concerned me that, once again, I was admiring a young, well-developed male body. We frolicked around and dove for freshwater clams. We dared each other to eat the contents and both with an open shell to our mouths, grimaced as we sucked the gross slimy meat and swallowed so as one didn't have bragging rights of outdoing the other. Both of us gagged and retched but did it not once, but several times.

We splashed and dunked each other, got into a wrestling match that escalated into groping which initiated erections and, in turn, initiated mutual masturbation. Even in the cool water, his hard cock was warm in my hand. We didn't let go of the other as we made our way out of the water and dropped to the sand. Jon took control and we lay on our sides at opposite ends.

The moment was surreal when I took him in my mouth and he took me into his. I was blissfully content, Jon's mouth was eager to please as was mine. We were equals, neither held any superiority over the other nor were we relentless in our efforts to please each other.

I was on the verge of explosion, my aching balls complained as I squeezed my groin muscles tight trying to prolong the inevitable. I could feel Jon's cock begin to throb on my lips, each pulse being accompanied by a volley of sperm which I felt hitting the back of my palate. I let myself go, every muscle in my body tensed, quivering uncontrollably.

It was as if we were one being with one mind. In unison we each lifted a leg and straddled the others head between our thighs. We pulled each other's penis deeper into the warm, wet confines of our mouths and throats. Our bodies trembled as muffled moans escaped from each of us as we greedily shared the fluids offered each other like starved gluttons. We remained in that position until long after the last moment of excitement waned.

Sand was embedded in our skin and sweat poured from our heads, another playful romp in the lake was invigorating. We found ourselves in an embrace and I forced my tongue into Jon's mouth. He didn't resist. It was life-changing; at that exact moment I knew that I was different, possibly a homosexual.

Jon and I found a shaded, grassy spot and lay down beside each other. He felt the need to reinforce his rationalization that it was war-time, that he wasn't a homosexual, but only utilizing his training to combat loneliness and stress. When I told him I thought I was one, he corrected me saying that we were simply venting sexual frustrations upon the other, it meant nothing. I concurred, if only to allow him peace of mind, but in my heart I knew better.

I wanted him to fuck me, an English slang term, he taught me amongst a host of others descriptive words. What we did in the sand was called a blow-job, in a sixty-nine position, another term followed by clarification as to its visual significance of the position that made me laugh when it finally made sense.

Jon was very gentle and considerate laying on top of me and asking often if I was alright. It was painful at first, but I was determined to take Jon inside me with no idea exactly why. It wasn't long before my bowel was full and much like the previous night with the Colonel, there was a pleasant sensation mixed with pain evolved.

Jon flipped me onto my back and I instinctively held my knees to my chest offering myself to him. He was neither rough nor was he gentle. I instinctively clenched my anus around his penis as he plowed deep inside of me. It felt so natural. The pace increased rapidly with excitement, a unified momentum ensued as I met his thrusts with my hips. His handsome face was blood-red, a vein protruded from his forehead above his ever changing facial expressions that displayed agony one moment, ecstasy the next.

My fingers dug into the grass and dirt and I screamed blissfully when he manhandled my genitals with both hands, pulling and squeezing until I could take no more and orgasmed which he captured and smeared over my belly and groin. Not long after, he shoved himself into me one last time and collapsed on top of my body forcing his tongue into my mouth in one last heated display of intimacy. I was in love, feeling that complex emotion for the very first time in my life.

Reluctantly, we disengaged our coupling and intimacy to dress and head back to the camp. I drove the jeep to within sight of the compound and then Jon took over. The guard at the entry gate screamed at Jon and the young man's face went white. We

were in definitely in trouble but that was very clear to me even before he explained why. We were late returning to the camp.

The Colonel was none too pleased when we presented ourselves in his office. He chastised Jon who stood straight and obedient accepting the wrath of his superior. He was finally dismissed. Jon clicked his heels and gave the Nazi salute before retreating from the office. I felt poorly for Jon but there was little I could say or do. I worried that he could be severely punished for his misdemeanor.

The Colonel must have somehow known that I drove the very jeep we were headed home with. He pulled over and motioned me into the driver's seat. Proud as a peacock, I switched places with him and drove while he snoozed in the passenger seat. My uncle's face was priceless when I parked the vehicle close to where he was mending a rotting front porch step.

He rose and beamed at the German as if seeing a long lost friend. As he led him into the house, he cautioned him to be careful of the steps and ushered to sit at the table where a fresh, unopened bottle of schnapps and two glasses awaited the special guest. His feet were still wrapped in gauze, a sad reminder of his activities from the night before.

I did my chores without being told for no other reason than to avoid my uncle for as long as I could. My aunt had prepared a plate which she had kept warm in the oven that I enjoyed later that evening. Beth was already in bed when my aunt told me to change into my nightshirt and excused herself after fussing over and serving my late dinner.

The men were well on their way to drunkenness by then, and when I arose to say good night, the Colonel grabbed my arm and pulled me to sit in his lap. His hand wandered up my nightshirt and began to fondle me in plain sight of my uncle who would have to be blind not to see the thin material rising and falling. I was embarrassed to say the least. An erection was coerced and the material exhibited exactly what was happening beneath my nightshirt as I was being masturbated. All the while, the men talked and laughed as if nothing was out of the ordinary. I felt the Colonel's own hardness against my bum through his trousers.

An eerie silence fell over the kitchen. Suddenly, the German said something to the drunken man. Uncle was clearly uncomfortable by it and didn't know where to look. He certainly wasn't going to look at me if he could at all help it. Another menacing volley of words was directed at my uncle that startled him into alertness. He tried to look at me but his eyes darting every which way as he relayed what the German told him.

The Colonel said that I was a born man-pleaser, the most beautiful boy he'd ever seen. Features and skin of a girl, genitals of a boy, semen like nectar. My uncle cringed relaying that last sentiment. He gathered his composure and went on in a monotone voice to say that I was a great lover, learning quickly to satisfy the needs of a man.

The Colonel stopped caressing me and leaned in toward my uncle. He placed his large paw on the nape of my uncle's neck forcing him to within inches of his face and said something that made my uncle go deathly ashen with a flash of fear in his eyes and a quivering jaw. My uncle must have been reluctant to relay to me exactly what the German had said to cause such a flutter and fear in his eyes.

Uncle looked at me with scorn and in a stuttering of words told me that the Colonel had warned him in no uncertain terms that should any harm be done to me by any man, regardless of who that man was, he would not hesitate to put a bullet in their head.

It was my turn for blood to drain from my face. How could the Colonel have known what transpired during the night at the latrine? He appeared to be sound asleep when I crawled back into bed trembling like a leaf and sobbing. Surely my dirt stained scraped knees and dark bruises on my left arm couldn't have given him any clue of what happened at least until the light of morning. Or had he been woke up by the commotion and peered out the window to witness the scene unfolding not ten yards away?

Suddenly, the large man released his grip of the bug eyed coward and backed away. A jovial laugh erupted and he raised a toast to his defeated adversary. Uncle recovered from the humiliation quickly and seemingly untarnished His alcohol flushed face returned as he raised a glass to meet the Colonel's own, a round of feigned laughter and false good-will ensued between the two men to carry on the evening as if nothing had happened.

His calloused hand again cradled my genitals while an errant finger meandered to locate and graze my anus. With the gentle persuasion of his hand, I laid back into his chest, spreading my thighs of my own volition despite Uncle being a witness to my submissiveness. To my astonishment, uncle actually observed the hand play under my nightshirt for a few moments. Then looking over his shoulder to ensure privacy before he commented, he chuckled and said something that I was sure was intended to be perversely flattering to the Colonel perhaps even complimentary of the man's conquest.

Well-assured by then that the women-folk of his family were out of harm's way of this homosexual only confirmed that he was selfishly looking out for his own best interests at my expense. He considered his actions were a great favor, he might have thought, which earned him some future consideration by not interfering but rather giving me to the Colonel like everything else his guest demanded from uncle's unconditional hospitality.

It was all an illusion I saw. After the fleeting exchange of laughs and words, perhaps I was the only one who had seen the quiver of his lip, the sly squinting and nervous twitch of his left eye when he met my stare. Nothing had changed, he loathed my very existence by then and, although my parents had trusted him with my care, I was now expendable, a mere bartering chip.

Perhaps through his guilt and shame of his actions of the previous night, he had somehow concluded and justified it as my doing. Maybe he had surmised that I followed him outdoors to the latrine naked with the motive of seducing him. Uncle probably had reasoned to himself that shoving me to my knees was merely meant to be a harsh lesson to humiliate and degrade me with no intentions of actually making me blow him. Sadly, I was beginning to realize everything for what it was but I fought not to hate him in return. I had been raised to turn the other cheek, to be forgiving of trespasses. However I hated him quite then, the bible be damned!

Once again, my bottom felt the unmistakable hardness upon which it sat, and the German's fondling became even more insistent. I was embarrassed when the colonel

hauled up my nightshirt to rub my chest exposing my privates which were being manipulated. More words and giggles ensued between the two men. My uncle now found an excuse to look away, to pour them each another shot of schnapps, to roll some cigarettes but the phony smile on his face never wavered.

In a mixed bag of emotions, I felt sorry for him. The German had crossed the line. I feared that the man would call my uncle's bluff, test him, if only to humiliate him further by offering him the opportunity to take me to the bedroom and use me. However much to my relief, the Colonel wrapped an arm around my waist as he rose, said goodnight, tossed me over his shoulder and carried me off to bed like a sack of potatoes leaving my uncle as stunned as I was.

He talked as he undressed, the uniform again being hung ever so carefully in the closet. I didn't understand a word of what he said but his tone was gentle and soothing. I pulled off my nightshirt and waited for him under the blanket. He was erect when he turned to look at me. Lifting the cover, he admired my prone naked body, growled with a devilish grin and joined me on his knees, his torso towering over me. His menacing erection was fully displayed and he deliberately rubbed it surely flaunting it for my benefit. His hands began to wander aimlessly over my body, even my toes he caressed, suckling each one before slowly slithering up my body with his tongue, leaving a cooling wet trail in his wake.

Lifting my bum slightly, he buried his face between my cheeks lapping at me like a dog who had found the hidden treat of marrow deep inside a ham bone. He took both my testicles fully in his mouth, his tongue again performing magical wonders. When he took my cock in his mouth I quivered in bliss, thrashing and pulling at the sheets. Before long I exploded mind and soul yelping like a coyote, my jism greedily coerced from my swollen cock.

He slowly moved up my body, paying no less attention to my skin on his journey until he found my mouth. Proud that I was experienced in such matters, thanks to Jon, I met his tongue with mine. Ignoring his pin-like bristles, our tongues swiped, each striving to suck the others, a hint of my semen lingered upon his breath.

The Colonel rolled off of me and reached for the petroleum jelly, smearing it on his cock and lifted me on top of him. I needed no explanation or instructions but, instead, positioning its girth, I lowered myself onto it. I relished the fact that I was in full control and was no less willing to impale myself upon him.

Patiently, he lay idle while I slowly adjusted and accepted it deeper until I finally felt his bristly pubic hair on my testicles. When he had no more length to offer and, after a short breather to compose myself, I rode him. He moaned, I panted. I reared my head back while my haunches did the work.

Most certainly my uncle had another angst filled night. By then, I really didn't care anymore and perhaps I was a little more vocal than necessary.

CHAPTER IV: DEFILED BY THE INTRUDERS

It was barely sunrise when I opened my eyes. The birds had taken over the serenade of the night crickets and a soft pink glow illuminated the bedroom. The Colonel's movements woke me as he got out of bed and walked to the window. His large frame blocked the light as he stood on his toes and rested his hands on the wall. It took only a moment to register that he was urinating through the window. I made a mental note to retrieve the urinal from under my bed. It was an oversight that once again, my bladder took pains to remind me.

What a novel idea! I thought, piss out the window; if I was only tall enough. Casting a glance around the room I spied a cedar chest at the foot of Beth's bed and decided that it would make an ideal perch. As I struggled to drag it over the floor to mimic his keen sense in answering nature's call, he laughed at my efforts and, picking me up, he held me at the window. I doubted that my aunt would have appreciated us watering her roses planted below in such a crude manner, but considering everything else over the past few days since the Nazi arrived, what we did over her rose garden was by far a minor offense.

The man began to dress as I stood watching not knowing why he wished to leave so early or even if I was invited along again. The answer to that question came when he picked up my trousers and shirt and tossed them at me. It was obvious that he was in a hurry that morning, foregoing his usual blowjob because of important military business, I assumed. Strangely, I wasn't sure if I was relieved or disappointed to be tagging along with my Colonel because each day of missed chores would be another nail in my coffin but, on the other hand, sticking around could also prematurely place me in it! That thought made me shudder. I momentarily wondered what my fate would be when the Nazi left for good?

We left the house in its quiet slumber and I was elated when he took the passenger seat, arms folded across his big chest and looking at me as if to ask what the hell I was waiting for. Proud as any boy would be, I jumped in the driver's seat. He reached over and placed a helmet on my head and, if I do say so myself, I did a slap-up job of maneuvering the jeep from the front yard to the highway and safely beyond toward our final destination.

The soldiers at the gate saluted not only the colonel, but looked at me and replayed the outstretched arm and clicking of heels routine. The colonel laughed, as did the two young men, pleased with themselves in earning their senior officer's

amusement. Careful to park the vehicle in front of his office tent and away from the mud puddles that a night rain had formed, he smiled and got out.

The scene was the same as the previous morning, the tall man rising from behind the desk to allow the colonel his throne. The men conversed, sometimes animatedly, while looking over papers. Shortly thereafter, two waiters arrived as if on cue to serve us breakfast. One, a boy of about fifteen kept looking at me expressionless as he went about fussing over our meal. Finally, a slight smile parted his lips and I returned the courtesy. I was flabbergasted when, in perfect Polish; he asked if my meal was satisfactory.

The men wrapped up their business a short time later. The tall man stood, his eyes met mine and no words were necessary. I followed behind him like an obedient puppy to the back quarters where we undressed. I performed the same ritual between his legs as I had done the day before and once his needs were met, I stood and masturbated as expected.

When I returned to the front of the tent, Jon was present, standing at attention at the door when I entered the office. Our eyes met and I knew that he knew what had transpired in the back room. I felt embarrassed and surely blushed. He looked directly at me and half-smirked - not in a condescending way - his eyes seemed to speak of compassion.

The Colonel looked up from his desk, said something to Jon, then scribbled and handed a note to the young soldier. In a harsh voice, Jon ordered me to follow him and we retreated. He was to be my guardian for another day, which I found most pleasing.

We walked leisurely about the base camp mostly in silence. Well away from the hubbub of the camp activity, Jon placed a finger to his mouth indicating silence and showed me the tented barrack where he bunked. It smelled of body odor and stinky feet. There were some twenty or so cots along each side of the dingy narrow structure. He explained to me that most were used as shared sleeping accommodations between the day and night shift enlisted men. Several other similar barracks had been erected side by side. The entire area smelled of stale urine probably because the young soldiers chose to piss outside the tent rather than take the long walk to the latrine. I thought about my aunt's rose garden.

The mess hall was nothing like the chef and waiter staffed officer's mess. There were rows and rows of bare rough tables with many young inhabitants seated with bowed heads spooning what appeared be very unappetizing porridge. Others were lined up with bowls at the front of the hall waiting for cooks to ladle the thin gruel. Jon was one. I passed, feeling terribly guilty for having bacon, sausage, eggs and waffles not an hour earlier. I did however; accept a mug of tea, not bothering to ask for sugar and milk when none was readily in sight.

What was clearly in sight and hard to miss was a group of boys in civilian clothes like my own seated at a table eating the same slop as two guards looked on nearby. When Jon and I had settled at a distant table I was immediately sorry that I had inquired.

He explained that an early morning raid had been conducted on an orphanage some fifty miles west where military intelligence believed underground resistance operatives were stationed. Finding nothing but priests and boys, and not believing the

priests denials, ten younger teen boys were brought back to base for interrogation purposes but it was all a ruse.

Jon looked around slyly to ensure privacy, leaned over and confided to me that on this day a local Inn would be the venue for several very high ranking Nazi officials arriving from Germany for meetings. The boys were to be provided for their entertainment, courtesy of the good Colonel himself. That explained the early morning jump on the day. The Colonel wanted to ensure his base was ship-shape for any potential inspections by the brass as well as assure himself that the predawn hunting trip was a success with fresh prime meat available on the menu.

We stopped next at the base commissary where he presented the Colonels note. Minutes later a picnic basket was handed off and we made our merry way in the jeep to the same little beach and wasted no time in undressing. We headed into the water where we spent a good long time before enjoying our lunch of cheese, pickled herring and bread with fruit for dessert.

Our cocks soon occupied each other's mouths. with Jon straddling my head, hovering just above me while his testicles warmly splayed over my nose providing me with a somewhat tantalizing glimpse of his rectum that my hands couldn't resist and dared me to part his cheeks for a better view. It was a darker pink than its surroundings with its puffy folds quivering ever so slightly; perhaps the result of his heartbeat, or perhaps the priming of his orgasm. I wasn't prepared to explore any further, though, at least orally, but I wondered what it would be like to fuck him.

I noticed the shadow first, then felt the cool metal end of a rifle barrel resting between my eyes that came into focus. Jon must have also been aware of company in our presence as my cock lost its warm cocoon sensation to a cooler one. A loud thud was heard immediately followed by an even louder grunt as Jon was kicked in the side and rolled off me. Two middle aged German soldiers stood menacingly over us pointing machine guns and yelling unintelligible foreign words that Jon screamed back in unintelligible foreign words.

Jon rose to his feet cautiously, his hands above his head with a gun barrel trained on his temple. I remained on the ground with the same unnerving threat. Spread eagle, I didn't flinch a muscle, not even to cover myself or even close my legs. Slowly and cautiously, Jon ambled his way to the tree where his uniform was hung and pointed. He had at least identified himself as one of them, surely that would show favor on our behalf.

The screaming only intensified directed at Jon who turned crimson and was obviously shaken up. The soldier manhandled him back to where I lay and shoved him to the ground. I hated not understanding what was going on. I could hear only the words but couldn't understand German. After leveler heads prevailed, smirks appeared on the faces of the two intruders. It was clear to them that Polish - and - pretty boy were either lovers or, at the very least, fuck buddies.

Jon looked at me, his eyes wide in fear; he was on the verge of tears and brought me up to date. Speaking in Polish he said that he could be in real trouble because he was, 1) on duty and out of uniform, 2) engaged in homosexual acts with an enemy civilian no less, and 3) breach of trust and duties as chaperon to the Colonel's pageboy. Each was a capital offense on its own and punishable by a firing squad.

A pageboy. So that's how the colonel's relationship to me was presented and accepted tongue-in-cheek by the rank and file. A pageboy with benefits no doubt but I couldn't dwell on that right then. Jon was in severe trouble and I was the center of it. I felt scared; no, paranoid for his well-being;

Jon buried his head between his knees and sobbed, his body convulsed uncontrollably. The men let up their sinister stance and lowered their arms. I presumed the soldier standing over the quivering teen was in charge. With three stripes on his shoulder and the more vocal of the two, he knelt down to Jon's level and conversed in a lowered tone with a devious grin.

Jon looked up at the man. I could see that the expression on his face clearly gave the impression that he was appalled. He glanced back down in a look of defeat. The man towering above me reacted with a ghost smile; his gun barrel gently skimmed down my torso and proceeded to prod my genitals.

Jon's foreboding eyes met mine, he looked away in shame. A deal had been struck, that I was sure of. I was the bargaining chip; the Polish pretty boy, - the colonel's forbidden fruit. That must have added an element of intrigue in itself.

Like the unfortunate boys in the woods, I was dragged over to straddle a downed tree. The men shed their munitions belts to the ground, downed their trousers, each began taking shared liberties upon my mouth. I wasn't a fool. I played the submissive role, not for fear of anything else except knowing that I was surely saving Jon's life. As far as I was concerned, it was a small price to pay.

The sergeant smelled atrocious, like rotten meat. The sight right under the foreskin was nauseating. As I was growing up, my father stressed the importance of cleanliness. He instilled in me a fear of infection which resulted in him having to undergo painful circumcision late in life. I wanted to vomit when the sergeant pulled my hair and forced me to take the gross flaccid meat back into my mouth. His long fat cock was slow to respond, unlike his impatient younger accomplice who was all but shoving his superior aside, his veiny member drooling a copious amount of slime.

Deciding not to share, the Sergeant ordered Jon over and down on his knees to service his subordinate. Both Jon and the soldier appeared contrite however neither made comment to the breach of ethics among the low level enlisted men. Perhaps the sergeant deemed Jon a homosexual anyway thereby justifying the order given.

Moments later, the Sergeant was fully erect and quite a mouthful. I wondered if the scene going on beside us had encouraged his excitement. Much larger than even the Colonel, the sides of my mouth were painfully stretched and it was almost impossible not to scrape the shaft with my teeth while he viciously mouth fucked me. But the facefucking did not last for long. My prayers that he would cum went unanswered when he pulled away from me and stepped over the log. I was going to be brutally sodomized; that, I knew was inevitable.

And brutal it was. He had made little progress entering me but enough to know tearing had occurred. The more frustrated he got; the more physical he became. He began punching me in the side and spine, or pulling my hair, as if I was somehow at fault. The tree bark dug into my belly and groin like dull razors but I just wanted him to stop hitting me and I would endure the other tortures.

I had one hope, a shot in the dark. I yelled to Jon to tell the Sergeant that the Colonel resided at my home and I was his fuck boy; that he would see the marks on

my body and question them and that I was prepared to tell him everything. Jon didn't hesitate to pass on my message and it worked. The beating stopped. I guessed that a third his cock was lodged inside me and going no further, it was deflating rapidly.

If the Sergeant's expression was anything like the other soldier, eyes bulging and mouth agape, he bent down and quickly pulling up his trousers. But, I couldn't see his face. Jon later said it was first, one of disbelief, maybe even a bluff about to be called. But he hesitated, then deciding there could be some credence to my status, the look turned to hatred more than fear, perhaps humiliated that his young enemy became the sudden victor.

A hard slap to my ass immediately followed the extraction of his mammoth cock. The void was a great relief, as was the loud fart that followed, but no one was laughing. I remained slumped over the log thinking it prudent to keep a low profile as long as possible or at least until the man had dressed and crawled over the downed tree that I felt served as a barrier between us.

The Sergeant was in Jon's face screaming, his forefinger jabbing Jon's forehead before a shove sent the naked teen splayed to the ground, his head striking a large stone with a thud. The men pilfered our picnic basket before heading down the shoreline. They were out of sight when I ran to Jon's aide. He was unconscious and bleeding profusely. My mom, a nurse, I remembered saying that a head wound always looked worse than it was, but his comatose state had me afraid. Holding him in my arms wondering what to do, he opened his eyes not seconds later complaining of a headache. I laughed, he snickered.

We cleaned ourselves up in the lake. The bleeding had stopped from the small gash on his head; a small bald spot marked the abrasion. I commented on his premature hair loss, he retorted that I could now securely sit on a fence post during a windstorm, we both laughed, dunking each other. The horror not long ago although not forgotten, now made light of;

On the drive back to base, Jon told me that the Sergeant's final words threatened that he, the Sergeant, and the subordinate would have Jon at their mercy for sexual favors any time they wanted thereafter. I felt awful and somehow responsible; however, even if I had left the man to brutalize me, the outcome for Jon would not have changed, I reasoned.

Jon premised that we should have been more cautious given that the Nazi's had recently formed a very tight two mile perimeter patrol to protect the base from possible enemy assault. They had not considered that the lakeshore would be a strategic defense point. In hindsight, it was logical.

The Colonel was seated at his desk when Jon delivered me late that afternoon and excused himself. He barely acknowledged my presence. He was studying what was a very large map, inking notations on it as I sat quietly off to the side twiddling my thumbs for what ended up being a very long time.

The cute waiter boy from breakfast knocked and let himself in, taking a seat beside me. Blond, blue eyed with finely chiseled features, he was dressed in civilian trousers that the bottom hems rode high revealing his stocking feet snug within a pair of well-worn shoes. His suspenders were snug over a knit sweater that I thought much too warm to be wearing in the stifling heat. I doubted he was a soldier, his appearance resembling that of a farm boy like me.

I wanted to make conversation with the Polish speaking lad, but the Colonel's demeanor was rigid suggesting that an air of expected silence dominated the office as he concentrated on his work. Like a couple of school boys bored out of our minds, we winked and made funny faces at each other. The odd giggle broke the silence causing the man to raise his eyes occasionally, but he didn't scolded us. Once, he even managed a hint of a smile.

Claus was my companion's name He was almost fifteen and definitely not military. As a member of the Nazi Youth program, he had been brought along as a pageboy to do domestic chores for the elitists; chores like laundry, cleaning quarters, cleaning guns or even polishing boots and, sometimes, waiter duties. It was quite apparent that the senior echelon spared no expense to make the best of the hardships of war.

I learned all this from Claus as we sat alone in the jeep outside an inn, the same inn that I was sure that great military minds were planning the final details of the destruction of my home city. These were the same powerful, prestigious men that would enjoy the company of innocent Polish boys most of whom were, perhaps, yet unawares as to the very carnal reasons why they were taken there.

I shivered in fear when the Colonel drove into the Inn's parking lot thinking that I would also be ensconced in someone else's bed for the night. Claus' presence was still a mystery. I wondered if he perhaps was a sacrificial lamb as well but that really didn't make sense since he was one of them. However, nothing made sense anymore; the Nazis seemed a whimsical, unpredictable lot. It seemed as if who did what to whom had no boundaries. I was beginning to rationalize that the whole structure was hypocritical from the top level down.

The Colonel wasn't all that long inside the stately, vine covered, mortar constructed building. I wondered about his status in the military hierarchy for his not being included in the strategic talks I assumed were going on inside. Perhaps he was only required to give a short moment in the spot light to offer his assessment and the state of readiness of the hundreds of troops under his command.

I was a bit put out when he directed Claus instead of me to chauffeur us to a destination that turned out to be my home. It was well past supper time by then; my uncle seemed distraught standing outside the barn when we pulled up. Still limping on his sore feet inside his well-worn boots, he greeted us with congeniality, yelling for his wife to prepare a late dinner. He looked at Claus in a curious way but it was no different than I was questioning the boy's presence in our home.

My uncle took on a rather sad look even before we left the jeep. Speaking English, that Claus interpreted; another multi linguist that I had to admire, he filled me in as we all made our way to the barn. Bertha, the cow, was in distressed labor. Once inside the barn, the Colonel removed his shirt and knelt at the rear of the animal which lay on its side. Placing his hands inside the beast's cavity he concentrated his eyes toward the ceiling as he manipulated the unborn calf from a breach birth position. Once the calf was in the proper position, he began pulling the tiny legs out until nature took its course. I swear Bertha looked up from behind at the Colonel and mooed an appreciative moo, seconded by my very relieved uncle, only in a different tongue.

It so happened to be Monday which was traditionally bath night. The large tin tub was hauled into the kitchen as my aunt fussed about heating kettles of water to keep it tepid warm. Beth had just vacated the tub and was standing wrapped in a large towel

when us men entered the soap scented house. She blushed at the sight of Claus who smiled, turning crimson himself at the sight of a near naked pretty girl two years his junior. My aunt shooed Beth from the kitchen to bed when she noticed the gawking young stranger in their midst.

I dreaded bath nights because of having to quickly strip naked and timidly submerge myself in a fetal position in the tub while my aunt washed my hair before leaving me to cleanse myself in semi privacy while she fussed about the kitchen. She was, still too close for comfort as far as I was concerned. I missed the huge claw footed tub back home where I could safely jerk off provided I, and not my father, was the last user and could pull the plug to erase the flotsam evidence.

The Colonel knelt before the tub to cleanse the blood and goop from his hands and arms. If my aunt had any plans of me taking a bath, I was grateful to the man for unknowingly tainting the water on my behalf. His action saved me from embarrassment in front of Claus, who most probably would have been subjected to the same humiliation had my aunt had her child domineering way. Thankfully, the tub was bailed and hauled back outside to serve as water trough for the animals.

Auntie prepared a feast of sandwiches from leftovers in the icebox. Hot soup, made from outdated meats and vegetables added daily to the huge ever-simmering iron pot to meld, was ladled into bowls. Always thick and delicious, it was impossible to name the ever changing concoction, referred to only as "soup". I would later learn that this practice of keeping soup on the stove and adding to it every day was a common practice in other cultures as well.

My uncle immediately saw the opportunity in having another set of strong arms to not only assist in my chores, but add other ones to the list. But my aunt quickly vetoed the idea saying that she felt it was much too late for us to be performing chores as she bid us goodnight and strode off to bed. It was a nice try though, uncle, I thought. Claus and I played chess at the table instead, much to my uncles displeasure that the drunker he got, the more irritated he became.

Claus interpreted and whispered most all of the conversation the two adults were having. One particular sentence I found particularly alarming. The Nazi casually told my uncle that he brought Claus home to lose his virginity and fuck my virgin cousin, a reward bestowed on Nazi boys loyal to the party, a rite-of-passage into manhood.

Uncles face immediately drained of blood. I thought he was having a heart attack as he gasped for air and clutched his chest. Claus' eyes were as wide as my own in shock; however I detected a certain glimmer of nervous pride in his demeanor seconds later. He sat up straight and took on a serious, mature masculine look. I had no doubt that he was keen on the idea of intercourse with my cousin. I wanted to beg him not to but the words came out garbled. Until that moment, I never realized how much I cared for Beth, - the awkward little girl with the noticeable developing boobies who was always under my feet asking stupid questions like how the chickens mated in comparison to having seen the obvious mammals in the act. It was typical farm life exposure to nature's ability to procreate that especially I, the city boy, was at first awed by. As for the chickens, I didn't have a clue but I suspected that, other than waking us up in the morning, the rooster had another purpose.

The little girl that sometimes found excuses to linger in the kitchen helping her mother, while I cowered modestly in my bath. I always waited for the right moment

to rise and don a towel usually just a split second away from both females' eyes that may or may not have caught an occasional glance of my bare ass.

I didn't need any interpretation as my uncle, shaking like a leaf, blubbered on in a mix of English and Polish in his confused state begging the man to have mercy, even offering his experienced wife to take the young man's virginity.

The Colonel templed his fingers to his face as if in great thought. A glance at Claus showed definite disappointment in the bargaining of his virginal fate. He peered at the Colonel with anticipation hoping that the man would not be swayed by the weeping bag of bones sitting across from him. There was no question that my uncle was so rattled that couldn't even pick up his tumbler of vodka without missing his mouth and finally dropped the glass to shatter upon the table.

The aura was thick with tension as we awaited the powerful entity's prolonged, nerve wracking decision. I prayed that my aunt would be the sacrificial lamb and my cousin spared. My bones and muscles ached in tense angst. I dared not breathe. No one expected what happened next.

CHAPTER V: ABJECT HUMILIATION IN THE KITCHEN

The Colonel turned his glare away from Uncle and toward Claus. He muttered a few words which perhaps caught the boy off guard. He looked puzzled, shyly shook his head, then rose, and walked to the Colonel's side. A smile cracked the stone faced man as he lifted a hand and with two fingers started to ever so slowly span the length of the lad's obvious excitement which was clearly apparent beneath the material of his trousers. Apparently the thought of fucking a woman in lieu of a young girl hadn't diminished his desire all that much.

The Colonel appeared pleased, reached up and removed the suspenders from Claus' shoulders letting them fall to his sides. Gravity played a role when the boy's trousers dropped to his worn, lace-less boots. Just as quick his bulky sweater was raised from his torso and off over his head.

Not having to be instructed, he kicked off his boots from his sockless feet and stepped free of the discarded heap of clothing moving even closer to the man who had stripped him naked without the slightest show of emotion. Clearly, Claus was used to being put on display, naked and aroused, in front of men and boys. He was a diligent valet by day to the very men that used him at night, I could only imagine.

I hated myself for thinking that my aunt was in for a treat. Claus reeked of youthful virility for his young age of fourteen. His had a muscular hourglass shape just like a farm boy. He was tanned from the waist up but a ghostly white below that accented his darker groin area, almost hairless testicles which were a bright pink and dangled in clear view below his long slender erection that appeared, curiously, void of foreskin which was not common, for a German that is.

The Nazi seemed transfixed as he fondled the testicles in his hand and caressed Claus' chest tweaking his nipples so they stood proudly standing out from his breasts, muttering how lovely the boy was. He then gazed over and smiled devilishly at the visibly shaken man who was still fearing his family's fate and, as if they were conspirators, solicited my uncle's opinion of the naked youth who, in return, raised his head up to look, his quivering mouth forming a weak grin. With a nod of his head, Claus concurred with the Colonel's assessment as was expected of him.

The colonel motioned Claus around the chair to stand between the two men, and resumed gently stroking the sleek young shaft. Uncle watched the spectacle which the

Colonel had so boldly been placed less than an arms-length away for no other reason than to further intimidate the shrunken man, and he had succeeded. Yes indeed.

The Colonel played with uncle's vulnerable emotions again mentioning the young girl that slept only a few feet away behind the curtain door. He said he was having second thoughts as to how it would be a shame to disappoint the very excited boy his earned rite-of-passage by denying him the pleasure of taking a nubile young woman and replacing her with a mere woman old enough to be his mother and already well-bred and defiled by the likes of my uncle.

It was clear that the man hated my uncle and was tormenting the man to the brink of madness. He cared little that my uncle was sobbing and shaking. My uncle, who was now resting his arms on the table, began to shake so violently that the vodka bottle would have toppled had the German not salvaged it, refilled their glasses and handed the bottle to Claus, encouraging him to drink from it.

The coward of a man pleaded for mercy, drooling saliva, his words stuttered and barely audible. A trail of fluid ran over the kitchen floor and pooled a short distance away. He had pissed himself in fear; the same as I had done that frightful night. I truly felt sorry for him regardless of all else when he looked across at me not with scorn, but with an appeal. Perhaps, for the first time, we met eye to eye because we had found common ground in Beth's well-being. He was somehow placing the onus on me to do something short of a miracle.

Grabbing a butter-knife, I rose from my chair sending it to the floor and yelled across the table at the Colonel telling him that I loved my cousin and to not harm her. I was not even sure if I found the correct words in a garble of English, Polish and German or whether I had sounded like a blubbering idiot. He peered at me sharply and I stared him down. My right hand was pointing the sorry excuse for a menacing weapon while my left was planted firmly on the table to support my leaning frame and to keep my trembling legs from deserting me resulting in my falling to the floor.

Suddenly, the Colonel's smug smile got wider, his blue eyes brighter, and he began to laugh, slowly bobbing his head as if pleased with me. I suddenly realized, he was very pleased at my brave outburst. Raising his hands, the man put on an exaggerated sign of defeat which I wasn't sure was meant to praise my heroics or to humiliate my uncle's cowardice. He said, "Anything for my pretty boy!" For once, I didn't mind being called a pretty boy.

He instructed the very disappointed looking Claus to refill his glass and raised a toast to me, a salutation that my suddenly recomposed uncle was only too pleased to partake in. Beth had been spared once again. However, my aunt's fate clearly remained in limbo and the Colonel wasted no time getting back to matters at hand.

He offered the man a deal. Bent over the table, he could get fucked by the boy or take the young man to his matrimonial bed. With only minor hesitation, the sorry excuse of a man was on his feet, his trouser fronts stained and soaked in piss, leading the way with naked Claus trailing behind. The Colonel looked at me, his expression none other than that of baffled amusement; I knew then that his bluff had been called. He had no intentions of harming Beth or my aunt. However, without a shadow of doubt, my uncle was the Colonel's true intended victim to be defiled.

The colonel smirked and shrugged dumbly, as if to say, 'so be it' for the old man's unexpected choice of personal sacrifice. He templed his hands on his face and shook

his head in what had to be disbelief of events but he made no attempt to stop what uncle, himself, had selfishly set in motion. Although I found no humor at my aunt's expense, I couldn't help smile back at the man accepting that he, himself, had been humorously duped in his perverted scheme.

I was sad for everything, but thankful to him for sparing Beth whether or not she was in peril. I went to him to show my appreciation without being summoned. He took me in his arms and with his large paw wiped the few tears that I had shed, smiled, and hugged me close into him. Without a doubt, he was indeed a manipulating evil man, a sadist; however, I was obviously someone special to him.

I wondered what kind of man he might have once been or would become after the war, if ever that was to happen. Perhaps he would be a staunch school teacher, or even a strict headmaster but, in my very soul, I surmised that men like him thrived on their god-like power over life and death and that war would never end as long as such men existed. That same ominous power intrigued me nonetheless. I, for one, was going to survive, thanks to him.

His hand found its way inside my trousers. I had sucked in my gut to give him easier access to where he wanted to place it. I was sure he wouldn't be disappointed at the discovery already waiting for his warm hand to encompass. I thought about the bruises on my back and wood splinter chafing of my chest and thought about what he could, … no, what he WOULD do to those men involved and the power I then held over them, if it wasn't for Jon, that is. He would certainly become a casualty for his role. I worried about him at their mercy at the base camp, and so did Jon. I saw fear cloud what was his usual happy, shining bright blue eyes.

A commotion of the unknown, but quickly pictured scenario had erupted from down the hall. My uncle would be convincing his wife to take the young boy in her bed and make love to him. She would be defiant of her husband's perverted request until she learned of the stakes involved and she would then concede in order to protect her daughter. If only auntie knew how her loving husband had so easily bargained away the violation of her body to save his own ass.

The man returned wearing his robe, having sense enough to change in order to regain some dignity of having pissed himself while throwing a boy into bed with his wife, my aunt, in order to save himself. I hated him all over again; the Nazi's side arm secured inside a polished black leather holster was, thankfully, a temptation that I resisted.

The Colonel ignored the intrusion and continued to fondle my genitals. Seeing this, uncle once again sneered at me. Nothing had changed the pathetic man's opinion of me and I sneered back at him with loathing hatred. I wanted to open the Colonel's trousers and shamelessly show my uncle exactly how I influenced the favor that saved his daughter. He sunk his head down onto his chest; I saw his shame, because he knew it, too.

The liquor flowed once again, but in silence, not in jovial camaraderie. I sat on the man's lap, his hand continued to sensuously rub me and if Claus hadn't bounced into the kitchen looking proud as a peacock, I may well have ejaculated. I should have hated the teen for fucking my auntie who did nothing to deserve that humiliation, but the man sitting to my right, who again hung his head in shame seeing Claus, was solely responsible. Strangely, I didn't even blame the Nazi at the time, he was

destroying my uncle without putting a bullet through his head and that was good enough for me. Why the abomination remained a mystery to me.

The Colonel summoned Claus to his side, bent over and sniffed the boy's cock and looked back up at him with a shit-eating grin. I didn't understand that then, however I could smell the faint scent of my aunt's usual perfume emanating from him to know enough that he had indeed been intimate with her.

Claus accepted the vodka bottle from the man and took a long swig. He was officially now a man, and the Colonel made a big to do about it, even having the gumption to force Claus closer to the idiot so that he could offer him a sniff of his wife's vaginal secretions on the boy's genitals. Again, the Nazi's side-arm caught my eye when the coward stooped to accept the offer and raised his head smiling at the Nazi; he then lowered himself in degradation again for no other reason than throwing himself on the good graces of the Colonel, rest assured.

I truly believe that that display of utter weakness to impress only infuriated the man yet, he remained composed, however his eyes spoke volumes to the contrary. He laughed, and asked my uncle if maybe he wanted to suck the handsome boy's cock and taste his wife's flavor. Uncle bolted upward in his chair looking like death warmed over. He almost keeled over backward in order to distance himself from Claus. Miraculously he regained his balance.

The Colonel's devious smile never left his face as he kept staring at the disheveled, blubbering wimp. He wasn't finished yet. He ordered Claus to sit on the table spread eagle in front of my uncle's seat. If at all possible, the blood that had already left his head sucked the minuscule remainder from his bloodshot eyes, his green pupils dilated to a pale, deathly hue.

I never regarded Jon or any of the young boy soldiers as true Nazis. They were along for the ride going into war and blindly following without a choice. Claus, however, was tangibly different. He seemed to enjoy the charade of emasculating my uncle. He was now leaning back on his elbows. His cock slowly snaked alive in front of uncle anticipating its part in defiling his enemy or, more realistic, the enemy of the puppeteer that held the strings of supreme power. Claus was again proving himself a worthy Nazi, not yet inducted into the army, but making damn sure he had the Colonel's attention and influence. I may have been young and naive, but on that conclusion, I rested assured.

Part of me wanted to try and intervene and save my uncle, however, I hadn't done so on my aunt's behalf for reasons unknown, and the thought of my uncle with a cock in his mouth of a boy my age, nonetheless, appealed to me in a sadistic way. The German leaned back and crossed his arms, his eyes glared venomously at the recoiled, sobbing man who knew there would be no last minute reprieve. He had no selfish human bargaining chips left besides his daughter, which wouldn't have surprised me in the least, had he next betrayed her.

More than ever, the gun situated in its shiny polished case one foot from my hand anticipated that last ditch attempt to save himself had he made that bad choice, and without hesitation and having never fired a gun, I swear that I would have put him out of his misery in a heartbeat. I could also swear that the Nazi read my mind. Unholstering his Luger and emptying the ammunition completely before placing one

bullet in the chamber, he handed the weapon to Claus. I prayed to God Almighty to instill some sense of reasoning in the blithering man before he destroyed himself.

The reek of shit became putrid in the air, he must have shat himself the moment Claus put the barrel to his forehead. Without any illusion otherwise, I felt that Claus would have loved to make his first kill to brag along with his lost virginity back at camp. I didn't like him anymore. The same kindred-spirited boy that I played "I spy with my eye" in the jeep as we awaited the Colonel's return from business inside the inn. Not the same boy at all, not even close.

Uncle leaned forward following the guided direction of the gun. Claus' cock was rigid; the teen was obviously getting off on his control over events. Uncle appeared disgusted; turning his face to the side and sighed just as he was about to take Claus' cock that brushed his lips. He retched and puked on the floor, adding to the already disgusting stench of the kitchen that otherwise always smelled of baked goods or soup simmering on the stove.

Claus put the gun to uncle's head again. A click. He actually pulled the trigger. The Nazi laughed, uncle screamed, sweat poured down his face. I wanted it to end. The man had been tortured enough. There is a fine line between love and hate; I came to terms with that right then. He was my uncle, my family, a provider, a loving father to Beth. I glared up at the Colonel with tears flowing down my cheeks.

His amused expression turned serious, he reached over and took the gun from the trigger happy teenager and laid it on the table. The Luger remained a menacing sight lying beside Claus' thigh, still too close for comfort should the boy pick it up again and find the single deadly bullet in the chamber. However, once again the man had shown me mindful respect.

Uncle came to his senses delaying the inevitable no more. Reluctantly, he took the boy's cock head in his mouth; his beady eyes focused on me sprawled relaxed over the Nazi's lap and chest with his hand still inside my trousers. I smiled back at him and for added effect placed my hands over and around the man's neck as he lowered himself to affectionately kiss me on top of my head. The message was clear as if I had said it aloud, 'you're on your own now; I ain't coming to your aid any longer, you swine!' His robe had fallen open and his cock resembled a dead mouse between his legs.

I felt the Colonel's manhood lengthen and began to lasciviously gyrate of my butt over it. The Colonel's hand moved forward, his fingers prodded my rectum in desperation to enter me. It was painful; the sergeant's large appendage had damaged me more than I had attributed to the lingering soreness that remained well after he raped me.

The Colonel fucked me with at least two fingers; his breathing was labored as he watched his sadistic handiwork unravel on the dinner table. It had excited the man well beyond what I thought were his intentions carrying out the ordeal. He screamed at my uncle and threatened to sodomize him with the broomstick conveniently resting near the door if he didn't put more effort into pleasing the boy who, in turn, had a handful of the man's hair forcing his head up and down.

Mental warfare was as much a part of the Nazi arsenal as guns, tanks and rocket launchers to intimidate and weaken their enemies. I believed at the time that the slobbering, blithering man would rather have taken a bullet over the humiliation. He

couldn't breathe; mucus flowed from his nostrils as he struggled. I don't know what made me blurt out in Polish that the Nazi might go easier on him more if he cooperated. I even said that the man himself liked to fellate boys. I had no idea how that was at all logical, other than maybe appealing to the man's latent homosexuality and his own preference in boys given what he had tried to do to me in the garden the other night.

Claus, of course, understood the language of my daring advice but, thankfully, didn't betray me. Cautiously he eased his hold on my uncle's hair as if to demonstrate good faith, allowing my uncle to at least gasp for air. Uncle rolled his eyes upward to look at Claus and a weak nod barely noticeable unless one was wise to the conspiracy, understood that a pact had been made.

My uncle wasn't as dumb as I thought and heeded my advice. He hadn't touched Claus with his hands until then. He reached up and gingerly took the cock in hand but he hesitated using the other until the liquor and fear, his hand found the boy's testicles. Claus released his grip on uncle's head and settled back on his elbows to watch himself being pleasured.

The Nazi certainly noticed the drastic change in the man's attitude from resistance to submissiveness. The uncertainty remained that he could very well have become angry being made a mockery of what he may have consider a failed effort to demean his enemy. What I didn't anticipate would be for the Nazi to crane a glance between uncle's legs as if that would determine the final outcome of the charade. I couldn't bring myself to look; instead, I stared at the menacing broomstick standing in the corner, fully aware of my own burning rectum and held my breath.

When the Colonel picked up his gun from the table and stared at it, my blood ran cold. Uncle's eyes widened in fear. He sarcastically asked the petrified man if he really liked Claus' beautiful Aryan-bred body. The question hung heavily in the air, either response could have been deadly. The Nazi was still playing the role of aggressor, still in control of events. He was certainly no fool.

Suddenly, he erupted in a roaring belly laugh, holstered his gun and motioning Claus off the table as he placed me on my feet. The Colonel then stood and without a word, picked up the lantern continuing to laugh as he led Claus and me to the bedroom leaving the bewildered, broken man to dwell in his own shit and shame in darkness.

The Colonel's planned sleeping arrangements did not come as a complete surprise. The moment we left the Inn and headed to the farm, I was certain that the man had sexual motives in mind. It had also become apparent that the man had spared my uncle further demise for no other reason than that of his hasty anticipation of having us two young boys in his bed. All the fear, angst and sex that he instilled, even at my aunt's expense as an added bonus, perversely fuelled his libido for the main event, perverse foreplay to him.

The Colonel ordered Claus to undress me. I stood before the boy who seated himself on the bed with a gleam in his eyes and a ghostly smile as he unbuttoned and removed my shirt. His erection stood firm pointing up at me from his spread thighs and his testicles splayed over the edge of the mattress. His hands caressed my chest and under my arms, an affectionate gesture I did not expect, causing goose bumps and tiny shivers wherever his soft hands roamed.

Moments later, the Colonel sat beside Claus, naked except for his trousers at his knees until he pulled off his boots and stepped out of them. His own erection stood proud and full, the shiny fluid beaded from the slit which he scooped up with a finger and smeared over my lips.

Claus had managed to open my trousers and slid them down my hips showing some amusement when my cock sprang free and nearly hit him in the nose. He lifted each foot freeing the denim and tossed them aside. His gentle hands massaged my buttocks and genitals and with a smile said something flattering to the man before leaning forward and taking me deep in his mouth. I could feel the hot breath from his nostrils on the base of my cock.

I was at odds with myself trying to make sense of what I fully anticipated would be me being used perhaps by only the man but, more likely, by both of them. Claus had to have been humoring the man, I reasoned, because there were no instructions given other than to strip me. He was seducing me on his own volition, a boy his own age.

When the boy invited me between his legs I fell to my knees in lust to taste him, but first, I glanced at the man for some kind of approval. The Colonel seemed pleased and nodded, his manhood flowing in juice as a result of his own hand contently stroking his meat as he ogled the scene being played out in front of him.The look on his face giving way to fervency in allowing Claus to take charge. If I didn't know better, perhaps the man was revealing a certain weakness in character that Claus was somehow attuned to.

Claus maneuvered me onto the bed like a rag doll and climbed on top of me with his cock in my face and mine quickly sucked into his mouth. The Colonel lay beside us, his head at our midriffs and I saw him no more once Claus lowered his pelvis and my tongue caught his crown guiding the way into my mouth. The raspy breath heard could only be that of the man between utterances of 'beautiful boys' over and over.

A stirring shook the bed a long while later in what had to have been the Colonel. A sudden blow to the back of my head caused me to open my mouth and roll my eyes back; the man had inadvertently kneed my cranium while positioning himself behind Claus, The man's salivating-like cock that at that obtuse angle appeared larger than I knew it to be towered menacing above his scrotum. It was so tight to his groin that the plump orbs within bugged at me like the eyes of a very large scary insect.

I took the liberty of spreading the firm milky white cheeks and the bright pink folds that I knew to be the intended target came into view briefly as it swallowed the thick appendage inch by inch. The excess accordion-like skin gathered down the shaft to finally mass near the base. Heavy panting from the man and guttural groans from Claus that pleasantly reverberated the length of my cock that remained idly lodged between his lips.

Once the man's cock had settled into the depths of Claus' ass and he had adjusted to it, Claus composed himself and began to fellate me with renewed vigor while the man fucked him. Beginning slowly but ever increasing the momentum, I watched the actual mechanics of the performance from below with awe. I had no real role of my own except to lay still with my mouth tight and concave cheeks sucking the cock that had a forced pistoning momentum of its own.

Claus' sleek cock spasmed twice before he jettisoned forth a succession of gushes of semen that lightly skimmed the back of my palate and pooled over my tongue. I

sensed the taste almost immediately as unique but very close to Jon's in bitter sweetness.

The Colonel growled like a mad dog and collapsed atop Claus who, in turn, collapsed on top of me. My nose was firmly planted between his taut testis and base of his shaft that was soaked wet and was pungent smells of body odor and feces. I struggled with the weight. Finally, I was able to turn my head with effort and dared to breathe the vile air.

What was almost funny was that the Colonel had fallen asleep. Loud snores assured that security as Claus wiggled his way free from beneath the man as I worked to free myself. Claus took the lantern and leading the way, I followed him outside the rear door in need of a pee myself. I thought about telling him about the Colonel and I peeing out the window but quickly dismissed the option feeling it would be another violation of my auntie.

We pissed mid-yard and, afterward, Claus made his way to the rain barrel. I showed him a bar of soap. The water in the rain barrel was used by the family for quick hygiene. Claus and I poured the water over each other in bucket fulls. We both felt invigorated in the stifling heat as we thoroughly cleansed our naked bodies. He next wanted to visit the barn to check on the newborn calf and its mother. Finding all well, we sat on a bale of hay and lingered staring at the newborn and remembering the Colonel's exhibited knowledge and kindness towards animals, as ironic as that struck me at the time.

Claus made it clear that he had a need to talk and I listened intently. He knew the Colonel well, in fact, intimately well. His guardian was a whore who ran a brothel in Berlin. A very unique brothel it was too in that not only did it cater the likes of pretty girls to those military men that desired them, but secretly provided boys for Nazi officials who would be escorted by a woman from the bar area to upstairs without raising the suspicion of others to his true pedophile tendencies. Claus was one of those orphan boys forced into prostitution by his own caregiver.

He looked as Aryan as any boy could conceivably be, except for the oddity of his circumcised penis. Why and when he was trimmed was beyond his knowledge. In fact, he told me that he was the son of a German Ambassador first posted in England for many years, and then stationed in Poland where Claus spent much of his childhood, easily mastering the language as he did his English in order to fit in with his peers.

His parents were murdered by unknowns. Some claimed that the Polish partisans had committed the crime while others, talking in conspiratorial tones, suggested that perhaps the Gestapo had a hand in it. There were no other living family members available to take care of him so he was placed in a German orphanage and 'rescued' at age twelve by Fraulein Mitzer, a widow, who had a very kind soul. His leaving the orphanage went unquestioned by the state run facility who welcomed almost anyone willing to take the burden of so many displaced children off their hands.

The Colonel blatantly took the Aryan looking boy from the brothel. Obviously his looks were his saving grace; to the naked eye he simply didn't belong there like some peasant child. Because the Gestapo had seized and sealed all the files on his parents, there was no way to prove the boy's lineage. To dig too deeply was to cause the spotlight of an enquiry and no-one in their right mind wanted to stir the Gestapo

hornet's nest. Claus became the Colonel's personal valet living in the man's home. Not much really changed for young Claus because the Colonel used him by night and shared him with distinguished guests whenever asked for.

However, Claus soon found out that he wasn't the only boy in the Colonel's harem. Periodically, boys were brought home and he was forced to have sex with them as the man watched. Claus was loyal, earning a special spot in the hardened man's heart. When war came along Claus was brought along as a boy whore for a chosen few officials with privileged access to him. He had lied in saying he was a member of the Nazi Youth. He was unable to join the elitist organization, although in his opinion, he was inherently entitled. Perhaps his father, the diplomat, had somehow shamed the party or had not agreed with party policies and made the mistake of speaking out, I thought, but didn't convey my thoughts to Claus. Why else, I also asked myself, would his heritage have been smothered by bureaucracy?

Back in the very cramped bed, Claus offered me a blowjob and I selfishly accepted; the night had been most excitingly raunchy and I had yet to be relieved. He was VERY talented, years of experience, his very survival depended on it. I wondered if the Colonel held my fate to be a whore-boy for powerful military men to enjoy. I immediately put the thought out of my head. It was a thought I would dwell on later but first, I intended to enjoy the moments of bliss until Claus would take me to orgasm.

CHAPTER VI: LOVE IN TWO FORMS

I lay in a corner of the bed and tried to make sense. Claus was strange. I wanted to like him, and did, when he wasn't under the influence of the Colonel. He had an evil streak no different than that of the man who ironically rescued him from the brothel only to make him his private whore-boy that he indiscriminately loaned to other men that the Colonel either wanted a favor from or, perhaps, even to wage blackmail against.

Claus had mentioned that so many men came to his bedroom and, when the men left, he would report to the Colonel the exact details of what sexual acts the men were into. Claus claimed that some men only wanted to receive oral or perform anal sex whereas others would perform oral on him or get fucked by him. Those, the bottoms or submissives as they were called, were the men the Colonel was most interested in. The Nazi's obviously had a double standard on what constituted homosexuality. Without a doubt, the Colonel was a secret homosexual himself; still, knowledge is power, the hypocrisy of it all notwithstanding. His motives were a mystery to my young naive friends who could not make sense of adult power games. That information only reinforced my theory that sex was indeed a double edged sword; on the one edge pleasure and on the other, power.

I thought again of the innocent children's game of 'eye-spy' that Claus and I had played in the jeep. Then I remember him holding a gun to uncle's head and tempting fate by pulling the trigger. I saw him anxious to molest my cousin but, ever the opportunist, he settled instead on fucking my aunt when she was offered up as the sacrificial lamb. I wanted to lay blame on the Nazi for this latter atrocity, but couldn't. I could only blame him for not interceding to protect the woman who fed him, albeit, she ended up a pawn and, unfortunately, collateral damage in his mind.

Claus had been very kind to me sexually. He could easily have taken advantage of me in the barn away from his handler. That thought had occurred to me when he wanted to check on the animals; instead he petted the beasts and uttered soothing words to them as he told me his sad life's story.

The offer of oral sex without expectation of reciprocation took me by surprise. Claus didn't stand to profit anything by it, on the contrary, perhaps even risked depreciating himself to me considering he wasn't being forced in any way. I mulled that over and over in my mind because there was something relevant that had to do with my relationship with the Colonel. Could the boy have detected exactly what my

uncle had perceived, and that what I was beginning to sense was the Colonel's odd benevolence toward his pretty boy? there certainly was no obvious display of jealousy but here clearly was an adversary that Claus reasoned was one to be reckoned with for whatever his reasons?

My final thoughts before dozing off were those of an immature fourteen year old boy stepping off a train, who was without a doubt intellectually stunted well below his physical age by pampering, well-off, protective parents; to that of a fourteen year old boy suddenly forced well beyond his years into a harsh reality of using his wits to survive.

I hated that damn rooster. I never got used to its annoying daily revelry that woke up everything avian and animal which, in turn, became an ill-tuned chorus of noise, all complaining to be fed. In the city I had had to put up with the clippity-clop of horse hooves on the cobblestone as street vendors made their way to set up their kiosks but, thankfully, at least at a reasonable hour after sunrise. Without a doubt, if ever a rooster found its way into the city it would be hunted down and strangled, or at the very least had its head chopped off, for disturbing the peace and would have ended up as the main ingredient in a soup simmering somebody's stove.

Usually what followed after the trumpeting call of the rooster was a clatter of pots and pans in the kitchen with my aunt preparing breakfast, the aroma being enough to drag me out of bed a short time later. Beth would be seated in her nightgown endlessly nattering about whatever was on her mind at the moment, her small boobies hinted under the material which was getting a tad too small for her. Nobody but me seemed to notice the petite perky nipples exposed every once in a while depending on her movements that I was mildly curious about and I would eventually beat myself up with guilt thinking about them when I played with myself.

My uncle would be busy reciting and writing out chores for me to perform over and above my usual daily doldrums. It seemed as if work on the farm was never ending and I wondered how he managed the upkeep before I arrived. Sometimes my aunt would intervene and allow Beth and I to go for a late afternoon swim in the nearby river, me clad in an old pair of my uncle's trousers that she cut off at the knees and that I had to tie with a rope. Beth would be in proper ladies bathing attire.

There was to be no breakfast that morning. The damn rooster could wail all he wanted but the small house was in a shroud of silence except for the stirring of three naked forms, none of whom bothered with the bed clothes rumpled at the foot of the bed. The air was hot and damp, our bodies clammy and the unique spicy redolence of masculinity was not unpleasing to the senses.

The Colonel rolled onto his back. Not having to be encouraged and without trepidation, Claus and I shared the man's cock and balls with mutual moxie, perhaps with rival enthusiasm, even. The whore-boy stole the competition by delving below the man's testicles that he held high above as he grossly laved the nether regions, his face glimmering with slick saliva. In unison, I mouthed and masturbated the very ecstatic, whimpering man, feeling pleased at myself for being a zealous contributor.

I couldn't believe my eyes when, as if on cue, Claus raised the man's legs and impaled himself in the man and fucked him vigorously. The Colonel yelped and immediately I tasted his warm tangy semen which gushed forth as the eruption rattled the man's body. His barrage of incomprehensible, throaty hoarse words I felt were

well-meaning. He had grabbed my hair in his fist but only as a reactionary impulse. Claus was not long until his own body shuddered and he mouthed a mix of English and Polish profanities. I envied him and began to second guess my inflated foolish notions that I held some kind of place over his homosexual boy-whore.

As we dressed, the Colonel finally noticed the bruises on my back and chafed chest as I knew he would eventually. I discarded my concocted story of falling on some rocks. when Claus was asked to interpret the cause. I saw the exchange between the man and boy as an opportunity to find out where I stood in the man's graces when Claus revealed that I had been raped by two of his soldiers. The man appeared ready to explode, the red and purple veins in his neck and forehead appeared quite pronounced as he seethed, digesting the unfathomable.

He regained his composure and asked more questions of who, where and what in a nonchalant demeanor while he primped himself after getting into his uniform while standing in front of the mirror. I regretted my selfish stupidity when the inevitable question was asked as to the whereabouts of Jon in his dutiful assignment as caregiver during my alleged rape. I hadn't thought that out and foolishly put Jon in harm's way.

I fumbled for an explanation to protect Jon and claimed that one man was a Sergeant, far superior to Jon. I told the Colonel that this man, who threatened him into silence and turning a blind eye, even though Jon had pleaded with the man to believe that I was the Colonel's valet which only seemed to compel the sergeant's desire even more, I was relaying a negative opinion of the Sergeant to his ultimate commander. I lied through my teeth to protect Jon. .

As we passed through the kitchen, the curtain was open revealing an empty bed where Beth had been sleeping. Obviously, my uncle and aunt were taking no chances having the madman and his young accomplices still about the house that they perceived as a legitimate threat. After we had gone to bed, they had removed Beth to the safety of their bedroom where the family remained cowering in fear until they heard the screen door slam and the jeep start-up. They needn't have worried because the Colonel was preoccupied with something far more important than breakfast being served.

Claus drove the vehicle which, once again, irked me. Amateur at best, he fumbled with the gears which required the Colonel to direct him. Jon had taught me well. I sulked in the rear seat. Halfway to base, the Colonel told Claus to stop the jeep and instructed me to drive, and I gloated, mastering every gear without a single metallic complaint.

I had to get to Jon to collaborate my lies in case the Colonel interrogated him,. I was certain it would happen sooner rather than later. I was scared to death that I would be caught in a lie and that both, Jon and I, would pay our own price. Him, I suspected would face a firing squad. Me, falling from the man's grace as a liar, even if only to protect Jon, would be subjected to becoming another boy-whore just like Claus.

I needn't have worried. The moment we stepped into the Colonel's office, the major stood, saluted and with a grave seriousness relayed something to the Colonel. Claus was perplexed and on the verge of tears. He told me that Jon had been severely beaten during the night and was in the infirmary under intensive care. The naked boy

was discovered at dawn by two mechanics in the munitions compound. He had been sodomized with a metal pipe.

The Colonel glared at me and the look on his face told me that he believed every word I had said. Through Claus, he reaffirmed the time and location of my assault, a detailed description of the men involved and then screamed orders at the bewildered man sitting behind the desk to get duty rosters for the previous day. The man flipped pages in a binder and had the information the Colonel demanded, the grid patrol location narrowed down to ten sentries.

Almost dislocating my shoulder, the Colonel grabbed my arm and pulling me, stormed us out the door. Claus and the man I served each morning were in hot pursuit. The enlisted men's mess was our destination. A hundred or so men and teens were eating breakfast and became silent, in wonder, at the sight of the Colonel leading me by the neck aisle by aisle. No one had to tell me why.

I spotted the younger man first; he looked me in the eye and started to cry shaking uncontrollably. He was the one who pointed out my aggressor seated not five chairs away looking like death warmed up. He immediately recognized me, his eyes were wide and white with blood webbing the tiny veins with his jaw flapping because he was unable to form words.

There would be no court martial, no trial, no plea for forgiveness. The Colonel upholstered his side arm and shot the man between the eyes. I had never seen such gore. His head exploded, blood and grey matter splashed everywhere splattering the men unfortunate enough to have been close by.

He abruptly turned his attention to the younger man stricken in fear attempting to flee from his chair and before I could tell the truth to spare the man's life, the back of his head turned into a crimson mush and he fell to the floor. I felt horrible. He never raped or beat me, I lied and a young man was executed for it. I would have nightmares over that for the rest of my lifetime.

The Colonel holstered his gun, put his arm around my neck and walked me away from the carnage. I was crying, sobbing heavily, telling him the truth of the other man's limited involvement that he didn't understand. Claus, hearing what I was saying, grabbed my arm and sneered. He told me to shut up as he was escorting me along with the Colonel away from the nightmarish scene.

After leaving the dining hall, we went to visit Jon in the field hospital. He was unrecognizable as the handsome young teen that he was; on the verge of death. I held his lifeless hand and bawled. I had an earlier premonition that he was in danger, I was remorseful for not having told the Colonel earlier. Jon died later that day.

When the news was delivered to the Colonel, he was working at his desk and I was sitting nearby, not really bored but indifferent to my surroundings, lost in thought. Claus had been dismissed earlier. The Colonel's face turned sad as he told everyone of Jon's passing and, when the messenger had left, he beckoned me to him, hoisting me on to his lap, wrapped me in an embrace. As God is my maker, it was the very first time that I ever saw the Colonel let down his protective guard as he cried with me.

Our grieving moment was soon interrupted by a knock on the door. A soldier entered and saluted. He said something to which the Colonel became alert and immediately ushered me back to my chair. Claus entered and smiled at me warmly as he took a stance beside the Colonel. One by one the ten kidnapped boys were

ushered into the office. The Colonel was extremely friendly to each one of them showing them a photo album. With Claus interpreting on behalf of the Colonel, the boys picked out photos of the officials they had spent with the night before and described what they had done with the men. Knowledge was power and the Colonel was again on a fishing expedition to gather Intel on some very powerful men within the Nazi party.

It was business as usual, Jon's death might have been forgotten by the Colonel but it was not forgotten nor would it ever be forgotten by me. In that brief moment in time when we knew each other, I had loved him. The Colonel assigned me another babysitter, an older, no nonsense type man. There would be no more joy riding or picnics on the beach. He ordered the guards to take eight of the boys down to the beach; obviously, the Nazi still had use for them. The two boys he held back were around my age. He told my chaperon to take me, Claus, and the two lads to the commissary for lunch and then to the lake for a bath.

Alex and Damon were just as baffled as to what was going on as I was. If Claus knew what the Colonel's motives were for holding them back, he wasn't saying. Neither boy was blond nor blue eyed. Alex had long jet-black hair, Damon was a brunette. I supposed that they were handsome, perhaps more so than the others, remembering that they were all selected and taken from the orphanage based on their appealing features in order to satisfy the lust of the men at the Inn.

The only indication of the eight other boys was a pile of clothing in the sand where I assumed they were stripped and bathed before being taken into the woods. A handful of soldiers were presently bathing and shaving and I guessed there were plenty more hidden away beyond the tree line. Alex and Damon had no idea how lucky they were and neither Claus nor I saw the need to clue them into the whereabouts of their friends whose clothes were strangely left behind. For some reason, I don't know why, but I saw a shred of hope in the fact that no bonfire was being fueled by trousers, shirts and shoes.

Our guardian, Heir Personality, watched us strip. Claus teasingly began a sexy strip-tease dance while lasciviously staring down the Nazi. I found the whole act hilarious and joined him in leading-on the man who was standing with his rifle butt hiding the strain clearly evident in his trousers. Alex and Damon couldn't possibly be wise to the effect that four naked boys' were having on the horny man. They were shocked that we dare make a fool of the soldier. We had absolutely no fear of the man We were the Colonel's valets and he knew it. Nothing would have pleased him more than to throttle us and haul our sorry asses into the trees.

I was enjoying debasing the soldier far too much, dropped to my knees and seductively motioned him to come closer for a blowjob. Claus bent over and spread his cheeks, begging the man to fuck him. The defeated man cursed us rather loudly, told us to hurry and bathe, then turned and headed for shade. We roared in laughter when Claus yelled after him to have a good wank and gave the frustrated man a solemn warning that jerking off would make him go blind.

We didn't hurry to bathe, much to the soldier's exasperation. He finally gave up shouting at us.

We frolicked and jostled each other in a game of shoulder-riding wrestling to bring down the opponent. For a long while I didn't think about Jon. We were simply boys

being boys and, as far as we were concerned, the rest of the world's evil doers could fuck-off and wait!

Marching the Nazi goose-step back to camp, we continued to ride the poor man's wits. Each time he swiveled his head to ensure his goslings were all in tow, we would stop and salute and sound off, "Heil Hitler!" We knew we were driving him fucking nuts so continued to do it; right through the security gate, to the amusement of the sentries. We kept it up all the way to the Colonel's office. The Colonel was none too pleased at the soldier for his tardiness. The man tried to explain our disobedience but the Colonel shouted at him and berated him for his incompetence at not being able to discipline a group of boys. He was dismissed in shame. After he was gone, the Colonel looked at us with scorn, then smiled and chuckled.

It was when he loaded us into the jeep and headed the way home that I realized his intentions. Somehow, I knew for a fact that his agenda was that I was going to inevitably have sex with Alex, Damon and of course, again with Claus. The thought wasn't unappealing to me in the least. The unappealing thought was for my uncle, aunt and cousin and their welfare. I dreaded another night of angst and worry.

I needn't have worried. Missing from the front yard when we arrived was my uncle's beaten old truck. No chickens scurried out of harm's way when we drove up to the house. The old nag wasn't at the fence bobbing her head and neighing a friendly welcome in hopes of an apple treat. Nor were the pigs in their pen rolling in mud. I could have sworn I'd seen Bertha and her baby in the neighbor's field up the road, a fact that was verified when I peaked in the empty barn.

The family had obviously fled their home unable to endure another night of their unwelcome guest. They had taken anything of value and, ironically, had left me behind. I was abandoned to my fate by my own family. I felt hurt. I felt insignificant yet, a part of me, was relieved that they were somewhere safe. I pictured Beth crying after me, my aunt's guilt in betraying her sister, and my uncle's good-riddance of me.

The wooden swastika that hung on their door and protected them lay on the porch burnt, my uncle's first bout of heroics before running away. It was an act of sacrilegious vandalism that would insult the Nazi. Somehow I knew it was the stupidest mistake the squirrel could ever have made. To his credit, uncle left an unopened bottle of vodka in the pantry. The Colonel beamed in delight at the sight of me holding it up in triumph. It was a gesture that I thought sure would calm the man's mood. He didn't seem all that put out by this particular turn of events; he was probably only disappointed that auntie would not be serving a nice meal that evening.

Claus and I decided we would make up for that, or at least we hoped as much. We prepared a large chicken for roasting and peeled up potatoes, carrots and celery. After dicing up the vegetables, we tossed them into the roasting pan with a good helping of butter and a variety of unknown spices found in the pantry. With the oven stoked and wood added, we all sat at the table and drank vodka hoping for the best.

Alex and Damon were relaxed. Little did they know that they were on the menu for dessert. The Colonel fancied each boy sitting on a leg. The conversation tables were turned, Claus was officially designated as the interpreter and it wasn't until then that I realized the similarities of the Polish and German dialects if one's ear was tuned into it and could grasp the not too distant analogies. Or hell, maybe the vodka spoke a unified language.

My first experience under the influence of alcohol left me giddy, and then melancholy. I fought back tears thinking of Jon. I had loved him, and he had loved me. Confusingly wrong as it was so right, I took solace in knowing that Jon never wanted to be a soldier. Oh Yes! My Jon walked the walk and talked the talk but there wasn't an evil bone in his body no matter what the doctrine was that was being shoved down his throat. He was a misfit in an army of misfits, all hiding their true individualities, bastardized as they were at the merciless hands of already brainwashed men.

Jon would go home in a wooden box as a hero, killed in the line of duty, returned with ceremony to his grieving parents. They would look at photo albums and reminisce. Jon's birthdays, the Christmas' they had spent and family vacations they had taken together. They would remember his graduation from the Nazi Youth, all so handsomely decked out in his uniform, a man at last, ready to serve his misguided country's belief in racial superiority.

Yes, I was well beyond my fourteen years. I also knew that I was expected to partake in the second rape of the two giggly orphan boys being tickled in the lap of a very devious man. This was the very same devious man that put a bullet in the heads of men that harmed me and who, without a doubt, killed Jon. If that didn't prove that he loved me, I didn't know what would.

Dinner was passable. The bird carcass was picked clean and the Colonel raved about our culinary skills. It was I that sat upon his lap after dinner. His tongue would occasionally swipe my neck and ears while, his hand seldom left my crotch. Only he and I knew the excitement that his petting had instigated hidden beneath the material.

He was noticeably relaxed and content within his company of boys. It was a jovial side of him never seen before because he never lost his pearly white smile. He could and did mysterious tricks with playing-cards and coins. How could it not be amazing finding a few of those coins down my pants earning me a squeeze of my shaft while he was down there. We learned that his grandfather was a magician and taught him the slight-of-hand while he was growing up and spending summers with the man on his farm. His knowledge in doctoring Bertha's breech-calf was now understood, not that I had given it much thought before then, but it was another feather in his cap in my ever-growing good opinion of him.

The master bedroom with the large feather-stuffed mattress was the logical choice of venue made by the Colonel. Alex and Damon looked on in confusion as the Colonel, Claus and I began to undress. Claus was blunt, coldly informing the two boys that sex was expected of them no different than with whichever man they had spent the previous night with. He then followed up by telling them about the fate of their clothes-less peers and about how the Colonel took favor upon them. He warned them not to disappoint the kind man and do whatever they were told without hesitation or he would be forced to strangle the life out of them. Claus said all this with a callous smile that frightened even me. The evil Claus was back, the henchman of the devil himself.

CHAPTER VII: LEARNING MORE TECHNIQUES

No one doubted that Claus was in charge. I, for one, suspected that he had a great deal of previous experience befriending, propositioning and coercing boys into his master's bed. Alex and Damon would be relatively easy. After all, I surmised, they had already been with men and were not much of a challenge for dear old Claus. He didn't really need his arbitrary threats to convince them of what was clearly in their best interest to comply.

Personally, I wished there were three less boys in the room. I would have loved to have had the man for myself to be made love to and, in return, make love to. I was truly jealous at having to share him with others. The man who proved his love to me in the most extreme ways; yes, the gruesome rape and beating of another comrade was most definitely dealt with as a capital offense and justified according to standard military protocol; however I preferred my starry-eyed belief that the Colonel merely used the unfortunate secondary event as an excuse to avenge me.

Thinking about it, I would rather have seen him sodomize the bastards with the same metal pipe that they used on Jon and then shot them dead. I might have even suggested the same in hindsight. I had convinced myself that the younger soldier was equally responsible in the beating and sadistic mutilation. The thought appeased my guilt laden conscience for falsely implicating him in my own rape. I would never forget the look of terror on his face when he saw me for the second time in his life and in the company of the Colonel, no less. I was the link to what may very well have been an unsolved crime. His futile attempt to escape convinced me of his guilt.

The Colonel stripped quickly and lay on the bed. I wasted no time in placing myself between his muscular thighs before anyone else could. He was already erect and I realized that I was the one unwittingly setting the precedent of expectations had traumatized Alex and Damon needed any validation of Claus' blunt edict as definitely being no prankish antic.

Claus lay the boys side by side and gave each one's flaccid cock equal attention. Who could resist Claus' oral ability. He was soon bringing Alex and Damon to erection whether they wanted it or not. I was already aware, after seeing him naked at the beach, that Alex was behind in pubescent development, having only a slight growth of pubic hair just sprouting along the base of his smallish, circumcised cock. Damon, on the other hand, had a full crop of hair.

However his testicles, thighs and legs were void of fur. His dick was thick and meaty looking, not overly long, but in a manly proportion in every way. Despite his erection, the foreskin slightly covered his dark pink knob, coddling it in some absurd, protective way.

The Colonel's cock grew stiffer in my mouth, his scrotum tightened in my palm, the excess skin which needed to allow a few more millimeters of inflation of his shaft slowly receded. He stopped my hand from masturbating him and held my head down not wanting any stimulation other than the stationary sucking of two-thirds of his cock. True to Claus' word, the man was indeed an 'obserwator:'—Polish for voyeur. He sat up with his back against the wall to observe the eroticism, all the while, twirling my hair in his fingers.

Claus moved the boys into a haphazard three way circular formation. Alex was sucking Claus; who was sucking Damon; who was sucking Alex. A wet, sloppy gurgle resonated not unlike a crèche of toddlers dozing and imbibing on their bottles or thumbs. Perhaps they were not overly keen participants, nonetheless, I was pleased that the two orphans were at least submissive and cooperative. I hated to ponder the alternative measures that Claus surely had in his arsenal of persuasive tactics.

I strained my eyes to look up at the man and saw his smugness. He appeared satisfied that Claus was competently directing and staging the sex show for his one-man audience. I wondered if the boy had ever put on such boy-orgy performances center floor for multiple viewers at parties hosted by the Colonel. Rational thought soon prevailed and I laughed at myself for even weighing the foolish odds of that as not a fictional scenario. I don't think that anyone can literally take a boy's innocence, his own logic of mind is sharper than thought once he tunes into life. Claus was a whore-boy with a survival mission and nothing he could do would shock me any longer. I understood that I was really no different than he was simply because, my life depended on it.

It was my first introduction into anal sex, me on the other end, that is. Claus squatted above Alex's head and held the boys legs up and spread them wide. With a devilish grin, he looked at me, his eyes beckoning. The Colonel shielded me from him. I was expected to fuck Alex who looked at me with sad puppy eyes knowing full well what fate lay ahead.

I had flashbacks of earlier that day on the beach where we were innocent boys playing innocent boy games and making insolent, disrespectful fun of our guardian that would have earned me a severe belt whipping by my father. It also reminded me of the one time I called my mother a bitch for not allowing me to go out and play because my homework couldn't somehow wait while an important championship game of street soccer was scheduled for that same, inopportune time. My bare bum was raw and very sore for days.

I wanted to prove myself worthy in the eyes of the Colonel, as well as, Claus. I looked away from Alex's disquieted face as he stared back at me between the vee of his secured legs as I vantaged myself peering down at my pink, puckered target. Claus straddled Alex so as he was almost face to face with me. His right hand aimed his cock and without hesitation, it was accepted by the boy's mouth.

Taking his time, Claus sensuously applied the petroleum gel as he caressed my cock, his hand giving me that added stimulative incentive, the grin on his face

malicious and, with a wink of encouragement, his fingers guided me to the rim but he didn't let go until I was deep-rooted enough to take matters under my own volition.

The tightness of Alex's ass smothered my cock as I literally strained to worm deeper. It was slightly painful spreading his resistance until I slid forth with only moderate muscle constriction thereafter. I was somewhat gratified that Claus' body, fucking Alex's throat as he was, prevented me from seeing Alex's face. I didn't think that I would be able to bear looking him in the eye. Little did I know at the time that Alex was a virgin. No man had taken him the night before as I had assumed. The only activities he performed for the man last night was to polish his boots and give him a blowjob.

Claus went down on Alex's small limp cock. However, his effort to inspire any apparent stimulus was futile and he quickly gave up. He moved across the bed and climbed onto Damon who's man-size cock needed no urging nor did he require any instruction on what to do with the goods dangling over his face. Damon was wise to his role and showed no adversity proving his willingness but, I detected a certain fear of Claus about him, I knew that fear well.

Alex had been crying. Tears stains tracked down his face from his puffy, red eyes. He lay like a rag doll; his legs that I held up by his calves were like rubber. The Colonel watched like a hawk, stone-faced and stroking his cock. I sensed that he was judging me; waiting amused to see if I would follow through with abusing the whimpering boy. Our eyes met for only a second or two, during which, a single nod so faint that I might have missed it, implied his will on me.

Instantly, I no longer cared for Alex's well-being. I only wanted to impress the Colonel. Alex screamed when I drove my hips forward and impaled him. A sense of power overwhelmed me. A few days ago, I would never have even squashed a bug and here I found myself deliberately hurting a boy. And, within the previous hours, I had sentenced two men to death by a simple point of my finger. I hardly cared when Claus screamed at Alex to shut up, muzzled the boy's mouth with his hand, and returned his attention to fellating Damon.

Unable to look at Alex, I watched the erotic scene being played out beside me as I fucked away like a dog on a bitch in heat. We were rocking the entire bed; the frame and springs both complaining loudly over the muffled whimpers of Alex. The Colonel leaned across Alex's torso to graze momentarily on the boy's genitals before lifting his head and opening his mouth, a sultry gesture that needed no clarification. My cock spiked and balls churned at the thought that his focus was to finish and taste me when he could have easily joined Claus and Damon whose genitals held much more of a masculine beauty than my own.

I didn't dare look down when I uncoupled from Alex. Instead, I stayed staring at the ceiling instead with my eyes closed fearing the possibility that filth on my cock might sway my man's amorous desire. The moist warmth of his mouth soon replaced the heat of Alex's snug cocoon. Unable to endure much more stimuli, I succumbed to a full body orgasm which I felt from head to toe and I howled like a wolf at the moon. Embarrassing though it might have been, but I ignored, Claus and Alex gawking at me, their cocks slick and not too distant from their jaws and lip. They were in awe of the cries of a lunatic whose both hands were clawing at the Colonel's blond

head, his nose mashed against my pubes and the day's growth from his whiskers on his chin scratching my scrotum.

Satisfied that I was tapped dry, the man rolled over the top of Alex to examine Damon's unique meat. Amused, he unsheathed the purple knob of its foreskin and brought it back up well over the crown to envelop a good portion of his outstretched tongue. It was truly fascinating how, at it being fully erect, excess skin remained ample by a couple of inches.

I could only imagine that the foreskin phenomena must have happened on other occasions with other boys since Claus began a vigorous pumping of Damon's shaft whilst the Colonel held fast on the head and tongue-fucked the sheath. Together, they brought Damon to heights that the lad had surely never experienced before. I envied him the attention and his blissful comportment until he could take no more of the agony.

Semen spilled from around the Colonel's cork-like, seated tongue, white as ivory it flowed like lava the short distance to where it was plugged by the circumference of the man's thumb and index-finger just below where I thought the base of the knob would lay hidden. I found it peculiar that the colonel didn't devour and feed from the offerings, only being content to observe the boy's orgasm instead. His lips did make contact with his fingers giving him the frothy white and drooling appearance of a rabid dog. I was very impressed by the amount of jism that Damon produced, catching myself wondering what it tasted like.

I hadn't moved an inch from kneeling between Alex's legs, who, with his arm draped over his eyes, was still sobbing. The weakest of the herd would soon be preyed upon. Claus easily manhandled the smaller boy onto his stomach and shooed me away. He wasn't in the least bit gentle, reminding me of the Sergeant ramming his large pole into me over and over until he had bottomed out. Alex was a sissy, and Claus apparently hated sissies. I was pleased that he wasn't physically violent any more than giving a few slaps to the back of Alex's head telling him to stop crying.

The Colonel now had Damon's rear end in the air. I wished it was me that was getting rimmed in preparation. I was green with envy at that display of affection. The Colonel's face was buried in Damon's ass but his eyes strained to the left to look at me as if he knew my state of mind, winked and resumed munching on the upturned ass. To make matters worse, he made me apply petroleum jelly to his cock which I did sparingly, out of spite for Damon, since the Nazi wasn't really watching as he was humped over the boy sucking the nape of his neck. All. I knew about hickeys was that the older boys back home sported them as a badge of honor.

It was a foregone conclusion that I was homeless. My uncle's family had left me to fend for myself. The thought that the Colonel could also grow bored with me and leave me to also fend for myself also scared the hell out of me. I was no fool to think I could ever have him for myself. There would always be other boys in our bed; I neither would nor could ever alleviate that. When all was said and done, the key was somehow making sure that he didn't fancy one particular boy over me. Damon was exactly the type of threat that I had to be vigil about.

All I could do was sit on my haunches and watch as Alex's head pummeled the wall as Claus hammered his ass and Damon's face winced in pain as the Colonel forced him to take his cock down to its base. The bed nearly knocking me over as it

It was an awkward position, I soon discovered. Perhaps if I'd had more time I could have managed a steady rhythm. Although I knew the effort was gallantly appreciated, the Colonel rolled us onto our sides into a rather painful half-nelson, jack knife position and took charge fucking me. I learned another valuable lesson, the man was always in control when it came to anal sex, and I was more than happy to let them have his way.

I was elated when the Colonel told me to pack some clothing, it was apparent I wasn't going to be coming back to the farm again. He watched patiently as I held, looked at and then tossed aside personal possessions First to go was a yoyo, followed by a Chinese checkers game; then baseball glove, and such. But they were not going to be left behind. Instead, he picked all of them up and stuffed them into my duffel bag. In another heartwarming gesture, he took the picture of my parents off the wall, studied it for a moment, then gazing at me as if qualifying a family resemblance, stuffed it in my bag.

The boys were sitting patiently in the jeep when the Colonel and I walked out of the house. He stooped and picked up the charred swastika. I could see hiss jaw clenched and face reddened in anger. He walked around to the rear of the jeep to unclasp the jerry-can of gasoline. I thought about begging him not to but it was easy to see his mind was set. We drove away from the crackles and pops that I couldn't dare look back at. My uncle, in his wisdom, had managed to rile the man one last time and paid dearly for it in the end.

Chapter VIII: Knowledge is Power

Much to my surprise, the base wasn't our morning destination. We went, instead to the Inn. No travelling tourists or travelling businessmen occupied the premises as one would normally have expected. Instead, men in uniform milled about. The Innkeeper had obviously made up for the wartime shortfall in clientele, although I highly doubted the Nazi's were full paying customers as the business and tourist sectors had been.

The 'Inn' was not really an inn as conjecture would have it, more of a small hotel. A quaint stone structure on which ivy had thrived and flourished over many decades encompassing some twenty-rooms. It was a three story building situated on what once must have been a manicured lawn with cherub fountains that had long since stopped peeing in the now moss covered basins. Whatever the name of the establishment on the sign high above the main entrance was, it was now obscured by a huge Nazi flag.

The interior lobby was tastefully ornate in dark teak wood. Scenic paintings adorned the walls and sculptured busts of men and women unknown to me were scattered about on shelves and tables. A huge fireplace wall allowed a view into what was obviously a dining room on the other side, decorated in much the same wood finishing as far as I could tell.

From behind the front desk, a very obese man dressed in a starched white shirt and wearing a black bow tie greeted the Colonel and his entourage of us young boys. Obviously the proprietor had spent better days welcoming a better class of guests who entered through his front doors. Even I saw through the phoniness and fear that the man tried to mask. His very survival, and maybe that of members of his family, depended on his extended courtesy. As lame as it was he reminded me of my pathetic uncle who had lost everything in spite of his groveling before this officer and representative of the occupying power.

Checking the Colonel in, he gave him a key as if all was a normal transaction. He rang a bell and a youth of about sixteen appeared. I recognized him as a busboy from the base camp officer's mess. Claus knew him, of course, and the two exchanged greetings in German. I was the only person with 'luggage' and felt a little uncomfortable when he tossed my duffel-bag over his shoulder and escorted us into the lift which took us to a third floor suite with two double beds.

The visit to the Inn was no side trip, I realized. It would be home indefinitely for the Colonel. His uniforms hung clean and crisp in the open closet, the bellhop also showed the man his socks and underwear in the chest-of-drawers. Clearly prearranged by the Colonel, someone had been ordered to transfer his effects from the base to his new residence. The only explanation I could come up with was that he had had premeditated intentions on vacating the farmhouse that day. I wondered if his original plan was to leave me behind with my family or if the unforeseen circumstances had forced his conscience to take me along. Sadly ironic, had he known, my uncle had only one more night to endure his nemesis' presence in his household.

At either end of the common hallway was a toilet, bathtub, and of course, running water. A luxury I hadn't seen since leaving home in the city. As if things couldn't be better, Claus directed me to the window. Below was a swimming pool that, above all else, appeared well-maintained on the otherwise neglected property.

We enjoyed a fine breakfast in the dining room. It came as no surprise that the fat proprietor was unable to economically maintain a staff. Instead, German soldiers and the valet youth substituted for the missing civilian staff. I would later learn that it was all part of the security precautions which were intended to eliminate the possibility of spies in what was the intended accommodations for powerful men who apparently came and went on a regular basis. Claus was no stranger to the Inn. He certainly was privy to much of its goings-on and a good ally for me to have.

The Colonel eventually left for the base leaving us four boys to enjoy the hot, humid day in the swimming pool. Claus was first to strip naked and hop in. None of us had a bathing suit or shorts or even a pair of underpants. Alex refused to strip. He was still very sullen and at odds with his treatment by Claus and I. Some of the men lazed around in towels or swam naked. Three naked developing youths drew plenty of spectators not only from those men, but also a few uniformed passer by who found a sudden excuse to linger about to enjoy a poolside coffee and chit-chat amongst themselves. They didn't blatantly gawk, however I would have to have been an idiot not to feel their eyes stealing lustful glances at us repeatedly as we used the diving board.

Claus, a young boy man in his prime, strutted like a peacock. He enjoyed taking a few more bounces on the springboard than was necessary causing his genitals to flop about. I followed his example whereas Damon remained modest and covered himself as best he could whenever out of the water. There was no doubt in my mind that he was fighting off his inhibitions in order to humor Claus' opinion of him. At the same time Claus berated Alex who sat on the deck hugging his knees. He did not give in to the peer pressure from the one boy to be reckoned with if he had any good sense of his own well-being.

Over time, most of the crowd had dwindled, the men having whatever business to tend to, unable to steal more time enjoying the view. There were only a handful remaining who I assumed had the day off. Claus meandered his way over to a man whose towel loosely covered his lower extremities as he sprawled like a beached whale on a lounge chair, one hand provocatively hidden beneath the terrycloth.

With a towel in hand only used to dry his hair, Claus straddled himself at the foot of the lounger with his legs spread wide. They chatted and laughed a short while before rising. The man nervously looked about as he adjusted his towel around his

waist from which jutted his unmistakable erection below his robust belly. He bade the teen a rather loud, overemphasized good morning and waddled his way indoors. Claus waited several moments, wrapped himself in his towel and made his way to follow the man, swiveling his head to give us a devilish smirk and a wave of fluttering fingers. Why Claus chose that man to rendezvous with in a tryst when he could have had a choice of a few better looking and well-built men who were ogling him was beyond me.

During his absence, Damon and I tried to console the withdrawn Alex. He was steadfast in being both obstinate and whiny. He sneered at me and pulled away when I tried to place my arm around his neck to comfort him. I couldn't apologize if that's what he wanted, nor would I. He was a victim no different than any of us. As a victim, he was just like the innumerable other boys that I witnessed enduring much worse treatment, not to mention his own orphan pals. He had been spared the living nightmare of the hell above the treeline. I tried to relay that in no uncertain terms but he seemed unable to grasp the reality. In disbelief, he told me to fuck off. I even questioned whether Damon took me seriously or not. Finally, I gave up in frustration and went for a swim.

Claus arrived back about an hour later looking smug, the kind of upside down smile that one wore when he had something of importance to reveal while awaiting inquiry from the very curious observer. He kept me in suspense for a long while to enhance the intrigue before giving up his coveted secret.

The man he went with was none other than an SS officer which, as he explained for my simple-minded benefit, the Fuhrer's hand-picked elite police unit was called. Obviously he held a rank more powerful in the Nazi hierarchy than even our Colonel or his superiors supposedly having the ear of the Fuhrer himself. In Claus' enthusiasm, he described to me what would be the Colonel's extreme delight when he learned that the man was a confirmed homosexual, even though he was a married man with five children who not only sucked Claus' cock, but got the boy to fuck his ass hard.

Claus had gained personal information for the Colonel and then acted upon the man's weakness albeit, unsure of what would happen in the man's bedroom. Luckily he struck the man's weak spots. I had no idea what all this meant, of course, however Claus was ecstatic and in such a good frame of mind with the outcome that he hardly bullied Alex for the rest of the day. Frank, the teenage bellhop, provided us with a soccer ball which we kicked around the front yard with our bare feet and dressed only in trousers. Even Alex participated in our two against two match.

Late that afternoon the Colonel's jeep could be seen stirring dust from the crest of the long windy road to the basin. Claus could barely keep his excitement in check. He even attempted to run up the dirt road to greet his mentor. However, the sharp stones under his feet persuaded him to gingerly retreat back to the parched brittle lawn to wait until the vehicle pulled into the circular driveway. We all laughed as Claus again danced, his feet burning on the sun-baked cement before hopping into the jeep. I was well aware of the information he had to so frantically tell the Colonel even if I still did not understand the significance of it. The Colonel looked intently at Claus showing no emotion as he was told the coveted information Claus had for him. Afterwards he

disembarked from the jeep hauling Claus with him like a sack of potatoes under his arm to the safety of the cooler lawn.

He asked Claus if we were given lunch. Satisfied that we were provided sandwiches at the pool, he led us upstairs, undressed and lay naked on one of the beds. His cock left no question of what he desired. Claus instructed Alex and Damon to tend to the Colonel's needs. I wished that he had chosen me for that task but I was more than excited when Claus shed his trousers, lay on the other bed and beckoned me to get between his legs with a smile. Claus thought of it as a certain privilege or perhaps even a reward that he felt he deserved to lie as the colonel lay as if not showing off his equality to us submissives.

Although I wished to swap places with Alex and Damon, Claus' cock was every bit as rewarding. Placing my envy aside to please the second-in-command, the unappetizing faint odor of scat reminded me where his cock had been hours earlier. I dared not complain when Alex wasn't living up to his expected task. The Colonel relayed his displeasure to Claus who, in-turn, screamed at the sniveling boy who had placed his burden on Damon. But Damon didn't complain at having to make up for Alex's apathetic approach if only to protect his friend. I admired Damon for that loyalty to Alex who remained stubbornly defiant.

With one vicious shove of his foot, the Colonel sent the boy flying off the foot of the bed to crash on the floor where he cowered and sobbed uncontrollably. Damon flinched in momentary reaction in his desire to tend to his downed friend. He was wisely prudent was his reconsideration of making that move because it would have placed both his and Alex's lives in jeopardy. I had little doubt that Alex's fate was sealed by then. I felt sorry for his foolishness but pleased that he hadn't brought Damon's wits down with him.

A knock on the door was the next disturbance. The Colonel yelled for the intruder's identity only to find out that it was Frank who had an important message to deliver. Entry granted, the bellboy blushed at the scene he had stumbled onto and hesitated, his hand still on the doorknob as if ready to withdraw, perhaps misunderstanding the Colonels muffled order to enter. He apologized for his intrusion. The Colonel beckoned him in and his stepping over whimpering Alex must have been an added peculiarity. The naked Nazi still receiving a blowjob from Damon asked Frank to recite the note which read that the SS officer requested his presence at dinner to discuss internal matters brought to the attention of the Schutzstaffel, the official name of the SS organization.

The blood curdled in my veins. After what Claus had told me about the SS, I feared that the Colonel was in grave trouble. It could only be the assassination of the two criminal soldiers that brought the fat investigator to town. Although Claus had forewarned him, the Colonel showed just a quiver of concern upon his lips now pursed in a ghost smile as he sat up in bed.

It was Claus who dismissed Frank, a liberty I thought astonishingly presumptuous when he instructed the bellboy to take Alex with him and detain him pending final orders from the Colonel. The Colonel raised his hand and halted Claus. He instructed him to advise the SS man that he would be honored to join him for dinner. Then, turning to Frank, he instructed him to arrange with the maitre'd for a terrace table close to the swimming area with no other diners within fifteen feet of the two

powerful men. My mother often said that she could see the wheels turning in my head when I was absorbed in something In this case, I could see those same phantom wheels spinning in the masterminds head.

Sex was no longer on the agenda. The mood had been stymied by the strategic need for planning which was now taking place in a hushed conversation with Claus. Meanwhile, Damon and I sat nearby and played a game of checkers. Both of us could sense the tension rising from across the room. I wasn't wrong in my summation that a wolf was in our midst. It was certainly a wolf much larger and definitely meaner than the evil one that presided unchallenged over his pack; the supreme ruler in his vast den of iniquity; the very man that finally showed a weakness to another man although it was well-masked.

Earlier, I had wondered about Claus' random decision to go with the vile looking man and if he had truly been randy. I also continued to wonder why that man and not others that he could so easily have seduced. I almost felt stupid and then laughed under my breath at how naive I was. I'd known the answer all along. Claus' role had been to ferret out potential adversaries of the man that he … well, loved; the man who was his guardian. Claus was no fool. He saw the SS officer as a threat the moment he discovered the man's identity, status and sudden presence in their midst which was more than a bit of coincidence.

The Schutzstaffel didn't usually make house calls to war bound encampments preferring, instead, to stay well clear of field operations. Although there were SS fighting divisions on the battlefields, the actual police officers didn't like getting their uniforms dirty while attending to business if they could possibly help it.

The Colonel dressed for dinner in his finest uniform complete with medals strung on his tunic that I had not seen displayed before. He was handsome as ever. Looking in a mirror, he placed his cap perfectly on his head as Claus fussed and spit shined his leather boots before pulling each over and up the man's calves tying them tight just below the knees. I caught the man's eye, smiled and clapped my hands just like a little girl. I was smitten in such a way that I felt a pang of shame wondering what the hell had possessed me to do such a foolish thing. He smiled back at me, chuckled with an amused look and, with his leather gloves in hand, he led his wolf cubs obediently trailing from the room.

We couldn't resist having a little fun in mimicking the goose step all over again just as we had tormented our chaperon the day before. Our bare feet slapping the tiled floor of the hallway gave us away rather quickly. He stopped, abruptly turned and caught us red-handed, sneered, then smirked and, finally, gave us the Nazi salute. We returned the salute while, at the same time, desperately tried to keep straight faced despite our muffled giggles. Now being well-behaved, we carried on walking in step behind the Colonel. We bypassed the lift in favour of taking the stairs down.

Claus and the Colonel exchanged glances as we paused in the ground floor stairway before he made his way into the lobby. Claus held me and Damon back for several minutes. Claus then peered around the lobby area making certain it was safe from whatever or whoever might be lurking about. He then quickly led us to the pool area and, once at the threshold, he cautioned us not to look for the Colonel who would be seated for dinner. A three-foot lattice fence separated the dining terrace from the poolside leisure area.

Inside, the dining room was rife with patrons. Only a handful of patrons, mostly officers, occupied tables on the terrace while half a dozen men opted to linger around the horseshoe-shaped bar that served both indoor and outdoor common areas. As we sat at a patio table, I found it impossible not to steal glances at the Colonel and his dining partner. They appeared to be engaged in what could only be construed as an intense conversation on the part of the SS officer if his red face was any indication. The Colonel's elbows rested confidently on the table; his fingers were steeped to his nose and chin in a bemused sort of way although he seemed to be listening politely.

When I heard mine and Claus' name called by the Colonel waving us over, I willed my wobbly legs up and forward to the lattice fence unsure what role might be expected of me. Claus signaled Damon to remain seated. When the SS man saw Claus' face, a look of sheer dread froze upon his red face turning quickly to a deathly pale. The Colonel made formal introductions.

He noted that Claus was a loyal member of the Nazi Youth program, handpicked by the Colonel himself as personal protégé and assistant to bravely accompany the Colonel to the Polish front as part of the young man's officers' training.

The obese man's jowls quivered, his brow sieved sweat that he mopped profusely with his napkin, falling deep into the Colonel's deceit. The Colonel next introduced me as his personal valet, a true Aryan, but of lower class parentage, but an aspiring infantryman. He went on to mention that I was the boy who had also been raped at the same time as the brave young soldier who had been assigned guardianship during a granted leisure day's picnic at the beach. The Colonel told the SS officer that both the young soldier and I were given the reward for exemplary service to him.

The Colonel had the full and undivided attention of his near-close-to hyperventilating adversary. He went on telling his concocted version of events, saying that I was distraught at Jon's murder and afraid of telling the truth of the prior circumstances leading up to his demise. He further stated that I had finally sought out Claus to reveal the horrible encounter that Jon was afraid to say anything about and had forbidden me to tell anyone after threats were made by the men. We had taken those threats very seriously because of rifles fitted with bayonets held to our throats.

The Colonel finished his well-thought out accounts and, for emphasis, he leaned across the table and venomously reminded the man that homosexuality within the Nazi regime was an abomination of military ethics. He also emphasized to his listener how especially hideous and repugnant was the raping of the Motherland's children not to mention the Fuhrer's own valiant young men fighting for the future that he, the Fuhrer, was counting on to uphold the Nazi vision of European superiority and dominance. He looked away from the man and deliberatly spat at the ground for effect.

Composing himself, he then took a serious chance and offered the investigator his own private interrogation of me for his records if need be. An offer that, if accepted, would highlight my lack of the German vocabulary and would have certainly raised some suspicion in the man's mind as to my Aryan status. The SS man never called the Colonel's bluff. He had been smacked down in his own private shame and wanted nothing more than to close his case without fanfare.

The SS officer probably took some comfort in thinking that Claus was also a homosexual and stood to lose his dignity and respect by his mentor, the Colonel,

thus, it was unlikely that the boy would expose him. The SS man suddenly came to the realization that the possibility of both of them being shot point blank by the man who so obviously hated homosexuals clearly indicated that it was time for him to shut up.

What a grand play of mental warfare the maestro had carried out to protect himself from the druthers of the protocol of a military investigation. I learned later, the SS often over-reacted in fearsome ways which were often unfounded. They were known to be very adept at manufacturing so-called true facts of events in order to pompously strut their importance to intimidate and discredit weak minded individuals who may or may not have had anything to hide. The officers serving in each branch of the military feared the protocol involvement and meddling of the Schutzstaffel in their command affairs.

The common, enlisted soldier would have had very little interaction with the Schutzstaffel whose existence was to maintain law and order of the officers corps, not the peons whose illegal actions usually fell under the responsibility of their own Geheime Feldpolizei (Secret Field Police) or GFP, a part of the German Wehrmacht until the end of the Second World War.

The fat officer complained of a sore belly, shook the Colonel's hand and assured him that his investigation was now closed. He said that his report would be conclusive and clearly state that the Colonel had acted rightly in accordance to military law dealing with homosexual rape. Case closed. He rose to his feet, nodded to me and gave Claus an extended, appreciative look and walked away. As far he as was concerned his homosexual secret was still safe. The Colonel never had to use that against him as a last resort, but I was confident that he was prepared to do so as hypocritical as it would have been.

It was easy to see how the Colonel managed to have young boys of his choosing brought along to the front by having the Hitler Youth Organization fast-track his beautiful boy-toys into the army and taking civilian youth under the guise of valets. He called in favours through blackmail of high ranking pedophiles that he had arranged interludes with to enjoy the forbidden Aryan boys. He also used Claus to seduce and weaken the morals and resolve of men who otherwise wouldn't have normally entertained the thought of homo-sex but by weakened inhibitions through alcohol or sheer emotional loneliness, maybe even peer-pressure during one of the Colonel's 'so called' sex parties. I could even imagine that a few generals unfortunate enough to have passed out drunk at the Colonel' residence would be too irresistible a target. They would wake up only to find themselves in bed with a naked Claus and there would be, of course, provocative photographs to prove what the man never did.

One way or another, they fell into the pedophile's arena and the Colonel was somehow aware that the Nazi party was rife with homosexuals. He had done his homework well and he had become invincibly powerful. Claus was in the Colonel's favor again. I wondered how many times this particular scenario had been replayed. There was always Claus, the dutiful envoy behind the scenes, always keen to potential threats against his master, the Colonel.

A feast of lamb chops, chicken and beef along with fresh vegetables adorned our table where the maitre'd, an obvious stiff-collared hanger-on of the Inn's staff, displayed an air of panic as three tatter-clothed, barefooted boys crawled over the

73

fence into his coveted dining domain. The Colonel's sneer at the pompous man was enough cause to encourage him to back off and he reluctantly set the table for his additional guests.

The pool side of the bar was gaining popularity and a rather jovial mood was developing. Men were singing boisterously while clanging mugs of beer that foamed and spilled over each other. The haggard barman did his best to keep up as men continued to flow in. It was a party I guessed; a celebration that brought officers from the base in numbers. German soldiers, like soldiers in any army, didn't need much of an excuse to revel it seemed; I soon learned that the celebration was in honour of Father's Day.

That realization made me heart sore for my home where I would spend weeks crafting a Father's Day card with ribbon and crepe paper. I would quill a beautiful poem in my finest penmanship on the inside, practicing the difficult scroll text several times on paper before daring to chance a misspelled word or an ink blotch. We would always go to my grandfather's summer house where almost all my relatives gathered to honor the family patriarch. I wondered if that was where my parents were right now and thinking about me. I was beginning to wonder if I would ever even see them again.

The drunker the men got, the louder they became. Many had shed their uniforms to swim in the pool. Some were clad in their underwear whereas others were naked as the day they were born. Apparently, a Nazi Officer party just wasn't a good party unless they had some entertainment on hand. Eight scared young faces, barefoot and topless, were being welcomed on their return to the Inn for another night of pleasure—boy duties—but to a far lesser degree of brass decorated men. Somehow, I wanted to believe their predecessors would have been far more gentleman like than the pack of ravenous wolves present.

Utter chaos ensued. Outnumbered by five men per boy, they were being manhandled and groped, passed around like potato-sacks and inevitably stripped of their trousers. It was all in fun at first, the soldiers didn't appear any more physically aggressive than slapping asses. Any man who wanted a blowjob didn't have to ask because the boys had been well-versed. They went from man to man, and in German asking, 'Kann ich suagen ihre schone Deutsche penis fur ihre Vatertag?' (May I please suck your beautiful German cock for your Father's day?), and there was plenty of cocksucking to be seen from our table as we awaited the delivery of our strawberry parfait dessert. While we waited, Claus made Damon and I rehearse the Father's Day phrase until we got it perfect.

No doubt, we would be joining the festivities in due course. Soon another troop carrier arrived. I wasn't at all afraid. If the Colonel wanted all his men to be sucked off, I would happily oblige his wishes. I just prayed that oral sex would be the only expectation of the ever growing drunk and disorderly crowd; a crowd that seemed content on getting blowjobs while standing around talking. The boys were on their knees in front of men fully dressed with their cock's exposed through unbuttoned flies, sharing a warm mouth between them as if it was as natural as sharing a bowl of pretzels on top of the bar. Other men lay on loungers or sat in chairs serious about using a mouth to get off promptly. But by and large, not a single man seemed overzealous abusers, however, the night was still young, and I was no fool.

After a dessert of strawberry-mousse, Claus looked around at our empty bowls and, with a nod from the Colonel, he summoned men close by the fence and Damon and I were eagerly passed along overhead by many men. When we reached the bar area, we were naked, shirts and trousers discarded somewhere along the way by what were many rough and gentle hands that either tickled or squeezed and, in some cases, hurt my balls. As we were passed around by almost every man present, the echoes of 'pretty boy' sounded in my head like warning bells that frightened me.

I managed to raise my head and see Claus sitting beside the Colonel with his arm around the man's shoulder, Frank had joined them. They were all laughing at me or perhaps I was imagining it. Regardless, Claus still had his man and had reinforced that fact with me. He was much to valuable to the Colonel and he was much too smart to let any potential threat from the likes of someone me to interfere with his and the Colonel's relationship. I was simply another expendable boy-whore.

I looked over at Damon who was now on his knees servicing a young Feldwebel or Staff Sergeant. As I neared the moment when I, too, would join the other boys on their knees servicing these soldiers. I wondered about the six-hundred or so Aryan German men under the Colonel's command who, because their wives and girlfriends remained back at home, were strongly encouraged to use and abuse the local Polish boys or, for that matter, boys of any other overrun country that they had previously set foot in. These boys were Slavs who were not fit to be on an equal par with an Aryan German soldier. They were there to be used in whatever way was necessary and, if chocking on a German sausage was a useful way, so be it. Their conduct was sanctioned by their leader. as acceptable wartime behaviour and without conscience so long as it is not mutual contact meaning, it's okay to get sucked by, or to fuck the enemy, just don't return any favours.

But what came rushing into my thoughts was the fact that neither Claus nor Jon, whom I had loved, were like me. They were not Polish. They were young Aryans; blond, blue-eyed Germans; members of the German race; young men he had somehow manipulated and sheparded through the system of red-tape. Could it be that Claus and Jon, and now perhaps even Frank were not the only ones in his private, secret stock of young cute, desirable Aryan Germans brought along for his carnal personal preference during his indefinite stay in Poland? I remembered Jon hinting that he had been intimate with the man, but he never elaborated and, I wondered, are there other young Germans back at base he is secretly fucking? Was this a monster preying on the youth of his own race against his own military rules? He was a shrewd man.

"Kann ich suagen ihre schone Deutsche penis fur ihre Vatertag, Heir Offizier?" I knelt and asked the shy looking young officer. He freed his hard cock from the confines of his trousers, and began pulling my head to his organ. Just as he slipped the dripping head between my lips, I could not help but feel hurt and even anger as I came to the realization of the Colonel's dark ambitions but, what was even scarier, was that it was a plan that was only now all making sense. Knowledge is power, but I wouldn't know what to do with it anyway! But, the Colonel did

CHAPTER IX: THE LIFE OF THE PARTY

Lucky me. The 'pretty' boy was the most popular of choices. My knees were scraped and sore from the cement after losing count of how many flaccid cocks I squeezed the final spits of jism from. Eight? twelve? fifteen? It was all a blur. My jaw ached. My lips were dry and flaky and my mouth was sticky, tasting exactly as it should, stale semen. Some men were hair-triggered, others took time and patience. It didn't matter to me, after getting one guy off, another penis would soon be replaced by another. The men were all on their best behaviour being kind to us whore-boys, a certain etiquette eerily prevailed.

I estimated the revelling crowd had gathered rapidly at near one-hundred-fifty or so by midnight. Every time a troop-carrier arrived an additional twenty soldiers filtered into the bar. The average age I noticed was around twenty-five. The shocked and excited looks on some of their faces led me to believe that the entertainment on the itinerary wasn't known prior to their arrival. The Colonel's added bonus was well-received with most of the soldiers indulging sooner rather than later. It became apparent that the older, more staunchly conservative officers showed no interest whatsoever in the goings on; rather, some displayed downright hostility and pushed boys away who approached them offering the "Father's Day" special.

Thirty or so were naked using the swimming pool to cool off from the stifling heat of the night. They didn't bother to cover up afterward preferring to sit around the pool in the buff talking. God certainly did not create man equally, I thought. There were many beautiful male physiques pea-cocking themselves to more than a few oglers. Waiters with trays of beer served those casual men so there was no need to walk naked to the bar where the majority lingered around chatting in their underwear while others were sweating profusely in full military regalia. Those were the stuffed shirts, pompous older men who, if they had had their way, would probably impose discipline within the unruly ranks. However, it was the Colonel's' soiree and they knew they were powerless to do anything.

The noise was deafening. The men were singing, playing mouth organs and accordions that couldn't carry a harmonic tone and, of course, boisterous men screaming over the din to talk to each other. Us boys on our knees were tripped over or stepped on by drunks. My calves smarted terribly and would surely be bruised in the morning. More than once someone would fall face first spilling their beer over

everyone and everything. Shattered glass was quickly swept up by a very efficient staff of teenage busboys who, along with the waiters, must have been commandeered from the base to keep steins washed and replenish the bar's inventory. The humid air reeked like a brewery mixed with the added smells of cigars, cigarettes and body odour.

Thankfully, there were plenty of lull periods in servicing men as the night grew older. The novelty had worn off or some soldiers simply bided their time. There was no urgency. The ten mouths weren't going anywhere anytime soon. I was resting after giving blowjobs under a patio table to three seated members of the nudist group. I didn't know if they were being discrete or if they didn't want to look me in the eye as I was servicing them, but it was certainly uncomfortable surroundings and I banged my head on the table several times.

It had been a few hours since I saw the Colonel. I peered through the crowd to see that his table was vacant; nor could he be seen in the throng of bodies. Glancing up to where I guessed our room would be on the third floor, I finally saw him, Claus and Frank leaning out the window viewing the scene below. The three were clearly bare-chested and, without a doubt in my mind, fully naked. The Colonel had his Aryan pets on either side of him and I know it wasn't my imagination when, soon after, I saw the movement of a fourth person behind the Colonel whose arms were draped over the man's chest only catching glimpses of blond hair randomly peeking over his shoulder. I could not clearly determine the features or the age of the individual. I just assumed it was another of his young playmates.

I was angry and hurt that the Colonel had abandoned me. I knew that Claus was his golden boy and that I could never compete nor be equals with him. He not only had history with the Colonel, but he also had earned the power to influence the man. Gut instinct told me that my not being upstairs with them was Claus' doing. The thought of him watching me from his vantage point was somewhat humiliating and for the first time I felt a loss of dignity.

Suddenly, a man stepped in front of me blocking my view. He was about nineteen, clad in underwear that noticeably jutted the material at ninety degrees which was enough to cause a gap in the waistband exposing a blond bush of hair that tapered and provided a nicely defined treasure trail upward to his navel. He led me away from the party to the garden gazebo situated in the darkness several meters back from the pool. Nobody seemed to notice and, if they did, they paid no heed. He appeared very nervous and somewhat drunk.

Once inside the darkness I put my hand down his boxers taking the initiative. He gasped. The heat that radiated from his thick meaty cock was feverishly intense. When I attempted to lower myself to my knees because I thought it was expected of me, his hands shot under my armpits to keep me upright. A hand gently fondled my genitals and I grew erect almost immediately. I felt his warm breath inches from my face and then his tongue trying desperately to bore its way into my mouth. I submitted rolling my own over his and soon enough we were in the heat of passion as we played with each other for a long while.

I was flabbergasted by the sudden turn of unexpected events even more so when he dropped to his knees and took me to the base with his nose pressed snugly into my groin. His inexperience was evident. He gagged momentarily and his teeth grazed in

his overzealous desire to perform fellatio on me but he was quick to master the act. The young man seemed even more eager when I began fucking his mouth. I could feel his drool saturating my balls that were molded into his palm and fingers kneading them tenderly.

My legs began to shake and my trembling knees barely held me upright when, moments later, I was spilling into his mouth which caused him to suck my cock harder as he simultaneously milked my shaft. I steadied myself on his shoulders and enjoyed one hell of an orgasm. I literally had to force him off me when my cock became overly sensitive. And, it was not a second too soon either. The moment I fell to the ground and slid my lips along his beautiful shaft, I found that, without touching himself, he was already past the point of no return and began ejaculating gobs of cock juice that I managed to capture from his intense orgasm.

When he started to relax from the intensity of his orgasm, we slowly slid down the wall and sat with our backs against the wall hugging our knees. He spoke slowly in German allowing me to filter his words as best I could. His name was Hans, a junior officer in training; the product of wealthy parents who bought favour as so many other parents had who were rich and influential members of society. Their position in the hierarchy of the Party enabled him to skip over many of the hardships of infantry boot camp after excelling in the private military academy's 'silver spoon' Officer's Program. He hated his years there. He even dared to further say that he hated the Nazi party as well and everything they stood for but had no choice in the matter other than to go along with the doctrine shoved down his throat. Obviously, the young man needed to talk. His candidness was perhaps brought on by the alcohol. I liked him. For a rich kid he certainly wasn't pompous or condescending.

Hans knew from the age of twelve that he was homosexual and began battling his demons. At age thirteen he was caught fooling around with a boy one year his senior. They were both naked and curiously touching each other. His father wasted no time enrolling him in that private military school to make a man out of him. Being cooped up with a hundred other boys the same age and older, his homosexual desires only intensified in an all male environment where nudity was a common sight as was mutual masturbation in the showers and oral sex after lights-out in the barracks. Most of the time the sex was consensual but sometimes it was forced by the older alpha males. It was widely believed that the superior officers turned a blind eye to such goings on and, as a result, none of the other boys dared complain to the authorities, therefore, they themselves turned a blind eye.

Many times he was propositioned by cadets; recruiters he called them, to engage in group activities but didn't elaborate. Although he admitted he wanted to, only once did he participate in a shower circle jerk. Hans was much too afraid to act on his impulses because he feared the wrath of his father if he was ever exposed. As I listened to his story, I wondered what my own father would say and do under those circumstances. I shuddered to even think about it. Hans chose to keep his distance from the corrupt crowd and befriended a few of the morally sound cadets. He excelled in school, graduated with honors and was recruited almost immediately into his current unit's administration as a warrant officer.

Hans went as far to say that certain regular boys were quietly taken from their beds during the night by officers only to be returned the next morning tired and mum as to

where they were taken and for what reason. However, while everyone suspected, they simply didn't talk about it. His story reminded me of Jon's confessed accounts of the Hitler Youth Organization. Although Hans went to a private military school, their stories were very much alike.

Hans said that when he noticed me that night he had to have me as I was different from the other boys He instinctively knew I was more experienced and he wanted me in ways he could not possibly have in front of the men. He claimed he watched and schemed and drank until he developed the courage to approach me during one of the few times I wasn't with another man. Taking a risky chance that all the others would be too drunk to notice and confident that no one else was venturing astray of the bar and pool area, he saw his opportunity as dangerous, but his desire to finally taste another guy was much too overwhelming.

We talked for a very long time. He was very honest about his life so I told him about the Colonel, about Jon, about Claus, about everything that had happened in such a short time since my leaving home in the city. He knew about Jon's demise and the Colonel's impromptu execution of the two soldiers, but he did not know the facts surrounding what were only rumours among the rank and file. Hans was taken aback when I told him about the Colonel being a homosexual. Even in the darkness, I could see the whites of his eyes as they bulged.

The sudden plodding of feet outside the gazebo had us both frozen in fear. It was two men, their figures silhouetted at the entrance stepping inside the rounded structure with latticed half-walls. Hans and I remained quiet, hidden in plain view should the men's pupils adjust to the darkness. They were whispering and snickering like two school girls. These were two soldiers not a soldier and one of the whore boys.

The men embraced and slurping sounds clearly indicated that they were sucking face. Grunts and groans and heavy breathing followed. They were dimly silhouetted by the glow from the festivities area, facing it in order to watch for intruders. One man leaned over the wall as the other stood behind. They were not in the least bit quiet. Guttural moans and brief squeals of pain gave way to wet slapping sounds. They were fucking! Bouts of oohs and awes and the creaking of the lattice wall echoed within the small confines.

Hans put his arm around me and held me close into him. I could feel his heartbeat racing with fear as we watched the ghostly asses and listened to the erotica playing out in front of us. I was hard as rock, reaching between Hans' legs, he was boned up as well and, as we watched, we toyed with each other's cocks.

Someone in the distance began to light off low-level fireworks. The gazebo lit up in flashes of bright white, red and blue tones. The two men, visible as day, immediately cowered to the floor. The looks on their faces was of horror when they saw Hans and I sitting on the ground across from them. One was baby faced, giving him up to be seventeen or eighteen while the other was slightly older probably in his early twenties. Their mouths opened and closed at a loss for words, as did our own.

We had caught each other red handed. It would have been difficult for us to have played down what Hans and I were doing holding each other close, our cocks clearly seen in each other's hand, and it would have been equally as difficult for Michel and David who couldn't deny their own lustful activity. Once the initial fear and shock

faded a little, Hans broke the uncomfortable silence. He knew the eldest as Michel who introduced his companion as David and Hans introduced me. Handshakes were not deemed necessary under the circumstances, the three were still quite shamefully frightened.

The fireworks ceased and we sat there in the darkness, the awkwardness of the situation still unresolved. I felt it important to clear the tension, they had to coexist together and face each other every day on the base. I could have left well-enough alone, I wasn't one of them. I was a Polish whore-boy. Perhaps it was the darkness, I had to look no one in the eye and blurted that they were not the only homosexuals I knew of in their vast deployment of troops on base. I didn't want to expose the Colonel as I did to Hans in case they were once active in his harem at some point. I was sure of nothing then.

However, I did confide that I had not only been intimate with a few low level officers, but that I was also sleeping with a very high ranking officer and through him, knew first hand of other esteemed men that were homosexuals. Mostly what I knew was hearsay and perhaps I had extended the truth a tad, however I saw no harm if it would ease their conscience knowing that they weren't the only ones harboring lustful same-sex feelings in their very own backyard.

David begged me to identify those officers. Naturally, his curiosity was peaked, there would be a certain safety-net knowing such things, knowledge was power, but I named no one, citing that my own well-being was at stake and, like I protected the identities of the others soldiers, it assured them that their identities would remain my secret as well.

The young soldiers talked openly about their sexuality and how difficult life in the military was for them. Michel and David had been seeing each other for several months, stolen moments no different than their presence in the gazebo that night were far and few between. They knew of a few other young men and would sometimes get together late at night in a parked troop carrier, always having one person as a lookout, or go to a secluded area along the lake if their leave furloughs coincided. David made an off-handed comment chuckling that he had had more sex back home in training within the Nazi Youth Program than he was ever going to have serving in the military, contrary to what he was led to believe. Michel concurred, being more blunt in thinking that he was going to fuck his brains out to help pass the time and endure the hardships of the impending war. I did the math in my head, Michel was twenty which meant that the conspiracy began at least six years earlier, if not longer, which also meant that conceivably thousands of youth had passed through innumerable private and public German military training facilities.

Point blank I asked the two teens if they had ever been forced into sex by authority during their tenure in the Hitler Youth Organization. Both admitted to being infrequently taken places to have sex with senior officers and told that it was their solemn duty to obey orders, a test of their blind loyalty to the Nazi regime, and they admitted an intense fear of those powerful men.

Michel elaborated on his plight claiming that his youth platoon was constantly told by superior officers that females were not necessary in a man's life, that women only distracted a soldier's spirit. A man was married to the Nazi party and his comrades. From almost day one of training at age fourteen they (his platoon) were told that

sexual alternatives existed for those who were shrewd enough to figure it out, and keep it covert and a well-guarded secret. Michel claimed that older boys were appointed as mentors for the new recruits in order to orientate and guide them into various aspects of their new military life. These mentors would also initiate sex in stages; mutual hand-jobs, oral sex, and finally anal sex and even group sex leaving them with the impression that it was normal activity.

David didn't hold back. His platoon professed almost the same. That women and family can wait until Germany's objectives had been met in the very near future. At which time, all Aryan males will be expected to populate Europe and cleanse the blood lines over time. His commandant made it laughably clear that fooling around with others in his platoon was a normal and healthy alternative for sexual release in order to put females out of their minds. David suggested that homosexuality was rampant in his Hitler Youth barrack and boys that didn't comply with the subtly laid out rules were squealed on and, at the sole judgment of the commandant, abruptly shipped off to infantry boot camps with no explanation given.

Hans, who went to military school and studied ancient military history as part of the curriculum, brought up that being a homosexual himself, he was especially interested in the ideals of the ancient Germanic Teutonic Knights. One aspect of their earlier and successful conquering of European nations was that they believed that homosexual behaviour within the armies inspired men to fight harder in order to protect his lover fighting beside him in hand to hand combat. One of the earliest and especially notable elite forces that was formed, The Sacred Band of Thebes, which comprised of one-hundred-fifty pair of male lovers who overwhelmingly defeated the Spartans in 371BC. He did not tell them of the battle of Chaeronea in 338BC when the Sacred Band died at the hands of the son of Phillip II of Greece known in history as Alexander the Great.

Hans joked that the Nazi Regime had adopted much of their own doctrine from the Teutonic Knights ideals and standards but must have missed the influence that homosexuals had on the great armies. Michel and David laughed and agreed that life would be a whole lot easier if they had. They may have been laughing but the wheels were spinning out of control in my own head.

Was it simply coincidental that Jon, Hans, Michel and David, who all attended different academies, yet had experienced the same basic clandestine doctrine in their formal training years. There had to be a connection between promoting homosexuality within military academies, cadet camps and the Hitler Youth and its eventual implementation into the mainstream military.

Was it only me, a simple minded fourteen year old boy, that was putting all the pieces of the puzzle together? The Nazi's may have used different tactics to promote homosexuality in the ranks. The various training authorities appear to have been tasked to use whatever subtle means necessary to achieve what would be the final objective. There may not have been blatant written procedural guidelines in their training manuals for obvious reasons. Such guidelines would provide proof of the subversive activity which was in definite conflict with the existing Nazi military code of ethics.

It was as if there was a secret faction within the Nazi empire that was promoting their own agenda for reasons I could not possibly fathom. Could it be a form of

brainwashing involving the young who would inevitably assume command from the old guard who were set in their old school ways of thinking but, for the moment, still held their views and power?

What confusion must have resulted in the minds of the young men living by the double standards being shoved down their throats. Being shot dead or patted on the back was what they faced not knowing who their allies were.

Hans brought me out of my trance and back to the real world when he asked me if I would fuck him. I had never fucked anyone before that night. Hans was more than eager to experience it and grovelled for it. Michel and David settled into finishing off what they had started, David atop Michel. The fireworks had resumed for only a few minutes and the glow in the gazebo allowed the four of us a sense of the erotic as we watched each other.

I bent and spread Hans' legs to his chest where he took the initiative to hold himself in place while I found his folds with a finger. I spat on my cock and directed myself into his tight opening. For once I was the aggressor and the realization that I was taking his virginity intrigued me.

Pushing forth and hearing him yelp in pain didn't stop me. I soon gained entry and shoved past his sphincter that I knew from getting fucked myself was the barrier to be passed quickly in order to take control. Hans screamed but I continued to drill further into his very warm body until I bottomed out inside him. I could feel my balls against his and when I laid upon him his hard cock was mashed between our bellies.

I fucked him slowly at first, then resumed the kneeling position and gave it to him fast and steady. Hans howled in what I guessed was delight. He never asked me to stop and I read that as a favorable response. I masturbated him until suddenly other hands relieved me of the burden, one of which worked its way between my legs pulling at my balls. Having finished off themselves, Michel and David saw fit to get involved in making Hans' first experience a memorable one. They were sharing turns sucking his cock that, in the pitch black, I had to blindly feel their two heads in order to confirm my suspicions. I came rather quickly. Unable to collapse forward atop the busy heads, I went backward onto my back gasping for oxygen.

My first fuck had been a memorable one. Hans' would also remember his first experience of being fucked. Michel was still ready for action and he assumed my place behind Hans. A much larger cock than mine, Hans wasn't prepared for the reaming Michel was giving him. He squealed and snorted like a pig but he endured even long after he came. David was in awe and commented on the force and duration of Hans' orgasm being second to none that he'd ever experienced. from other guys. Michel's breath became labored and before long he let out a few blissful yelps that I imagined Hans was most probably happy to hear because it signalled that the end had finally come.

The sounds of the party brought me back to my senses. I was the Colonel's whore-boy and belonged at the bar. The 'pretty boy' would surely be missed and I didn't want the Colonel to somehow find out that I had been negligent in my duties. I had Michel, David and Hans manhandle me back to the common area to give the impression, if anyone noticed, that they had used me. I never got a chance to say goodbye to Hans, or Michel, or David, but I had little doubt that the three would become great friends after that night.

Things had certainly deteriorated in our absence of no more than an hour. The older crowd had left the Inn leaving the young bucks to party into the wee hours of the morning. Several boys were laid atop patio tables being fucked from behind as well as in their mouths. One boy lay on his belly atop the bar screaming for mercy as a man was impaling him with a wine bottle while onlookers cheered him on.

It was Alex who I identified as the victim. I was shocked by his predicament, but not surprised that he would eventually be thrown to the wolves at some point. I felt terribly sorry for him. His face was contorted in agony as he was being violated in such a sickening manner. I wondered if he had remained pig-headed and managed to rile the wrong man.

I didn't have time to weep for Alex. Two men brought me to the cement floor scraping my already chafed knees. On my hands and knees I was soon taking a cock in my ass and another in my mouth. The man behind me wasn't very large and had no problem entering me. My aggressor pummeled away and I sucked the one in my mouth easily meeting his thrusts at the base of my throat. He was thick and stubby but not exceptional in length.

I saw Damon squatted on a semi dressed man in a lounger facing him. They seemed to be getting along well. Another man in boxer shorts knelt alongside and sensually massaged Damon's back. I recognized both men in their mid-thirties as guests of the Inn that I had seen about that day in full uniform. They were majors and obviously both were drunk. What was out of the ordinary was the fact that they appeared openly enamoured with Damon. I was glad that he'd accepted his fate, unlike Alex, and was being equally flirtatious with his admires.

Not long after, I saw the three leaving together. I naturally assumed that the two men shared a room and it was their destination. Half the whore-boys were now noticeably absent. There wasn't any question in my mind that they, too, had also been taken to rooms by higher ranking officers staying at the Inn. Many of the enlisted men would have returned to base via troop carriers. Many were plenty drunk but not drunk enough or foolish enough to smuggle boys into camp.

Both men assaulting me had short fuses. They had probably been building their excitement all night for a final nightcap before going back home to base. They were probably just following in the footsteps of several other soldiers who had apparently waited and were taking advantage of the remaining whore-boys before the final troop carrier returned to shuttle them safely home. It was the military police who, rather roughly, collected the bodies of those who were passed out while others were ushered staggering to the awaiting vehicles, many of them stark naked. The MP's then searched for and bagged discarded uniforms and boots that were scattered about to be identified by the owners when sober minds would prevail tomorrow morning. The party was over.

Three of us whore-boys remained along with six half-dressed men who were obviously residing at the Inn. Alex was lifted and slung over a man's shoulder and taken away with another man trailing behind. That left me and another lad's fate in the hands of four young officers in their mid-twenties. Also present was the bar staff cleaning up the mess. One of the officers pinched a busboy's ass as he was passing by. The two exchanged what could only be described as flirtatious smiles. The fifteen year old turned red and kept his eye on the vivacious man as he cleared his tables.

Fritz was the name of the other whore-boy. He was thirteen if a day older. He was shy and covered himself. He was still not comfortable with his nudity although he had been exposed to the eyes of many men during the night. I, on the other hand, could care less about my own modesty.

The four men remaining were sitting around a patio table and beckoned us over. An officer pulled me onto his lap and nonchalantly felt me up. He had a huge grin from ear to ear, and took to twirling my hair in his fingers. He was handsome in a rough sort, Germanic sort of way with deep blue eyes, unruly blond hair and a flat nose that may or may not have been punched or broken several times. He was shirtless and his chest and arms were muscular. Ironically, I noticed a gold wedding band on the finger of his left hand that was exploring not only my groin, but my belly and chest as well.

Fritz was also hoisted onto a lap and being fondled. The other two men then leaned over to cop a feel of both Fritz and me. Not that there were many witnesses left milling about, but their promiscuous behaviour I found rather daring should the wrong pair of eyes happen to notice. With the telltale signs of rising dicks in all four pairs of uniform trousers, there was no question in my mind where Fritz and I would be spending the night or that we were going to get fucked, probably at both ends.

Five minutes later; the men finished their beer and rose from their chairs. Fritz and I were draped over shoulders like sacks of potatoes. The men danced around singing a lively boisterous German tune and slapped my and Fritz' bare asses carrying on their antics as they ascended the stairs to a second floor room where we were tossed onto one of the two beds.

The soldiers continued to party sharing a bottle of vodka among themselves and, intermittently, forced some of the raw liquor into Fritz's and my mouth. Not used to hard liquor, we gaged while the four men saw the humour in it. We were fed swigs of vodka more than once. One of the soldiers drizzled the liquor over our genitals, with hoots of laughter the men tried not to waste a drop. It would have been difficult not to get an erection when more vodka was poured liberally and all four men, not wasting a drop, began slurping and licking us from navel to anus. More young homosexual Nazi officers, convinced me that my theory was right when the busboy from the bar entered the room along with another boy I recognized from the bar staff. Both had changed out of their server whites into their junior officer uniforms.

The four men were not at all bothered by the arrival of the junior men who walked in on the display of paedophilia, nor did the two young officers seem concerned. It was almost like they expected Fritz and me to be there. I laughed to myself. It seemed like the after party had been prearranged. It looked as if the impromptu party would have consisted of just the four soldiers until Fritz and I were an unexpected bonus to the planned orgy. I wondered if any of my knowledge of the subversive homosexual activity would benefit the Colonel in some way? Would that earn me a place as one of his spies like Hans? .Although they were young officers, in my reasoning they were important enough to be housed at the Inn and not the base. All I had was a room number, easily traceable to the registered occupants,, but I would endeavour to find out the names of all four men. The junior officers were of no importance in the grand scheme of things.

Two men shoved the beds together and everyone soon disrobed. I wasn't expecting an orgy of that magnitude. Men sucked men and boys sucked boys often indiscriminately depending on whose cock was in who's face at the time. The eight bodies wiggled and moved around to get into in a very awkward and contorted orgy position. We finally settled into two groups of four so that all participants were being serviced contently and comfortably, but nonetheless, it was humorous trying.

I had the second fuck of my life that very same night. It was with the soldier with the peculiar nose, no less. His ass was high on all fours as I was guiding my cock to its mark. He breached back to meet my thrust and that surprised me because I was able to enter him so easily without using spit or lubricant. I rode him like the stallion I was at that moment while being well-aware that beside me was the busboy, turned back into a junior officer, fucking the soldier who had pinched his bottom when he'd been cleaning tables. A quick look around saw the other four were all joined together, limbs intertwined, sucking each other.

I came in the man's ass and fell onto his back exhausted. He whimpered as if disappointed that I was finished so quickly. Rotating his ass and clenching his anal muscles on my shriveling cock was the very last sensation before I slithered out of the warm cocoon.

We spent the rest of the wee hours drinking and having sex. I fucked one other older officer and was fucked by Fritz. I can only describe being fucked by Fritz as a side show because the men were cheering on the boy whose enthusiasm was really keen Unfortunately, in his over zealousness, his short erection slipped out often and, at times, he didn't notice that he was fucking my crack to the humor of all.

Eventually everyone had passed out asleep on the joined beds. I awoke and had no idea of the time other than daybreak hinted through the window. I crawled out of the bed careful not to disturb seven other intertwined bodies. I wanted the Colonel; no, I needed the Colonel. naked. It wasn't by choice because my clothes were somewhere around the pool. I cautiously walked the one story up hoping beyond hope that nobody happened to be awake to see me naked. I was also hoping beyond hope that the Colonel's door would be unlocked. I had no idea if I would be welcome. I feared knocking on the door only to have Claus wake up and shoo me away.

Holding my breath in anticipation, the door knob rotated to the left without resistance and the door gave way. I listened a short while. I heard nothing from the interior so I stepped inside quiet as mouse. In the semi darkness I saw the beds joined together exactly the same as the men I spent the night with had done.

My eyes focused after a few seconds and I saw bodies sprawled about. My eyes adjusted to the semi darkness and I counted five blond heads in a slumber. The Colonel lay in the middle. I froze. I expected to see only the Colonel, Claus and Frank so I was somewhat taken aback to see two more young bodies.

I was distraught. Tears came to my eyes. Yes, I was jealous, and I felt I had a right to be. Okay, I was blond, blue eyed and, yes, pretty for a boy. I could at least admit those facts to myself. I searched around the room and found my duffle bag. I dressed and threw it over my shoulder. I decided that my destination would be my home city and I was determined to walk the distance. I didn't want to be a whore-boy any longer. I had a taste of that and was ashamed of it.

Half way down the hallway I heard bare feet slap the floor. Suddenly a hand painfully grasped my collarbone. I froze, grimaced and turned my head to the left where the pain originated. It was the Colonel, naked and glaring at me in a quizzical sort of way. He spun me around and peered into my eyes. I could not read his mood. He was stone faced as usual. When he lowered his head to meet my lips I turned to rubber, my duffle bag fell from my shoulder onto the floor and I met his tongue with my own. I wasn't going anywhere after that, I was the Nazi's boy again!

CHAPTER X: DEALING WITH A RIVAL

The last face I wanted to see when the Colonel released me from his bear hug was Claus', expressionless, standing naked just outside the threshold of the room. The Colonel suddenly began to berate me, talking so fast that I understood little of what he was saying He went from loving and caring to a parent chastising a child, his finger pointed and poked my nose.

Taking the liberty, Claus moved closer and filled me in on any details that I missed. The Colonel was very worried about me when I didn't come back to the room. Claus, himself, was sent to look for me several times. The Colonel thought that some drunken soldiers had stowed me away with a few of the whore-boys so they could take me back to camp to rape He even ordered the camp be searched. And, just in case I was laying somewhere hurt, he then sent a search party to scour the grounds of the Inn.

.Room searches were currently in progress after a lengthy delay in locating the Innkeeper for a passkey. The obese man was eventually found passed out drunk sitting on a toilet in a staff bathroom off the kitchen.

As if I needed proof, four soldiers burst through the fire exit door at the end of the hallway, machine guns not slung from shoulders, but held at the ready meaning serious business about to search the third floor rooms. The Colonel called off his dogs just as a few doors began to open with heads peering out to investigate the commotion. The Colonel apologized and ordered them back inside.

A proud looking middle aged Sergeant, briefly scanned me with a slight grin and assured the Colonel that he had now accounted for all the whore-boys all of whom were located within the safety of the Inn and in rooms with men. Many of the men were roommates along with perhaps a few invited guests, all legitimately using the boys for pleasure. None of the boys appeared to have been beaten except for one, although not severely, who all three men concurred was disrespectful and uncooperative and in need of discipline. The Sergeant assured the Colonel that he believed the men, he himself had witnessed the boy's insolent disposition.

The Sergeant then lost his proud demeanor of finding all the boys and appeared nervous and sullen. He hesitated finding the right words and relayed that the search party also came upon numerous other men in rooms who were engaged in homosexual group sex. In two other rooms they discovered the roommates sleeping

in one bed, provocatively, naked. All twenty-one of the guilty men were detained and currently being held in the dining room awaiting the Colonel's orders.

The Sergeant wasn't finished. He looked down at his boots as if in shame, the bearer of further bad news, he conveyed that he received word that another forty-eight homosexuals had been arrested on the base, caught red-handed in barracks, latrines and vehicles engaged in lewd acts. Some claimed to be innocent bystanders, nonetheless, those individuals were also being held as guilty by association pending investigation. The base duty Sergeant suspected that those men loitering around the latrines and in the motor-pool compound did, in fact, have premeditated designs of seeking other homosexuals for sex.

The Colonel's stone face fell and he turned ashen, collected himself and told the Sergeant to record the names of all to be submitted to him. He told him that no written reports were to be made and to release all the detainees. He told the Sergeant that he would personally deal with the situation in the morning. He sternly warned the Sergeant that he and his three young subordinates were not to mention a word to anyone. He informed him that the investigation was a matter of utmost importance and for internal security to handle. He told the Sergeant in no uncertain terms that he would hold the man personally responsible if rumours leaked. He was then instructed to contact the base and relay the same message to the commanding officer. With a look of fear the Sergeant saluted his superior.

There was definitely an awkward moment when I believe, the Sergeant preoccupied with events, realized for the first time that his commander was in front of him stark naked as was one of the two boys, oddly enough, all standing in the hallway. The Colonel ordered the soldiers to stand down on anymore searches and dismissed them.

I knew in my heart that the men I had been with one floor below were implicated. Even worse, Hans, Michel and Damon may have also been among those discovered back at base. Michel had mentioned the parked troop carriers as popular venues for sex, although risky. I thought how ironic the situation was. On the one hand, the twenty-one men staying at the Inn would have felt safe having sex behind closed doors while, on the other hand, those at the base had no choice but to gather in dangerously vulnerable locations that offered darkness and a semblance of privacy, always looking over their shoulders and keeping their ears alert.

What was supposed to be a search for a missing boy, namely me, as ill-ordered as it was, turned into a witch-hunt for homosexuals? The number of men within the battalion who had been exposed was a significant number; however, something told me that it was only the tip of the iceberg.

The Colonel stood for a few moments digesting the information before surprisingly chuckling in private amusement. He then herded Claus and I back into his room, a venue where ironically another homosexual orgy had taken place that night.

My conspiracy theory surfaced in my mind again. If I was correct, the Colonel was a very large cog in the machinery. A piece of machinery that must have been huge and powerful enough to either gain or influence various levels of power to support the carrying out of the clandestine agenda to create a modern day chapter of the Teutonic Knights. It was beginning to make sense to me; the same dumb, naive Pollock who

was protected all his young life and never had to think for himself, let alone make any decisions or form any conclusions who perhaps had an overactive imagination but.....

It was going to be a long war, everybody said so. The Nazi occupation of Europe was a huge undertaking covering a huge territory. It would be years if, and when, they achieved total domination. Not unlike the Teutonic Knights of old, men would be away from home a very long time; away from wives and girlfriends, if they made it back home at all. Many of those young Teutonic Knights may not have even had a girlfriend or experienced the pleasures of heterosexual sex.

I was a good example. Fourteen years old and had never kissed a girl. However, I was shown how to kiss another man. Obviously, I had never had sex with a girl, but I was taught how to pleasure a man sexually and enjoy his pleasure in return. It was all I knew about sex and I learned to adapt to it as a way of life, really a way of survival, at the time. Had circumstances never exposed me to homosexuality; if my comfortable life at home had gone on uninterrupted; I doubt very much I would ever have been subjected to it. I would have continued to think about the mysteries of girls and hetero sex and beat my cock for years to come in fantasy.

Uncountable committees of experts, at all levels of their field, had been hard at work for years planning this war of all wars. The military contingent was no different, charged with the strategic planning that was no more important than the logistics committee whose planning was needed to house and feed thousands upon thousands of troops, or the transportation committee whose job it was to develop the plan needed to keep vast fleets of vehicles of many different kinds fuelled and operational. There were various other departments needed; finance, procurement, engineering corps, intelligence and the list went on. However, beyond the humongous task of military strategy, the very wise and powerful men chosen to oversee the work of the committee had collectively agreed that a dramatic social reform of the military's troops was crucial.

Blackmail, threats, and the sheer blind and unquestioned orders from superiors that the subordinates were obliged to follow fearfully, despite all logic or personal reservations, were all contributing factors for the success of the scheme once initiated. No doubt, promotions and transfers of the scheme's supporters into positions of authority right down to the very core was essential. The eventual success of the scheme was to start at the beginning of the education of the recruits into any army. Therefore, the training instructors, who were very crucial in instilling the mental conditioning, were the implementers of the objective and, unquestionably, were at the root of this schemes ultimate success.

Evolving, parallel to the scheme, would be the internal politics to turn a blind eye to the increasing popularity of same sex being practised. If my theory was correct that the inception of homosexuality within the training institutions had begun a few years prior, the younger soldiers, those sixteen to twenty-one, comprised a great percentage of the troops now deployed. Even if it lay dormant, those soldiers were already conditioned to the idea and would easily and quickly resort back to it, as perhaps was happening in the Colonel's own battalion.

I recalled asking Michel why the academy authorities would turn a blind eye to boys having sex. Perhaps not far from the truth was his cynical reply that 'they probably preferred boys fucking than fighting each other all the time.

By what I learned going to an all boy's prep school for one year was that, for many, male aggression seemed to be a way of survival in a cohabited all-male environment. The military would surely be the same. Harmony among the rank and file would be very desirable during the foreseeable years at war with one country or another. One and the same, sexually contented men would be good for morale.

I concluded that sex was very important to men; they liked it often, were promiscuous and even shared their bodies in group settings without inhibitions.

Another question occurred to me then. How did the Nazi's gauge the success of their initiative after the training camps when the boys were dispersed and drafted into the military whose policy on homosexuality was clearly defined as negative? Even I knew from school that experiments had to have a measurable, conclusive result. I surmised it was more like planting acres of seeds, initially caring and nurturing the crop before letting Mother Nature take her course in hopes of a good harvest. The training institutions had planted their own seeds and could only wait and hope that those seeds germinated when the time was right.

Or had the sly man, the Colonel, planned his party well. Free flowing alcohol, a rare commodity and privilege, in order to loosen inhibitions of the predominantly young officers, knowing that the men would hook-up in numbers, then used the room and base search results as his measuring stick. The man was no fool, assuredly he had his spies on base and had prior knowledge of the illicit meeting places and a premonition that a drunken bunch of horny soldiers would conceivably flock there that night.

Others from the base would be invited to stay the night at the Inn by those young officers that the Colonel deemed worthy of such comfort, odd in itself that overall, very few senior officers occupied the Inn other than those in transit.

Albeit, the paramount question was how the Colonel would handle the crisis. Would he somehow manage to cover it up, or would he sacrifice those individual lives to protect the greater cause.

Back in our room, the Colonel turned on a bedside lamp. Strewn on the floor in a heap were two low level khaki infantry uniforms that obviously belonged to the two sixteen-year-olds who had been disturbed and now stirred looking groggy and bewildered. I thought I recognized one as being from the Inn's perimeter security force and assumed the other was as well. Obviously, both were off duty and had not been transported back to base. I would learn later that Frank had, on the Colonel's orders, invited them to 'party' with the Colonel. How could they, who were two beautiful, well-built and well-endowed specimens of manhood, refuse such an offer? They couldn't and the two young soldiers were then plied with liquor and seduced into sex by Frank, Claus and the Colonel.

The three, Frank included, were the most beautiful specimens of masculinity. Chiseled facial features, muscular, but in a softer body tone; with long flaccid cocks whose loose foreskins protectively sealed their glans. Slack, loose scrotums protected testicles proportionately weighted which caused the masses to droop over, or hang between well-shaped taut thighs, the spectacle ever changing as the lads stretched and rolled about complaining of their disturbed alcohol induced slumber. Before they fell asleep, Frank had made sure that he sampled both those firm asses riding one and then the other to his personal satisfaction.

As I fully expected would happen, the Colonel's third degree interrogation of my whereabouts began. He sat at the small table pouring himself a healthy vodka while I stood in front of him. I could tell that Claus, who joined the others lying on the bed intently watching, was relishing it. I would have liked to have had him interpret for me rather than me struggling to be sure that I spoke well enough German. But, in truth, I did not trust him. Somehow I knew that he had manipulated me into believing that the Colonel had sanctioned my being tossed into the ring of whore-boys.

I told him the honest truth of where I spent the better part of the night. I admitted I went with men to their room for sex. Suddenly a brain storm struck me; I told him that I went with them in order to gather intelligence for him because that's what I thought he would have wanted once I suspected that they were homosexuals. He was only mildly curious but became more so when he saw through that lie and condescending asked if any of the men held significant enough rank to veto his orders of my returning to the room by midnight. I was dumbfounded. No such orders were given to me and I bluntly told the Colonel that. He glanced over at Claus for only a second then asked me why I was attempting to run away. With tears rolling down my face I replied that I no longer felt welcome and that I didn't want to be a Polish whore-boy as he made me do that night. I told him that I felt unwanted and was set on finding my way home to my parents where I belonged, even if I had to walk the distance.

The Colonel was aghast. His face went ashen. I could see the throbbing of the angry purple vein prominent in the middle of his forehead that I knew so well. He placed his hands on my shoulders and with all sincerity said that he only ordered me to mingle with the elite crowd at the bar for a short while; his pretty boy, perhaps give a blow job or two if the men were worthy enough. He questioned how I could have possibly misread those instructions.

I heard Claus gasp. The self-satisfaction I felt on hearing that almost made me laugh aloud and to turn and gloat at him. Instead, I shed some more tears and sobbed through a sad story explaining that I was abused by many men that night. Having nowhere to spend the night and fearing that other men would force me to their room and rape me, I saw refuge in the kind men that offered to take me back to their room. Yes, they had sex with me, but it was consensual and gentle, I added that they also had sex with each other. I fell asleep; and woke up and made my way upstairs to dress and gather my belongings. I told him my clothes had been lost somewhere around the pool area.

Claus went from gasp to choking. I would have loved to have seen his face as the Colonel grasped me into his arms and rocked me soothingly telling me how wrong my thoughts were. For dramatic effect, I let the floodgates of tears pour sobbing breathlessly. I had to wonder what the other three teens made of the scene being played out.

The Colonel kissed me and then laughed. He switched into a jovial mood as if nothing had happened. He slowly removed my clothes as I stood before him, caressing me from head to toe. I was like butter in his hands. I became erect even before he focused on manipulating my genitals. I saw that he was also hard and I reached for his manhood. His tongue entered my mouth and I bit and sucked it. Of

all the other beautiful boys present, I was his special one, never having lost his love after all.

The Colonel was in a good mood and inspired another party passing around bottles of vodka. Claus met me eye to eye, he smiled holding the bottle to his lips, I smiled back. Some kind of truce had been forged; I was very much a part of the Colonel's life as he was. He had set me up earlier that night and naive as I was, I fell for it; shame on me!

The boys didn't need much liquor to be feeling good again. I needed very little myself to feel the effects from the strong spirit. The Colonel ensured that I was the centre of attention by lifting and placing me on the bed. Peter and Boris, as they were introduced, along with Frank swarmed me into an orgy as the Colonel looked on from his chair content to be the voyeur for the time being. He sat there stroking his long, fat cock that I so badly wanted to ravish with my mouth. I wanted to prove to him that I loved him and that I was such a fool for thinking of running away from him.

Claus attempted to sit on the colonel's lap and was pushed away. He also refused his attempts to masturbate him. Instead, Claus sat on the floor between the man's legs and sulked paying very little attention to the activity on the bed. He was in shit and he knew it.

I lay prone on my back. My cock and balls sucked and licked and manhandled roughly as my bum was fingered, painfully double fingered, yet it was sensuous. Frank even kissed me intimately when I didn't have one of the infantrymen at either side of me filling my mouth. But if I did he would lick their balls or the base of their shafts that my mouth had travelled the length of and left exposed. I found that extremely arousing, my lips meeting his when I went downward, or feeling his tongue on my cheeks.

Both teens were beautiful. Their foreskins were impressive and ran fluid up and down their shafts in my tight mouth and hand that collected the mass of flesh at the tip. My tongue periodically explored the depths within and was rewarded each time with a hint of the sweet nectar. Especially so was the offering after each teen waited a few moments while I serviced the other. Their rich fluids built up in their shafts that I keenly squeezed forth to savour before going down on them.

I couldn't seem to get enough of their secretions and the masculine scent where groins and scrotum's merge and a slimy-sweat manifests itself over the working day. I found the pungent odour intoxicating in all men. Grazing my nose in the oily texture, it would always linger in my nostrils long afterwards like my father's strong manly cologne would remain with me a long time after a hug sending me on my way to school.

Frank positioned himself behind me hoisting my legs to his shoulders. I interlocked my feet around his neck and prepared myself to take him, wanting it so badly. I was being greedy because I also wanted Peter and Boris to fuck me. Both boys were settling in happily as they took turns fucking my mouth while Frank worked his large cock inside my ass. He wasn't gentle. Pain, however, quickly turned to pleasure soon after he spread my anus wide and was lodged deep inside me. He was gyrating his hips as he slowly pumped gaining momentum until he was thrusting, sweat dripping off his head onto my groin, his face contorted as if he himself was in

agony. He retracted his cock to the brink of exit but, at the very last second, propelled his lower body forward with vigour. He kept that momentum going for a long time.

I presumed it was his own technique based on lots and lots practice with lots and lots of male asses. In any event, it was by far the best fuck I'd ever had so far in my young life. I was meeting him at every downward thrust of his piston clenching my rectal muscles around his girth in reverse and releasing him to plunge forward again adding to my delight, and surely his as well. He certainly didn't hold back vocalizing his pleasure with a long string of obscenities and panting like a dog. With one last scream he buried his cock, that I was positive had increased in size, deeper into me. Frank gave into exhaustion, his sweaty body collapsed upon me, his hot breath panting in my ear.

During my fuck frenzy I had lost track of who was sucking my cock and whose balls were slapping my chin and fucking my mouth, but Frank's pleasure was never denied him. I was fully conscious of my obligation the entire time Frank was ram rodding me. If not carnal, my excitement of our four-way was of each knowing his role and performing in unison like a well-oiled machine.

It was Boris who came in my mouth. He gave no indication or warning. His cream gushed over my tongue until I tasted it collecting in the pit of my lower jaw. Bitter sweet, I rolled it around in my mouth before I swallowed the mass. I was again amazed at how every man and boy tasted so slightly different.

The Colonel clapped his hands. He then held his drink high in salutation. Obviously, we had put on a good show for him. His true admiration was measured by his glistening cock and fingers of his right hand. At first glance I thought that he had cum until I noticed the clear fluid still bubbling from his slit and flowing down his shaft. I remembered that he was, in fact, a heavy secretor of seminal fluid.

My view of the Colonel between my legs which I continued to hold to my chest anticipating another sure fuck was suddenly blocked by Peter's body. He was quick to take Frank's position and plunge his shorter, but much thicker cock deep into my ass without much resistance. Frank had surely eased the way, but nonetheless, Peter's girth was like fire spreading me open as it forged ahead and quickly bottomed out. He wasn't quite content reaching his maximum potential and repeatedly attempted to drill deeper using my hips as leverage, his large testicles warm upon my cheeks as his bristly pubic hair tickled my balls.

Peter began in short strokes, his cock so fat that it seemed to remain stationary. I doubted anything more than his bone glided within the casing of his shaft being held snugly in the confines of my rectum. The feeling was not all that bad, quite different from Frank's fuck, but his constant fullness was pleasurable. There was little I could do to contribute but lay there as he virtually masturbated himself inside me. Peter came without much fanfare and pulled out to lie on his back leaving a large void that I could feel the cooler room air invade.

I was hoping the Colonel would make love to me next but it was Claus appeared between my legs with a look of scorn. Our eyes met for a moment and I was in no doubt that hatred burned in his. He had obviously claimed his turn to fuck me. He knelt between my legs and immediately slammed into me. Unfortunately for him and his motives, his cock, as nice as it was, barely had an impact in the well-used, cum filled abyss and I lay there like a rag doll letting him have his way. There was no

question that he was trying to hurt me. Getting no response from me, he became violent. He forcefully slapped my face and punched my chest and stomach as he continued to try and fuck me hard. He became a mad man reaching down and squeezing my testicles until I screamed in horrific pain.

I saw the Colonel through my watery eyes tower above Claus and grab his armpits to haul him off me. I saw the man drag the boy down off the bed to his knees and backhand his face several times. The force of the blows was so hard that blood shot out from Claus' nose. Peter and Boris jumped off the bed and bravely intervened. They were holding the Colonel's arms to prevent further beating of Claus telling the man to calm down. He easily shoved both of them away. Knowing better than to make another attempt to subdue the man, the two young men cowered in fear.

I jumped from the bed landing with my arms around the Colonel's neck. We were face to face and I begged him to stop. He could very well have beaten me as well in his state of mind. Instead, he looked into my eyes and pulled me into an embrace, rocking me. As sure as the day I was born, I knew beyond a shadow of doubt that I WAS still the Nazi's boy!

CHAPTER XI: THE COLONEL'S ORDERED ORGY

Men important enough to be entered into the Colonel's little black book of powerful men were seduced into having mutual sex with a young boy. This information was stored away for later use. Men who could be blackmailed, if necessary, to further the cause either by turning a blind eye, or even lending influential support to the secret 'Teutonic' agenda. I doubted Claus even knew the extent of the master plan. He probably thought that the Colonel was merely gathering intelligence on men in high places to protect himself from the potential exposure of his own homosexuality.

Obviously, the Colonel ordered Claus to translate his wishes so that there were no misunderstandings. He understood this as being his responsibility in their relationship although he never had a second thought about deceiving the Colonel in playing me against the man. After all, he had learned from the master of deceit himself!

This approach had backfired. Shrewd young Claus had fucked up, maybe for the very first time in his devious life. Then, it hit me. It had dawned on Claus that the relationship I now had with the Colonel was becoming more than sexual. Claus had come to the realization that I wasn't just another whore-boy that the Colonel took a passive liking toward. I suspected this scenario between the Colonel and a boy might have logically happened in the past and, in each instance, Claus would have found a way to sabotage those relationships.

Until now, that is. He had met his match and he knew it. I wasn't going anywhere anytime soon. I knew I had nowhere to go and I was under no illusions. I simply had to survive. Through the process of elimination of the various options, I realized that running away was not a practical solution. I reasoned that had I run, I would have been captured, or worse, shot dead within two-hundred yards of the Inn, something I really hadn't thought about at the time. I decided then and there that I would remain and stay under the protection of god himself.

The Colonel sat on the floor with his hands covering his face. He was a troubled man deep in thought. Claus had long since scurried away on all fours and cowered in a corner. He nursed his bloody nose. His face took on the look of shock as he saw his blood on his hands. He glared over at the Colonel not wanting to believe that the man had attacked him.

I felt sorry for the Colonel again. He was a man of many burdens. I felt that if we were alone, he would hug me tightly and cry on my shoulder and reveal all his dark secrets. I, in return, would hold him tight, rock him gently and tell him everything would be alright; that he was a strong minded man with a lot of responsibility. I would wipe away his tears and smile reassuringly. He would make love to me, spooning, the way I liked it most.

The Colonel eventually rose and walked over to Claus who, with tears welled in the corners of his wide open eyes in fear, cowered at the naked man towering above him. The man stooped and gently tweaked Claus' nose. Satisfied that no real damage was done; the Colonel leaned into his ear and said something in private.

Claus appeared proud all over again. He stood and hastily made his way to the door. The Colonel laughed and called after him to put on his trousers. The boy thought for a moment, foolishly giggled and, after finding his trousers, was gone.

The Colonel smiled at all us dumbfounded lads like nothing had happened, saying the party must go on. Diving like a kid onto the bed, he lay on his back and asked whoever was going to fuck him first had best put their cock in his mouth to get it hard. The invitation was unexpected and totally out of character for him. As it was I didn't hesitate to give it a second thought and before anyone else, I scrambled onto his chest with my hands on the headboard supporting myself and fed him my cock. Not one second later I was hard. I was excited by the thought of actually fucking the Colonel, the powerhouse, the mover and the shaker, the man feared by many but most of all, the man whose masculinity was being surrendered to me.

I knew now, without a doubt, the Colonel was a homosexual because, other than performing blow jobs, I had never witnessed the final confirmation of it. I had never seen him take a cock up his own ass. And, after all I'd been through, I felt it was my deserved right to take advantage of the offer. I worried that my size would not compete with the other older teens and that he would politely excuse me from the invitation. He didn't. Instead, he swallowed my cock and his tongue began to do wonders as it moved around my crown and lower shaft. Before long, I had the audacity to fuck his mouth.

In my overzealousness, I slipped out of his warmth more than a few times. But, rather than search for another partner, the Colonel searched me out with his tongue and delved back onto it.

I strained my neck to look back and saw that Boris and Peter were going down on the man. Frank had lifted the heavy legs and buried his face in what I could only guess was the Colonel's ass. It was all about the powerful man then and I believed that the teens were only going through the motions to please their commander, not because they wanted to but, because they had to.

With all the hot action going on below I dreaded that I wouldn't get the opportunity to fuck my Colonel after all. I could see that Boris and Peter were now semi erect. The only cock I couldn't see was Frank's which was hidden behind the scene. I feared that he was in a better position and would be the one to plunge his cock into the Colonel first.

I gave up hope until; once again, I got carried away and slipped from his lips. At that moment he didn't endeavour to take me back in his mouth. I wasn't sure I had heard him correctly when, in a breathless whisper, he told me to fuck him.

I was proud, excited and very scared all at the same time. I moved down his body quickly. I used my ass to shove Frank's head away but when he didn't move fast enough for my liking, I gave him an extra hip powered-shove to clearly send him the message to fuck off! The Colonel lifted his legs to his chest. I got into position on my knees anxious to do the deed but, at the same time, scared to death. I poked and prodded, prodded and poked. Frank took the liberty from behind me to direct my cock to the target. I fretted a moment in after thought wondering if I should have, at least, spit on my seemingly longer and thicker excited cock which was ready to explode when Frank saved the day by lubricating it with the Colonel's gobs of fluid.

I had to think of strangling puppies and smothering kittens as Frank's touch almost brought me to the point of no return. He then took the liberty of positioning me, rubbing my sensitive knob over its mark a few seconds before slapping my ass as a cue that I was on my own.

I could feel the heat of the man's anus enveloping my cock as the head forced its way inside and through the protective ring. I drove further needing only to shove, pull back and re-shove once before I felt my groin firmly against the mound of flesh. The Colonel yelped causing me to have a sense of pride, I wanted it to hurt him but only a little. He was giving his ass to me, not Frank or Boris or Peter who were all blessed with greater endowment. I was not going to pause for even a single breath. It was my conquering moment and I had a lot to prove as a worthy sodomist. My balls were tingling and drawn up toward my groin. I could feel them dangle in the warmth of his spread cheeks.

While Boris and Peter continued to service the Colonel's genitals; Frank had climbed atop to straddle the man's chest and shoved his cock in his mouth. I fought off the urge to orgasm but the effort was futile. A moment later I came and I poured forth my essence into the man if only to prove my virility to him and, thankfully, my erection didn't let me down. The Colonel was humping me back and moaning.

Boris knelt behind me, his cock toying at my hole followed by a sharp pain. I was about to be fucked while my own cock was buried in a guy. As if the erotic nature of that scene hadn't piqued my senses, Frank lowered himself down the Colonel's torso and Peter guided the man's slimy cock head inside the teen who squatted to be impaled and began to fuck himself.

Peter completed the orgy by standing in front of Frank for a blowjob while he assisted greatly by holding the Colonel's legs up and apart allowing Frank a little more room. The spontaneous four-way fuck fest was awkward at first and, while we laughed at our foolishness, we soon developed a harmonious rhythm. Five sounds of passionate grunts, groans, gasps and skin slapping skin charged the room's aura in an electric frenzy.

I came again and yelped like a coyote. Soon we were all howling as one by one orgasms were reached and the sex pyramid collapsed. Peter was the last to spill his seed. Taking matters in his own hand, he began jerking off in Frank's mouth. The teen was obviously thirsty for it because he endured Peter's fist smacking his mouth as he maintained a portion of the cock in his lips and devoured it once the teen had released it for him to finish milking with the suction of his mouth. What happened next was beyond comprehension.

The Colonel made a remark that Frank shouldn't be a cum hog. On all fours the young officer crawled to meet the man face to face. They kissed. A slobbery, open-mouthed kiss in which Frank shared the collected spunk over the Colonel's tongue. Us onlookers stared in disbelief at the exchange, both faces covered in saliva and semen.

Frank's ass was high in the air. I watched as his not so puckered hole suddenly spewed the Colonel's off white load. Runny and thick, it ran down to his balls. I never gave a thought to what Boris or Peter would think. I wasn't a big fan on performing analingus but, I couldn't resist. Spreading the soft milky cheeks wide, I sucked and prodded the cavern with my tongue as deep as possible. The liquid was bitter and the odour was a little foul but intoxicatingly manly.

After I had licked Frank's crack and balls clean, I lifted my head to find the Colonel face inches from me smiling. He tousled my hair as if I had done something extremely pleasing and proud. I had crossed over a great line of sexual deviation to show him that I could be just as, if not more, perverted than he. I succeeded.

The Colonel started the contagious laugh and congratulated all of us on our sexual hi-jinks and prowess. He rose from the bed and sat again at the table and, reaching for the bottle, he poured himself another vodka. He then handed the bottle to Boris, who drank and passed it around. Only after my swigs did anyone wipe the top of the bottle.

The Colonel gave a short lecture to Peter and Boris on the virtues of homo sex and how they were still masculine and had proven their loyalty as fellow comrades in being willing to do anything for each other in such times of hardship and loneliness. What all of us had done that night was nothing short of man's extreme need for sex and each one had contributed beyond reproach in assuring the overall pleasure of each other.

It was more like he put the words in their mouths in getting each to admit that they liked the sex and wanted more of that. He went on to say that it was a comrades duty to share their newly acquired perspective with another peer or two who they liked and trusted and felt would benefit from the doldrums and sexual frustrations of military life as they now knew it compared to life home.

The powerful man of influence claimed that he would take great favour upon those who would join him and strive to make the battalion a better place, even promotions were possible. He ended his sermon by telling them that Frank would show them places on base where men gathered for sex to relieve wartime anxiety and stress, that he turns a blind eye to.

I was stupefied. My heart missed a few beats and I gasped out loud. That sure had a familiar ring to it. My theory was far from proven; however the Colonel certainly added credence. What I found even more shocking was his promoting the use of clandestine sexual venues when he presently had one hell of a mess yet to be resolved over that whole issue!

Suddenly, the door was flung open. It was Claus grinning from ear to ear. With him were the three young, armed infantrymen who had been involved in the Inn's room searches. They looked around at the naked bodies sprawled atop the bed, each with a look of puzzlement and perhaps embarrassment. Boris and Peter both sought pillows or blankets to hide themselves even though it was much too late for modesty.

Frank had sat up against the headboard, legs spread wide with his erection prominent, the vodka bottle at his lips not caring that company had arrived.

The Colonel rose to welcome the three young men graciously displaying a wide smile. He extended his hand for a courteous handshake. His cock was still half erect and it swayed to and fro with each step he took with his long hanging balls slapping his thighs.

The three were red faced, unable to mouth the polite and usual reciprocated greetings in return. It was almost comical how they looked everywhere except meeting the Colonel's eye. There was nowhere else to look without seeing male nudity.

Claus brazenly unshouldered the rifles of the seemingly paralyzed teens who paid no attention to being disarmed. He leaned the guns against the wall. He then stripped off his trousers which definitely caught their attention. He stood nude at the foot of the bed and smiled back at them.

The Colonel sat back down. Frank looked from face-to-face of the fresh meat. Since he had not cum yet, Frank was determined to get one of these newly arrived teen infantrymen to either wrap his lips around his cock for a good face fucking or he would shove his cock up one of their tight asses.

Frank now moved like a man on a mission. He rose from the bed, his long, hard cock was pointing north with a slight curvature near the tip which, I hadn't noticed before, strained to point south. None of the lads could possibly miss that. Each young man briefly stole a glance at this magnificent piece of Germanic male flesh while shock was clearly displayed on their faces and some uncomfortable fidgeting ensued.

The fidgeting became even more pronounced when Frank slowly began to undress the youngest of the infantrymen. The young teen stood frozen in fear as his jacket was removed, his shirt unbuttoned and his utility belt unbuckled and let drop to the floor. The boy was literally shaking in fear as Frank knelt and slowly removed the soldiers' boots and socks. The trousers were unfastened next. Not unusual for soldiers in the battlefield, he wore no underpants. His flaccid cock shrouded in foreskin was impressive. The boy's sac was long and his testicles flared cradling half his length.

Frank's hands were firmly planted on the young teen's slim hips as he licked the underside of his cock and balls; then, each was taken gently into his mouth for what I assumed was a tongue bathing. We definitely heard the wet slurps. I never thought it possible because he was clearly embarrassed in front of an audience but, ever so slowly, the young man's impressive cock responded.

Frank was fully aware of what was happening to his quarry. His hand soon manipulated the growing cock into a full erection which he slowly stroked exposing the boys reddish head time and again only to hide it again in the mass of skin. He then went down on it right to the base. The teen's body trembled and he gasped audibly.

Without words or speaking volumes, the Colonel motioned Boris and Peter to undress the other two young men. They looked at him in what could only be described as disbelief. It would only stand to reason that the soldiers all knew each other having the same security detail at the Inn. Only a moment of reluctance later, they obeyed their commander and chief.

I had no misgivings on his authority when be beckoned me to sit on his lap. In a split second, I was content in his strong arms, my face against his muscular chest. I

was more than a little perturbed when he called Claus over to stand by his side. He slid an arm tightly around the boy's waist hauling him into a closeness I could have done without together as we watched the scene unfold. The door to our room remained wide open and anyone passing by would have seen us.

But, in reality, the shrewd Colonel was taking care of business. The three soldiers would never speak a word of the homosexual activity they witnessed earlier. There was no lecture necessary from the powerful man to ensure their silence.

The three naked soldiers must have found some kind of solace among each other as they were being serviced by their peers. Realistically; in fact, each was receiving his very first blow jobs. There was no display of inhibitions, each pawed the head of his provider, eyes cockeyed, heads thrown back, all grunting and moaning that, together, sounded like a very bad choir in practice.

The Colonel had enough. It was time to move on. He ordered the boys onto the bed. Whether they wanted to or not, the three infantrymen were about to get their first taste of cock. Two went down on their partners and lay side-by-side in a sixty-nine without the need for a threat from Frank of the Colonel to comply. Apprehension, however, developed in the oldest teen. He held Boris' cock near his mouth with a look of disgust. I don't know what possessed me but I got off the comfort of the Colonel's lap and, with my boner leading the way, used all my might to force him onto Boris' cock.

What a proud moment it was that followed. The Colonel peered at me, his eyes wide and his mouth even wider in awe. I had impressed him. As if testing my heroism, I was taken by surprise when he told me to fuck that same, reluctant boy. Suddenly the image of Alex came to mind. He'd been the weakest of the original litter.

Names were never cordially exchanged. He spit out Boris' cock and looked up at me with sheer fear, his eyes begging me not to violate him in such a manner. I looked at the Colonel who, with a nod of his head, told me to proceed.

Clause manhandled the teen to where his ass was upright and his mouth was poised above Boris' rampant cock. He spit in his hand and rubbed my cock in it. I really didn't want or need his help. I would prove to the Colonel that I could commit rape on my own volition. And, rape it was. The teen sobbed as I forced myself into him. Then when I forced my cock through the defences of his tight cincture, he screamed. His head reared back. His hands left Boris' body and he grasped the mattress. Boris held him tightly around the neck to keep him from moving forward away from my penetration.

All sexual activity ceased, almost. I momentarily became the center of attention and saw them all staring at me. Drool hung precariously from Peter's mouth linked to his partners cock. Frank held the youngest boy's cock in his mouth just staring intently with his own zealous partner sucking away on his thick cock seemingly oblivious as to what was going on around him. Frank's boy was definitely a player. I had to wonder if he had not already been indoctrinated in the art of man love. He was cute as a button. I wouldn't doubt that some senior officer or two had used him before. The tell all was later when Frank laid him on his back, lifted his legs to his shoulders and mounted him. The boy had definitely been there and done that before.

For the first time, I was merciless. The young virgin ass I was working on was much more of a challenge. I was wise enough to recognize that my victim was clamping his sphincter to prevent me from entering him. That's where the rape came into play. My cock hurt as I gained precious centimeters until my head felt a final void making room for my shaft to enter. He was still tight, his anal muscles clenched in resistance even though I had punctured and defeated the barrier. If he wanted to continue to clamp my cock, all the better it was going to be for me. He screamed bloody murder throughout his ordeal but Boris silenced him forcing his cock between his lips. At just the right moment, Claus saw fit to pinch off the teens nostrils.

Eventually his mouth opened and Boris sent his dripping cock deep into the boy's throat. A few slaps by Claus soon had him subdued enough to convince him not to bite down on Boris' penetrating weapon and perform the oral sex as expected.

Glancing behind, I saw the Colonel hard and rubbing his cock. Damn, I wanted to lick the fluid I could see on the tip and then give him a blow job. I had never felt such an urge like that before. If possible, the thought made me harder. As if reading my mind, he did something even better. From behind and totally unexpected I felt his hands clamp onto my hips as he rammed his cock into me.

I got over the initial shock and pain. It felt like the Colonel's cock was my own and, without letting up, I pounded away at the boy beneath me. He stayed perfectly still and let me ride him as I face fucked my victim. The Colonel's cock was long and fully inside me. I had been fucked many times that night and was quite sore, but the Colonel inside me was like being in heaven. I didn't even mind when Claus stood over my fuck buddy laying beneath me and had me suck his cock. Fucking, getting fucked and sucking cock was too much excitement to endure. I came again. It never deterred me. I was still hard as steel. The Colonel's sudden thrust drove me into whatever his name was devouring my cock while Claus stood over him and enjoyed forcefully fucking my face. We were together again and I was happy.

I know that it was quite impossible but, I swear, I felt the Colonel blast my innards. He screamed profanities and took hold of me around my stomach pulling me deeper onto his cock. Then Claus, pulling my face and lips tightly into his crotch, came with a hefty load flooding my esophagus. As he shot his load, his hands were holding my head so that my nose, deeply embedded in his pubic bush, was mashed so tightly against his lower belly that I couldn't breathe. I knew that he enjoyed the fact that I had choked on his cum and it burned my throat afterward.

The Colonel got up from the bed and returned to his seat, Claus and me each leaning into him on either side and watched the Colonel's ordered orgy take place. Even Frank stood back as the five infantrymen were encouraged into an orgy to suck each other's cock. The Colonel had insisted upon it. It was his final assurance that there would be no leaks. I had a gut feeling that eventually Frank, the Sergeant and the junior officer among us, would probably find himself transferred to the front!

Everyone stayed over the rest of the night. The three soldiers had long missed their shuttle back to base and the colonel would ensure that no AWOL charges would be brought against his guests.

I slept on the edge of the bed with the Colonel's arm around me. I awoke sometime in the wee hours, his cock hard against my back bone. Everyone else was asleep. I did what I wanted to do so badly, I rolled over and sucked him off. I wasn't

sure if he was awake or not until I felt his fingers twirling my hair. A few minutes later, he pushed me off him. I thought he didn't want it. He lay me back down on my side facing away from him and cuddled me. I thought I was going to die when I felt his cock at my hole. He made love to me slow and gentle. He masturbated me and I felt the rush. My toes curled, I shivered and spasmed as if having an epileptic fit. He brought his hand to my mouth and I licked off my own cum. He stained his neck down to meet my own and bit and sucked it. He drove deep and planted his love inside me. I no longer had any question; I was definitely the Nazi's boy!

CHAPTER XII: A TASTY MORSEL DEVOURED

Even with the two beds pushed together, the nine bodies sprawled every which way left little room for comfort. The air was strong with body odor. Peter and one of the new boys were giving each other a blowjob. Everyone else was sound asleep. It still amazed me how the three had been seduced and so easily complied with having group sex. They were reserved participants, no less, but not as relaxed about it as Boris and Peter who adapted rather quickly to the newly discovered benefits of same sex. Of course, the Colonel's presence and active participation was a great influence, not to mention his position of power and the psychological impact of that in and by itself.

Considering that men like him order reluctant troops into perilous front line war situations of life and death; well, I guessed that encouraging them into same sex would be small potatoes in comparison.

Sleep was impossible. It didn't take much effort getting out of the bed, I would have fallen out in the blink of an eye. The Colonel's limp cock had long since slipped out leaving an empty feeling. Males get erections in their sleep. I had hopes that his would come back to life and that I would feel it grow inside me.

I needed to piss. Short of falling out of bed, I simply stepped out. Frank was awake lying at the foot of the bed and together we made our way down the hall to the toilet. I don't remember ever sharing a toilet to pee. We might not have bothered with toilet etiquette because a sword fight ensued and we pissed all over each other and the bathroom floor. The chambermaid, the fat owner's wife, would certainly be horrified when it came time for her to clean up the mess.

The allurement of the deep, claw-footed bathtub that I had little respect for back home in the city was suddenly very desirable. However, Frank's suggestion that we first go downstairs for an early morning swim was also intriguing. The bath could wait.

We went back to the room for towels to wrap our waists. We giggled when we saw that Peter was lying prone atop the teen and giving it to him fast and furious. Both were oblivious to our gawking and our humorous exchange of words before we let them be and hit the stairs in a race for the pool.

I won when Frank had to backtrack for his towel that had slipped from his hips. Unfettered, he ran through the lobby nude stripping me of my own towel and

whipping my ass with it while in hot pursuit. A few security soldiers mingled over coffee while on their break. They laughed at the sudden, but welcomed, break in their five-thirty in the morning monotony.

Once we arrived at the pool, we stopped dead in our tracks. The Sergeant who led the room raids was sitting on the edge of the pool naked as the day he was born with his legs dangling in the water, a bottle of vodka planted between his thighs, obviously stolen from the bar. The man was obviously very drunk, singing and laughing to his own amusement.

No one else was visible. The only sounds heard was the clanging pots and dishes by the kitchen staff preparing for breakfast. The man saw us, focused on me in his drunken stupor and called me a 'junge hure', a boy whore, grabbed his cock, laughed, and told me to come over and suck it for him.

He became quite irate as Frank and I ignored him to use the pool. Frank had had enough of the man's drunken belligerence because of his continuing to insist that I suck his cock. Frank told him to fuck off more than once. He even told the man that he wasn't permitted to be where he was, that he was not an officer, was truant, and should have returned to base after his shift. I didn't know if Frank's status as a junior officer held clout over an infantry sergeant regardless, out of uniform, the man wouldn't have identified the young man as a superior anyway.

The Sergeant eventually succumbed to the alcohol and laid back on the pool deck sound asleep. His cock was small, shrivelled up and only peeking a pinkness from his thick mat of groin hair. Even his balls were tiny, his genitalia certainly ill proportioned in accordance to his large, muscular body. Frank and I gathered at either side of the Sergeant's knees and got a great kick out of watching his cock, like a turtle's head, expand an inch and recede back into his cavity with every deep snoring breath.

Frank took on a sinister look, hoisted himself out of the pool beckoning me to follow. We gathered up the man's uniform, boots and gun belt and tossed them into the pool. His trousers and shirt floated on the surface, the rest settled at the bottom.

I didn't know until then, however it did make sense, that a soldier was to respect his uniform and any desecration of it is considered an insult to military protocol. Even greater still was his disregard for his weaponry.

I understood the ploy immediately when Frank went running back into the Inn and returned with a duty sergeant to witness the insubordination of the passed out man. Regardless that he was naked, he had managed to pull rank screaming for the man to take action or else he would awaken the Colonel himself, who would be none too pleased at the interruption due to the Sergeant's ineptness should he even try and protect his drunken counterpart's blatant insubordination.

Frank and me frolicked in the pool, doing handstands, racing ends, or simply laying on our backs treading water to gaze at the stars and point out the dippers and the North Star oblivious while military police arrived from base and two officers, not so gently, dragged the inebriated man by the arms out of sight. A third officer asked us to gather the paraphernalia from within the pool.

Another game ensued; who could dive and gather the most. I won with two socks, underwear, a tunic and cap to Franks gathering of boots, gun belt and trousers. Unsuspectingly, he dunked me jokingly for outdoing him. I came to the surface choking having ingested a mouthful of water. I played drowning, splashing my arms

wildly, submerging for affect until he came to my rescue. When he did, I caught him off guard and held his head under water while he flailed his arms and legs under my playful, but relentless grasp of his head. A sudden pain to my balls made me instantly surrender.

We were both ecstatic although we didn't gloat or even mention the episode to each other. The colonel would be most pleased learning that the Sergeant would no longer be a threat. I learned later that with no provisions for imprisonment, the man was shot dead for treasonous acts against the Nazi regime. Frank and I had set the scene for the man to be sentenced to death. I live with this horrible, haunting fact to this very day.

The bathtub took forever to fill with hot water. Frank and I sprawled neck deep with our backs resting at either end of the tub. A foot found each other's groin. Our toes acted like fingers stimulating us to erection, after which our feet began masturbating the other gently. The intimacy was nice, not urgent, during which we talked about our homes and how much we missed loved ones.

Unable to resist, I asked him about his homosexuality. He venomously denied he was one and claimed he was only practising the 'alternative' sex until after the war when he would marry his longtime sweetheart, Maria. Of course my interest into how he was initiated into the 'alternative' sex was piqued. I had already surmised in my mind what I had learned from the other teens.

It was at a Hitler Youth summer camp where his platoon of forty thirteen year old boys were sent the very day after school let out. From the first day of arrival at the basic training camp the agenda was introduced. The boys were told to strip their clothes and all activities of the day were to be carried out in the nude. The reason given was to shed any inhibitions they may have harbored about their bodies. Living in an all-male environment there was no room for modesty. They were informed that they would be sleeping in the nude as the military did not always issue underwear, one less piece of clothing in need of laundry. It was recommended that soldiers save the two pair of issued socks for cold weather climates.

The following night was an introduction into open masturbation. Each cadet laid upon his cot and jerked off for all to see. Masturbation was normal and healthy, the instructor advised insisting that all males do it so why try to hide the fact. The young teens were assured that they would witness plenty of men masturbating during the morning showers at the advanced training bases.

That became a nightly ritual before lights out for a week. It only took a few nights for the teens to lose all inhibitions. The air in the small cramped barrack with cots spaced a mere foot apart took on a heavy odor of semen that, in itself, the boys were told was ninety-eight percent protein. They were told that in a survival situation, semen and urine could sustain their lives, so they should get used to the taste! Jerking off became a routine event during the morning showers. Their lessons had been well-learned.

The abasement of women was soon planted in their minds. Women were beautiful and sexy, but their value was limited to sex, raising babies and housekeeping. A soldier needed his comrade during war more than he could ever rely on a woman for his well-being. Soldiers were married to each other. Men also needed sex in lieu of an available woman.

That's when alternative sex was introduced and suggested. While never actually being forced into it, the commanders were relentless in their encouragement of it. At the morning revelry line ups for inspection, the commandant asked, with a show of hands, who enjoyed mutual masturbation or oral sex the previous night. Day after day the hands being raised increased, the teens were giving into the pressure. It became common to hear boys getting into each other's cots, giggles and bed springs along with the unmistakable sounds of wet slurping in the darkness. Some became brave using the showers for early morning mutual masturbation sessions.

That was where Frank met the Colonel, a regular visitor to the preliminary training camp. He and three others spent many nights at the man's residence and in his bed. Sometimes other boys were required to sleep with guests of the Colonel, but never Frank. Claus filled the void once Frank became too old for the man's tastes. However, he maintained a very good relationship with the Colonel ever since. So adept was he in seducing young boys within the Youth program, as well as civilian youth, that he became a pimp for the Colonel's needs.

The sun was coming up and we were interrupted a few times by men entering to piss, however, never did we stray from each other's cock. We got odd looks as the men held their dicks pissing. They nodded and made small talk in polite acknowledgement at the strange sight of us, although it was doubtful any paid enough attention to see what we were doing hidden in the depths of the tub. Knowing there would be no more privacy, and as the sign on the wall clearly advised, we went to the room leaving the tub full for others to enjoy. Hot water was at a premium during the heavy usage of the early morning hours.

The Colonel was sitting at the table along with Claus, both naked. The teens were all fast asleep. I regretted leaving the room. Claus had probably had sex with the man in my absence and had regained his place in the man's heart. I beat myself up over that. My place should have been with the Colonel when he awoke and needed his usual morning blow job to start his day. What a fool I had been to allow Claus the privilege. Maybe it was my imagination but I thought I saw sprinkles of dried cum at the corners of his mouth.

Not angry in the least, the Colonel was obviously curious where Frank and I had wandered off to. Hearing the highlights of our absence, he remained stone faced; however, I detected the slight form of his dimples at either side of his mouth suppressing a smile. Frank nor I told him that we were the ones that threw the Sargent's clothes and utility belt into the pool. Frank was wise in keeping that fact away from the man, whereas I selfishly wanted to brag about how he and I had taken care of business on the Colonel's behalf. I followed Frank's lead and shut up. I highly suspected that the man knew the truth but didn't want to hear it.

The Colonel ordered Claus to go down to the kitchen and arrange to have a few carafes of coffee, juice and a tray of Danish brought up to the room. No one was going anywhere any time soon, that was clear. He also told him to tell the staff to feed breakfast to any of the whore boys that may have been tossed from rooms, their usefulness having been served. I was glad that the Colonel was showing compassion toward them. Maybe he would send them back to the orphanage before too long.

The room service waiter was young, perhaps fourteen but short for his age. Dressed in all white with shiny black shoes, the blond, blue eyed lad was Adonis like.

I had not seen him around before. I was shocked to learn that he was the obese proprietor's nephew spending the summer working for his uncle. The Colonel was all eyes on the boy who was scanning the room with his jaw and eyes agape. The boy was definitely taken by the scene of five naked boys sprawled on the joined beds and a man with three additional teens all sitting just as naked at the small round table.

Claus and Frank clearly read the colonels mind. Both were quite used to getting the man what he wanted and there was no question that he wanted this boy. It didn't take them long before they were on their feet on either side of the dumb-struck lad who was nervously unloading the contents of his busing cart on top of the long dresser of drawers. His face turned a bright red when he realized he had two naked bodies standing so close to him.

Frank asked the boy if he knew who the man was. He was visibly in fear learning that it was the powerful Colonel. The man smiled broadly and waved when their eyes met. Claus suggested in a friendly manner that the boy join us for breakfast. Frank held the cart in place when the lad made excuses and prepared to exit the room. I was aghast fearing the young Adonis was about to be raped.

Frank somewhat soothed the worried waiter urging him to join us for breakfast as a guest of the man himself. He pointed out that it was an honor that his uncle would be very angry with if he found out such a privileged opportunity had been shunned. I could see his eyes lower and flutter. He knew that he had no choice but to stay and feigned a shy smile with a slight shrug of his shoulders ceding to the demands.

Claus suggested that he get comfortable and remove his clothes like the rest of us who were carefree and relaxed. Fear returned as Frank and Claus began undressing the young teen. His jacket was removed followed by the unbuttoning of his shirt which they pulled from his trousers and took off his torso. He was trembling but did not try to resist the removal of his clothes. He knew it would be pointless.

The Colonel continued to sit and watch but had not said a word. However, his hard cock which he continued to stroke clearly indicated his approval at the disrobing of the strikingly handsome young teen. He reached out for and poured himself a vodka almost overfilling the glass. His attention was preoccupied as he gazed at the beautiful young boy to his left. I took the liberty of relieving him of the bottle and took a swig myself.

The white trousers were unfastened and lowered to his knees. In his nervousness and fear, the boy had pissed himself and it flowed down his right thigh. As Frank and Claus were removing his shoes and socks, the wet underwear clung to his genitals revealing a long pinkish cock angled to the right straining the thin tight material. It was very clear that he was circumcised.

When he was finally asked by someone what his name was, the boy responded by saying that his name was 'Franz'. He told them that he was the result of a Polish mother and Austrian father. With a pronounced stutter and a hint of pomposity, he claimed that his father was the Polish ambassador as if that information would somehow sway matters in his favor. It didn't. Frank did the honors. Franz's underwear came down in one swipe that, once they hit the floor, he stepped out of on his own volition. With just a hint of arrogance, Franz kicked them forward with his left foot.

Any male that denies he sees beauty in another male's body is a liar. I couldn't deny the fact any longer. The five awakening teen physiques displayed in all their splendor whether laying on their backs, or in full frontal observation, were each beautiful in their different ways. Claus and Franks bodies held their own masculinity and were appealing to the naked eye.

To me, the Colonel was still the epitome of rogue manliness. However, Franz's body was so perfectly constructed with all the assets of being handsome, muscular, toned, and sun tanned except where a small fitting bathing suit might have covered his equipment. His beauty was not unlike that one might see in the pictures of Olympic swimmers I once saw so sparsely covered. I wondered if he wasn't a swimming athlete.

I envied Claus and Frank on their knees sharing the beauty of Franz's genitals, nonetheless, there was another tantalizing feature left open, inside the boy's firm rounded butt! Why I, myself, found that area strangely intriguing, I didn't quite understand. Frank's pink rose bud had been alluring. Franz's cherry plug was once again a curious fetish to me.

I scooted over and onto my knees to join in the seduction of Franz. His cheeks were soft as velvet with only a slight buoyancy. There was hardly a handful of meat to grasp as I spread them apart. The wrinkled pucker was much firmer and tighter than Frank's fucked chasm. It reminded me of chewing gum. Only the tip of my tongue could enter between the metallic tasting folds no matter how resolute I was to gain entry.

A gasp resounded. One was Franz, the other was the Colonel. I took a moment to look over my left shoulder at him. He was beaming from ear to ear with his juice flooding over his thumb. The voyeur was in his glory. A virgin boy was being had. I could not see what Claus and Frank were up to, but judging by the sound of the slobbering, smacking lips. I felt a face at his balls when I reached under, and his rocking to and fro, clearly indicated that all was well up front.

Franz grew suddenly frigid. I felt his hole clench and his body become rigid. The five soldiers had all risen to stand around. They were focused on devouring the pastries and fixing themselves a coffee or juice. They mingled around us seemingly oblivious to what was going on around them. All I saw was legs and their swaying genitals, a testicle festival from my vantage point as they scratched their balls and pulled at their cocks.

Apparently coming to terms with the sudden crowd, Franz resumed fucking someone's mouth and enjoyed his balls and ass being licked. I heard the Colonel give the five soldiers hell for blocking his view and while they moved off toward the window, they kept within reaching distance of the Danish pastries. I hoped there would be some left over for me.

For a second time, I felt Franz's ass close tight by my licking and prodding tongue. He was cumming. His legs shook and his ass quivered. I peered upward and saw his head rear back into his shoulder blades.

The Colonel summoned me over. He removed his hand from his cock and spread his legs wide. I knew what he wanted and I got on my knees again. I happily obliged the man. Frank came over and straddling me, he leaned over to share Franz's jism

with the Colonel. I was soon tasting his offering which pelted the depths of my mouth from his spasming cock.

In the background I heard a commotion, Franz was refusing to get on his knees and service Claus. The ever diplomatic Frank had finished feeding the Colonel like a mother bird feeding her hungry chick. Frank immediately took control of Claus who appeared ready to force the young civilian through violence if need be.

Observing the scene before him, the Colonel called Claus to him and had a quiet discussion. The next thing I saw was Claus dressing and the man writing something on stationary. Obviously, Claus was being sent on another errand.

Frank had leaned in and spoke a few soothing words that I could not hear into Franz's ear but, from the corner of my eye, I saw the boy kneel in front of Frank. The other teens cheered the lad on and chanted, "Suck! Suck! Suck!". Franz gave in and accepted the cock nudging his pursed lips.

The three infantrymen stroked their members fully prepared to rape the enemy civilian once Frank had had his way. After all, they had been taught and shown how by the very man seated in their presence. Surely he would expect nothing less. However the Colonel had other ideas. He looked at me, then at the teens. Looking at them, he told them that I would be the one to do the nasty deed first. Was this yet another test of my loyalty to him? Except, the problem was that I didn't think that I could do it!

Chapter XIII: Taking of a Cherry Trophy

The three young soldiers seemed relieved when the colonel intervened and told them to use the lad's mouth but not to fuck him. Perhaps they had no more need to rape to get their rocks off. Technically, they had been raped themselves from the moment they stepped into the room and then all night long, but in a different obligatory kind of way. Survival!

I was apprehensive. I did want to fuck him, Franz was gorgeous, but not under duress seeing his pleading eyes communicating with mine I wasn't sure if the tears forming were out of fear of me or the large-cocked-teen suffocating him soon after choking and spitting out the result of Frank's orgasm onto the floor in angery, bitter disgust. Perhaps he was over emphasizing his distaste for affect hoping for sympathy and a possible reprieve. He'd cooperated with Frank and thought that should have been enough and wanted no more part of it. He thought wrong.

Franz was sucking his third cock when a polite rap was heard at the door; an unobtrusive type knock, perhaps sounded with a key, like the chambermaids did whenever I occasionally stayed at the finest hotels with my father while on his business trips. Mostly, if they received no answer, the maids would let themselves into the room.

The Colonel looked at Frank and gestured silently with a head motion toward the door for him to see who was interrupting. He quickly returned his attention to the scene being played out before him. Frank got out of bed, opened the door cautiously to partially block his nudity. The voice that sounded from behind the door was none other than the Inn's proprietor. He was looking for his nephew who hadn't been seen in over an hour after he was charged by the kitchen with delivering room service to the Colonel's suite.

Frank lied and said the boy had left long ago after setting out breakfast, elaborating the sham by complementing the young waiter's astute service shown to the Colonel and his room guests. I saw the man's head squeeze between the door and frame, a sudden look of horror on his fat face registering first the naked bodies lying on the beds and then the bare rear-end of his nephew on his knees in front of an older teenager whose cock was being driven back and forth in his cherubic face.

Frank, thinking quickly, opened the door a few inches and then slammed the man's head with it. Stunned by the impact, his face turned ghostly white and his eyes rolled back in his head. He lost his balance and fell forward. The motion of his large

frame was more forceful than Frank could hold back with the door and the innkeeper soon landed sprawled on the floor inside the room.

The man's obesity didn't hinder his getting back on his feet quickly. At first staggering, he quickly regained his senses and then lunging toward the seated Colonel. Peter and Horst didn't waste a second jumping off the bed and tackling the man to the ground just a second before he made physical contact with their commander. I had to give him credit, the fat man had guts. I thought back and could only wish my own uncle had had the balls to stand up and protect me, not to mention his own wife.

The Colonel was amused. He laughed out loud. Suddenly, I could only grimace. He took on an evil look that I had seen before. Grasping the sparse hair of the subdued man at his feet, he forced his head upward, spit in his face and turned him viciously to look toward his nephew's rear view. What he saw was obviously what the man suspected before busting through the door. His nephew was sucking cock.

I felt horrible and sorry at the same time. The man had done nothing wrong other than try to protect his nephew. He struggled once more to get at the Colonel but Peter punched his head repeatedly. He actually hit the man's face only once but, when he did, the force of the blow caused the poor man's nose to deform and explode in a bloody mess.

With a simple nod toward the door by the Colonel, Peter, and Horst, with the aid of Frank, dragged the mass of blubber out into the hallway with his trousers seemingly wanting to stay behind, revealing gross hairy testicles but no visible cock. The door slammed behind them. The boys returned and Franz started calling for his uncle until someone told him to shut up or the next cock he would be sucking would be the fat mans

Peter and Horst had certainly earned themselves a place in the Colonel's good books although the lank and muscular man could easily have overpowered the threat in his midst. Right then and there the Colonel promoted both foot soldiers to Obersoldat or 'Private - First Class,' earning them a slight edge of superiority over their peers.

That same minor edge of power might even come in handy should either completely cede their morals to become loyal disciples of the Colonel's agenda, and should that happen, they would only enhance their opportunities for further promotions. Why wouldn't they if it made their life in the lower ranks easier?

No doubt, the Colonel's power to arbitrarily reward service with promotion sent a message to the other three lowly infantrymen. All of a sudden, the fat man barged into the room again however he never made it three feet before those same naked teens pounced on him and began to beat on him again. Again, I had to admire the man's protective instinct and felt very sorry for him. He was helpless in his effort to aide his nephew and, once again, my own cowardly uncle came back to mind.

The Colonel ordered the soldiers to bring the man into the room and keep him subdued. The innkeeper was going to witness the abuse of his nephew first hand. Boris and Peter tossed Franz onto the bed belly up and wrestled with the squirming boy to keep his legs against their chests. Everyone looked at me as if asking what I was waiting for.

The Colonel suddenly shoved me from between his legs. The erection I had sustained while blowing him never subsided. He had kept it aroused with his hand

even during the crisis' dealing with the obese man. It was my time to perform, and I thought it best not to delay too long or I risked losing my erection and wouldn't be sexually motivated enough to gain another.

Frank leaned over and basted my cock in grease At least Franz wasn't going to get dry fucked. I was justifying Franz's ordeal to appease my conscience by thinking that he was very fortunate to have my much smaller cock take him when compared to the sizes of the others in the room. Nor would I be too rough. I was only hoping that he would soon settle down and cooperate, otherwise his rape would be his own doing and so I absolved myself of any wrongdoing.

Poor Franz was well-restrained and muzzled. Frank was whispering something in his ear that seemed to calm him. It was apparent that the two knew each other. Logically, it was Frank's work assignment behind the scenes of the Inn was the link between them. I didn't doubt that Frank had designs on the beautiful boy. He no doubt saw this shrewd opportunity by exposing him to the Colonel whom Frank knew would salivate over the Adonis. He would have had to pull some strings in the kitchen in order to have Franz deliver the breakfast.

The obese Innkeeper wasn't blind. He would have deliberately kept his nephew well out of sight of the homosexual perverts who had taken over his domain. When he learned that Franz had been sent upstairs to the room of none other than the wolf himself, he knew it was a setup. He surmised that his kitchen staff were either none the wiser or, more likely, pressured into it out of fear.

I didn't have to worry about my erection. Franz's legs being held up and spread wide. His prune-like hole and his respectable genitals were displayed and vulnerable. This sight of beauty was enough to rush additional blood to my cock which was secreting a dew-drop of clear fluid My self-image of pride and prowess was certainly boosted because of having so many eyes focused on me.

Franz was tight. His anal muscles struggled to prevent the one-way anatomical valve from being forced to conform from its intended design. My rod hurt from the pressure meeting the resistance. I had never heard of anyone sustaining a fractured cock. I pictured mine in a cast with all the guys signing it just like my friends did the time I broke my arm.

I remembered the Colonel fucking me the first time. I was relaxed, my ass in the air enjoying him tonguing me. I remembered the sharp pain when he rammed into me. I wasn't expecting that because my anus was loose enough for him to gain precious inches before I knew what was happening. Looking down into the face of the beautiful and scared boy below me, I knew I needed Franz to let his guard down just for a second.

As I started to withdraw the laboriously gained inch of ground, I cried out that I didn't want to fuck him after all because my cock hurt too much. That did it. I could feel his rim give up the pressure surrounding my cock. Not wasting a precious second, I plunged into him merciless gaining at least two inches It was just enough to make the rest of the journey still difficult but enabled me to force my way inside him, inch by delicious inch, as his warm tunnel closed around me.

I had gambled using deceit and risked it all by giving up that precious inch of headway and appearing as if I were a coward. Peter and Boris were certainly convinced and releasing Franz's legs. Frank had uncovered his hand from the teen's

mouth only to hear a barrage of profanity, followed by a guttural scream when he realized that he'd been had. I think Not only had I gained some additional experience for future use but I also gained a great deal of respect and admiration from all. My co-participants in the taking of Franz's virginity scrambled to regain control of the teen who was flailing arms and legs. How I managed to stay embedded during that brief interlude was beyond me. I even suffered a random knee blow to my nose that smarted terribly.

No more Mr. Nice Guy, I fucked him hard. The more excited I became, the more adrenalin pumped through me, my breathing intensified spewing blobs of snot-slimy blood down to his groin and belly. His goods I fondled, so soft and fluid, he would never become erect under the circumstances, but that wasn't my intent. I was somewhat envious of the slightly younger boy because I did admire his manly perfection.

I looked over my right shoulder to see the Colonel beating his meat He gave me a proud smile and a wink which sent me into a euphoric state. I heard faint muffled complaints from the fat man Someone had silenced him with his own belt looped around his head and through his mouth like a bridle. He was still being held down on his knees by the three infantry teens.

After I came, Frank couldn't wait to take my place. He'd probably dreamed of that moment for a few weeks. One of the infantry lads took his place holding Franz down by the shoulders. There was no need to gag him, he had suddenly became quiet. Even when Frank entered him, he only flinched and let out a loud grunt. Peter, then Boris, took liberties. By then there was no restraint necessary, Franz held his own knees to his chest. I knew the feeling he was experiencing, numbness, his threshold for pain being maxed, his body finally fighting off the sense of pain and succumbing to some kind of oblivious state of mind.

The Colonel rose, found his gun belt and extracted his Luger. He ordered the belt removed from the fat man's mouth and immediately replaced it with the gun barrel deep enough to cause him to choke. The Innkeeper began to sweat profusely, his bloodshot eyes bugged out of his head and he wheezed like an asthmatic. In no uncertain terms, he told him that Franz was now his personal footman during the remainder of his stay, with the finest compliments of the Inn, of course.

Asking the man if he had any reservations about the new arrangements, he violently shook his head clearly indicating no. The Colonel smiled and thanked him for his respectful hospitality and released him. The weak kneed fat man was aided to his feet, turned and stumbled to the door. With his hand on the doorknob, the innkeeper again turned to the Colonel and stuttering, asked if the colonel would like lunch delivered to his room, Franz would be more than pleased to make those arrangements. My admiration of the man's integrity was instantly shattered; he was just as much the coward as my uncle was. I hoped that Franz would not endure the false sense of shame as I had done, as if we had a choice.

Franz was used three more times, even performing oral sex on the Colonel afterward. Once again I feared the new competition in my midst. I had best get used to it; the man would always have a fresh beautiful young boy at his disposal. Unlike Claus, I would accept that fact. There would be no sense in showing animosity toward them, and even if one could be shamed from the Colonel's graces by us adversaries,

another would surely follow. As my father often said about his business ventures that I never understood until then, it is prudent to keep your friends close and your enemies even closer.

Claus walked in, a stack of files under each of his arms that he handed them over to the Colonel. He looked strangely curious at the new face being cuddled in bed by Frank while the other soldiers lazing around looking dazed and satisfied in semi sleep. We were playing chess. The Colonel asked me to retrieve my game from my duffel bag to teach him. I didn't say it but, as far as I was concerned, the Colonel's life was a chess game that he crafted so well. There was no question in my mind that the actual game would be child's play for the him.

The Colonel breezed through the ten files separated from the other stack. His interest seemed to be centred on one particular identical page of each file. He would give the hint of a smile at each one and then stacked them in a single pile once he had perused them. I saw typed, printed names on the tabs similar to those my father was often seen with. Claus had been sent to the base to collect personnel files which surrendered to him by the Colonel's secretary under his written orders. He obviously wasn't planning on going to the base that day.

He summoned Frank over. The teen had just gotten Franz's cock hard and was no doubt planning on going down on it But an order is an order and, reluctantly, he obeyed his order and joined the Colonel at his side. Frank was asked to look at the names on each file to see if he recognized any of them. He selected six. Two, he said, were currently bunk mates, two he had worked base security with and the other two had spent time in the same training unit outside of Munich. Then he dropped the bombshell without being asked. He told the Colonel that he'd had had sex with four of the ten soldiers at some point.

The soldiers of interest to the Colonel were all involved in the base searches the previous night. He commented that all ten young men had attended training and holding camps awaiting deployment where he knew for certain the same sex agenda was endorsed. Although he remained stone faced, I was learning to read his eyes. He was elated by his discovery.

The Colonel had to have detected how smitten Frank was of Franz. He laughed and told him to get back in bed with his boyfriend and give him a blow job, afterward, Frank would have an errand to run. The thicker stack of files he didn't bother to sort through, I just knew in my heart that they were of the many men caught in the late night raids.

The Colonel was a busy man. He ordered Claus to round up the ten whore boys. Once gathered outside, one by one they entered our room and he quizzed them as to who they spent the night with and what sexual activities had transpired. Alex also entered. He was still naked, as they all were. No one knew where the boys' clothes had ended up during the party. Poor Alex was black and blue, his eyes swollen to narrow slits, his lips fat and scabbed. One look at him and the Colonel was on his feet demanding to know who had beaten him so badly.

Claus was dispatched again, this time to direct the three infantrymen along with Peter and Boris to room five. Telling them to dress, he ordered the men to kick down the door if necessary and rifle butt the officer occupants in a flash raid that they had

been trained to carry out. I believe the five truly relished the thought of beating the snot out of officers, many of whom treated lowly infantrymen very poorly.

Frank was instructed to drive back to base and make quiet arrangements with the Colonel's Adjutant to have all the parties involved in the base's search raids; the search team members, as well as, detainees alike. They were all to be delivered to the Inn later that afternoon.

Next, he ordered me to find a duty sergeant and have him report to him immediately. I returned to the room not ten minutes later and found the virile Colonel on top of Franz fucking him vigorously. Leaving the Duty Sergeant to wait in the hall with the naked whore-boys, I sat at the table, poured myself a vodka and watched until he drove the final thrust into the panting boy. I know it wasn't the alcohol but I definitely heard Franz breathlessly mutter, "thank you, Sir!" While his sincerity may have been doubtful, at least he was smart enough to know that his survival, and perhaps that of his aunt and uncle, was at stake.

After filling the boy with his essence, the Colonel didn't wallow atop Franz. In no time at all. he was on his feet still semi-erect and dripping semen when he opened the door to usher the sergeant into the room. Doing up his trousers, the red-faced NCO had been getting a blow job from one of the whore boys while biding his time. The Colonel ignored the man on-duty's indiscretion and got right down to business. He gave him a list of nine rooms to be vacated by the inhabitants who were to be sent back to base accommodation. The excuse given was that the rooms were needed for unexpected high rankers arriving that evening.

It was the list he drew up while interviewing the whore-boys, a list of occupants who restricted themselves to using the boys, and not each other. Only one boy claimed that the two men he spent the night with engaged in sex with each other, as well as, enjoying their young guest. Their room was spared eviction.

Also on the 'hit' list, were the rooms that the search party had found no sexual activity taking place in except for the two occupants who were innocently sleeping in their respective beds. I was confused as to the Colonel's motives. He hadn't mentioned anything about the pending arrival of high rankers, as he called them but, then again, why would he?

Franz was even tasked with notifying his uncle, the innkeeper, and the kitchen staff that the Colonel would again be hosting a soiree that afternoon. It was to be a pool party, not for officers but for a few of his valued infantrymen.

The Colonel's squad of vigilantes returned laughing so hard they could hardly remain standing. The four officers had been dealt with. Two to a bed, sound asleep and naked, they never knew what, or who, had hit them, only hearing that it was in retaliation for beating a little kid. The Colonel would later have to deal with the four child-beaters who would register complaints of being assaulted in their beds. The Colonel, being the Colonel, would assure them that the matter would be looked into, and that would be the end of that.

Their next mission was not as savoury, perhaps even demoralizing. The five were told to return to base, each was instructed to seek out peers whom they knew had been trained earlier in the year and then housed at remote camps awaiting deployment. They were to be invited to the Colonel's party. It was an invitation none dared refuse.

Everything became clear to me then. The Inn was being cleared of hardline military seniors to make room for younger homosexuals, as well as, potential 'alternative' sex friendly troops in a blatant, cocksure, even risky master plan to push forward the secretive Nazi agenda.

I didn't have to hope that the Colonel knew what he was doing, I was absolutely sure of the man's capability to initiate his daring endeavour and seeing its success to the end. The Colonel's very own endorsement of 'alternative' sex would cause a ripple effect, then a tidal wave within the young battalion ranks secure in the knowledge and knowing that there would be no severe repercussions any longer! However, deep down, I had a strong worry that the man would become a target of opposition forces within his own battalion. I feared for his life and, as a result, my own!

CHAPTER XIV: A PARTY AT THE INN

In the Colonel's opinion, all the pieces were falling into place. He no longer had use for the ten whore-boys and ordered the duty sergeant to arrange a troop carrier to take the boys back to the orphanage. In the meantime, while we awaited the transport to arrive from the base, Claus and I were told to take the boys, who were still loitering naked in the hallway, feed them lunch and allow them the use of the swimming pool.

Both Claus and I knew what the man's motive was. He wanted time alone with Franz. To say that I wasn't jealous would be a lie. Claus, on the other hand, was furious. He moped and sulked and frequently gazed up at the window. We were both sure the Colonel wasn't taking a nap as he claimed. Franz had gone to get him some lunch, his beautiful cock would be dessert before any nap, rest assured.

The Inn was eerily quiet, the dining room empty, save for the few perimeter security soldiers on their lunch break. The remaining officers were obviously in their rooms as ordered, awaiting their fate. Many would have been base residents spending the night after hooking up for sex with the privileged ones with rooms. To my knowledge, the Colonel, whether an oversight or on purpose, had not dealt with them as yet. I felt sorry for them, especially the men I spent the night with and had to fight off the urge to go to them and put their minds at ease.

Two of the diners came outside to while away the remainder of their lunch break. They sat and watched the nude boys playing in the pool. They were both in their late twenties, fairly handsome, and began making lewd comments to me and Claus, who were dressed and supervising the others. Claus laughed and told them that we were not whore-boys, but should the men wish, he would send two over to give them each a blowjob.

The soldiers trousers were open in an instant and Claus lived up to his word. At least the men left us alone to continue to dwell on our sorrows after that. However, one of the men had a very appealing display of manhood leisurely suspended from his trousers. I was a bit envious of the boy who knelt down before the seated man and obediently serviced him. Sadly, the scene and its effects on his full endowment were blocked from my view so I was left to my own imagination.

Perhaps it was my sour mood that caused me to take stock of myself and re-evaluate my fixation for the male genitalia, especially my preference for masculine men. It wasn't normal. I realized then that I had come a long way from the

philosophy of only doing what I had to do to survive. Truth was, I loved cock, and shamefully, it really didn't matter who the man was, I would be willing and eager to give him a blowjob.

The desire to suck my own father's cock was not too far-fetched from my imagination. Where that sudden sick thought came from scared the fuck out of me. But truth is, I would! I would want to blow my own father and show him how good it was It was probably a pleasure that mom wasn't giving him. Other than whores, I doubted wives did that. I would even go as far to admit that I would like him to fuck me, make love to me like the Colonel does. I found myself erect, visualizing my dad coming into my room at night like he used to do on rare occasions in order to kiss me goodnight. Instead, in my imagination, he would take off all his clothes. I would smell his manly cologne as he got into bed beside me. Finally, he would have a good reason to pay attention to me instead of locking himself in his office all night.

Claus nudged me and brought me out of my semi-conscious state. The troop carrier had arrived and the boys were being herded aboard. I was happy to see the end of their nightmare and that they were leaving the Inn in a cloud of dust. The many men assigned to the simple task made me laugh. The boys were in for one last sexual adventure before their journey home was complete. I had gotten cold hearted, another fault that I had to reckon with.

Claus and I bypassed the pool and continued on to the gazebo, each feeling the need for each other's company without words being spoken. Inside, we undressed and in a standing position, held each other crushingly tight to grind our crotches together. We didn't kiss, however, like two vampires our mouths bit and sucked each other's neck. Hands joined as one that we fucked in heated mutual masturbation. How we remained standing defied gravity, dizzy from an erotic kind of spinning waltz, we bounced off the rounded walls or rolled along them. Neither had the need to suck or fuck. What we were doing was uniquely between us, a much different sex than we were accustomed to. One body, one mind and one terrific orgasm that oozed between fingers to a sloping wet final few weakening fist fucks.

Some other place, in some other life, we may have had to explain the red and purple hickeys applied to each other in passion, however there was no fear of that embarrassment in the company we kept. Nor was there shame at the obvious fact that we had given them to each other in some sort of sexual contact. Never in my wildest imagination would the boys at school put two and two together and then slap our backs in unbiased good humored support. Yes. I had been transported to another world, another way of life far removed from the values and standards once known to me. I wondered if I could ever go back to it.

Sweaty and slimy, we had a dip in the pool. Returning to the room, the Colonel was nowhere to be seen. I didn't realize how tired I was, it had been a very long night and an even more interesting day. It was going to be another long but an even more than unusual night. I was certain of it. Claus and I laid down and slept for several hours.

I awoke startled. One of those few-second episodes where you don't know where you are, or if it is morning or night. Seeing Claus beside me, my mind sorted itself out and returned me back to reality. A voice emanated, resounding loudly. An angry voice, screaming his words that echoed from what had to be a public address system

outside. I identified it seconds later; it was the scary man in Berlin that I had heard on my parents RCA Victor.

I dashed to the window and saw rows of soldiers below. All at attention, perfectly still as mannequins in a department store. They were listening to an amplified radio broadcast address by their Fuhrer. The sound quality was so poor that I could not comprehend a word.

Claus stood at my side rubbing his eyes, turned away back toward the bed and said offhanded and carefree with a hint of sarcasm, 'It must be Saturday; the lunatic is speaking to his loony-bin again!' With a yawn, he climbed back into bed.

He added with a chuckle, for whatever reason, that the men hearing the speech live from outside Berlin would clap loudly long after the man had left the podium; none wanting to be the first to stop applauding among their peers because it would be seen as disrespectful. The silliness went on for eons, according to Claus. Who was I to disbelieve him? More so, where had he learned the callus opinion of his country's leader and his followers; perhaps the Colonel himself was a Judas?

It was what happened immediately after the broadcast that had me call Claus back to the window to witness. The smiling and waving Colonel, wearing his dress uniform supported by an extremely attentive impeccably dressed Frank, made his way through the throng of at least one-hundred rather sedate almost humiliated men to a small riser stage where he was given a microphone.

The Colonel addressed his men about the long, path they had travelled victoriously and how the treacherous road lay ahead for all. He exemplified that men must do what they had to do to in order keep their sanity for the betterment of their units and survival of all; even if their thoughts strayed not only from old-fashioned military codes and doctrine, but also, in times of war and duress, nature's own rules of decency and conduct could be bent with God's blessing shining on his favourite military machine.

His words sent his command into a frenzy of cheers and jubilation. He was exonerating his men for giving into the carnal needs that even he desired in such lonely times and found unrepentant comfort and solace in an alternative to fulfill man's instinctive desires when normal options were so sadly unavailable! Raising his left hand he laid it on Frank's shoulder. Frank bashfully looked up at the man to meet his warm devil-be-damned smile.

These words were so carefully structured. Never once did he blatantly cite that he was advocating homosexuality. His words were ambiguous enough that some men could be seen scratching their heads in confusion, whereas most others absorbed the full meaning of his speech.

The Colonel had kept his cards close to his chest all day. The 'guilty' parties thought they were being assembled not only to hear their final throne speech, but for disciplinary measures that would surely follow, perhaps even firing squads. The euphoria that erupted was deafening. I could only imagine the relief felt by so many, their hours having been spent fretting what unknown fate awaited them. I learned later that two had already taken their own lives while many more contemplated that tragic action to end their nightmare.

The Colonel excused himself telling the soldiers to enjoy their evening because the Inn was theirs to enjoy. Tents had been set up on the lawn for sleeping overnight as

there would be no transports back to base that night. He chuckled mischievously adding that no military police would round up drunks and that the Inn was temporarily off limits to perimeter security forces. The message was clear, they were to police themselves, a cautious reminder that any man trying to leave the Inn would be shot, as per standard security orders. The Colonel had ensured that there would be a very captive audience at his party.

Liquor flowed freely, music blared from the tinny sounding PA system diligently installed for the Fuhrer's speech. Modern American swing tunes were sung and danced to despite the sound quality. Who cared? They were the personal guests of the Colonel's gala to enjoy without the strict day to day supervision of superiors, a much needed social event to forget reality if only for a night.

The host mingled in the crowd, shaking hands, exchanging pleasantries with Frank close by his side keeping up the mystique of their true relationship. Frank had become somewhat of a celebrity himself, a minor officer and a very high ranking officer would certainly lend to speculation; however, the illusion would also be that rank had no protocol when it came to forging interpersonal relationships.

Little did they know that they were guinea pigs in a Nazi experiment that could change military morality thereafter. That very night would reveal how well the Colonel had orchestrated the agenda within his own battalion. All the Colonel could do was sit back and hope that the stage was set that night, no holds barred.

Claus, Franz and I squeezed for a vantage point either side of the Colonel and watched the festivities from our room window. Frank, Boris, Peter and the three, still unnamed infantrymen, partied with their peers, lost somewhere in the crowd. I searched for Hans, Michel and Damon, hoping so much that they were present to enjoy the Colonel's party.

Of course, in the sweltering heat, the allurement of the swimming pool was prone for stripping off clothing along with the horseplay that resulted in the shedding uniforms after being thrown into the water fully dressed. Unlike the night before, nudity took precedence as the booze flowed and the night progressed.

Frank came in the room bearing gifts for the Colonel. A boy whose uniform hung from his smallish, slender body as if he was childishly masquerading in his father's clothes. Of course, the boy was blond as blond could be with piercing blue eyes and red rosy cheeks that I was not sure was a natural boyish hue, or flushed from shyness.

He would have had to be at least fifteen years old to be enlisted, but didn't look a day over twelve and a half. How he could possibly support a Mauser rifle over his shoulder, let alone hold and point one at an enemy was beyond comprehension.

A new unit had arrived at the base that day to join the Colonel's battalion. All I could think of was that recruiting was getting pretty desperate. The Nazis seemed to be strengthening their forces in numbers by lowering the age of recruitment to supply demand. Even the Colonel had to subdue a chuckle at the sight of one of his newly supplied infantrymen.

When the boy literally marched over to his grand superior, a stocking foot completely exited his ill-fitting boot as the overzealous lad performed the foot stomp in conjunction with the out stretched arm salute and screamed, "Heil Hitler!"

The Colonel couldn't hold back his amusement. He looked at Frank as if he was up to a silly prank but Frank smiled smugly and shrugged his shoulders, his arms

potential victims. Rarely, if ever, did a 'treat' leave the residence without having had Claus' cream swimming around in his belly and the Colonel's little soldiers embedded deep in his rectum. Without a doubt, the two made a great team in the seduction of vulnerable children. I resolved then and there to find a straight razor and remove my own sparse pubic hair. I would be one up on Claus. He was much further into puberty with hair on his legs, I didn't. The Colonel would find me irresistible!

CHAPTER XV: A DEATH AT THE PARTY

The soiree was very festive. I could feel the aura of relaxed and happy people around me. The four bartenders and numerous waiters and busing staff supplied from the military base appeared to be having just as much of a good time compared to the previous evening's party.

A late evening buffet fit for a king was a definite treat from the infantrymen's usual grub. Roast beef and hams were being sliced by the Inn's own two chefs. An assortment of hot vegetables warmed in chaffing dishes accompanied by breads, salads, pickles and fancy desserts. Claus and I gorged ourselves. Our plates were piled high that we started from the top and ate our way layer by layer. We even returned for seconds. We washed everything down with a couple of steins of ale each.

We sat in the grassy area across from the pool which began to overflow because of so many bodies frolicking or horsing around. From what I could see, the gods must have favoured the Germans with handsomeness and such fine physiques. Everywhere I looked, naked men were swimming, standing around talking or grazing on the buffet. I thought how my mother would be horrified if I ever came to dinner in just my underwear, never mind naked! Semi-formal attire was the norm at suppertime in our house.

Being on the outside looking in, Claus and I saw many beautiful looking teens and young men being intimate with each other. There was plenty of touching, groping, and mutual masturbation going on in the pool and, as the night went on, there were definitely meetings in the surrounding bushes for blowjobs and a good fucking. The large tent erected for sleeping arrangements saw a constant stream of men coming and going.

We decided to sneak to the back of the tent, lift up the canvas from the ground and stick our heads inside. It was dark, but my vision adjusted enough to see twenty or so soldiers either on their knees in what Claus called, 'pulling train,' indiscriminately giving blowjobs to anyone who stood in front of them. Others were on hands and knees taking it up the ass and sucking cock at the same time. The din was that of pants, grunts, moans, groans and the slapping of skin-on-skin. The smell that permeated the air was of canvas, body odour, and sex. The smell was intoxicating and a nice blend indeed It was a smell that I soon came to appreciate.

I was extremely excited by it all. My cock was so hard and uncomfortably restrained in my trousers. When Claus suggested we join in the massive orgy, I was

the first to remove my clothes and crawl under the canvas. That was the last of Claus that I saw for a long while because I eagerly 'pulled train,' as Claus called it. The interior was dark enough that my youthful features would not have been detected except for perhaps my long hair, an oddity considering military regulations. There was a probable curiosity on the part of the many men who held my head to fuck my mouth but not one questioned it.

I lost track of time and exactly how many blowjobs I gave. The tent was crowded with men. I opted for a position along the wall to prevent my feet and calves from being stepped on. My jaw ached and my sinuses and sense of taste detected nothing other than semen that had been deposited down my throat or in my mouth and swallowed quickly before the next impatient cock materialized.

I had been fucked three times, that much I was aware of. I felt the ooze leaking from my rectum and over my balls. Although my ass was numb, it wasn't nearly as sore as my jaw. Even my inner ears hurt for some strange reason. I had been a slut, a whore, and enjoyed every minute of it. The complete and utter darkness assured anonymity and added a sense of intrigue not knowing or caring who was doing what to who. I thought again how I would never again fit in back home. I loved cock and to be denied it would be like an alcoholic without his liquor.

I needed to cool off; the tent had to have been a stifling ninety-five degrees. I removed myself by easily rolling under the canvas and disappearing after my final fuck. The man I had been sucking would just have to find an alternative mouth to cum in because I was done. I found my clothes behind the tent and carried them to the pool area. Claus had already gathered his stuff and gone long before me. He had only sought after a quick blowjob or someone to fuck.

I didn't see him anywhere. A gander up and I did see the colonel leaning from the window over Zane. There was no sign of anyone else present in the room. Boris and Peter were sitting at a patio table with two young men. Two of the three unnamed infantrymen each had a very young soldier that they were leading toward the gazebo. These were conquests that would make the colonel proud and their own lives would be enriched by his blessings.

I caught a glimpse of Frank handing over a room key to four naked soldiers who leaned on each other in an intimate drunken camaraderie. Each sported states of arousal from fully hard to semi-erect. Frank exchanged words with them and the four trotted inside the Inn grateful for their good fortune of privacy. Frank looked for more candidates, I last saw him heading toward Peter and Boris. Their seduction of the two obviously younger and nervous men in their company would be made much easier in the confines of a room. Frank had obviously concluded that, after the time Peter and Boris had spent participating in the Colonel's private orgy, the teens had earned the right of a room. Just by the look on Peter and Boris' faces when Frank handed Peter the key, I knew that the two young novices in tow would be right royally fucked by morning.

Four men stood naked huddled near the bar belly to belly in mutual masturbation, others fully dressed sat at the bar, their arm movements giving them away to what they discretely attempted to hide, hand jobs.

Later that night, inhibitions were completely lost by many. Men lay upon loungers or on the pool deck receiving blowjobs, many were in sixty-nine positions. One

couple was fucking with the bottom's legs held high by two visibly excited soldiers awaiting their turn. The large tent remained a popular venue, discretion was still paramount for most, perhaps finding the sudden sexual freedom in public much too intimidating, especially those being exposed to alternative man-on-man sex for the first time.

By night's end, there didn't appear to be a person dressed, liquid courage seemed to have alleviated inhibitions. Open sexual activity around the pool was still evident however, it appeared to be kept to a minimum. I watched as men continued to pair off and head into the darkness within the garden. Two stood in the pool engaged in a very passionate kiss. They were lovers, I thought, finally able to expose their secret affair.

Even the waiters and busing staff dared to take in a blowjob or give one. Two very drunk bartenders sat on the bar with their trousers down sharing a bottle of vodka and enjoying the customers servicing them.

The Colonel would be very pleased. The night had been very well-planned and orchestrated. Where I had expected to see men distancing themselves, there were none. They either took an active role or were selfish in their own sexual needs, it didn't matter. All that mattered was the end result; tolerance. In my opinion, the Colonel's 'litmus' test was a huge success.

There would be plenty of men willing to service those strong willed naysayers who relented their morals in need of pent up sexual release. Guys like me, cock lovers, who got off giving more than receiving or bending over to receive our gratification. All those reluctant to participate in what they might considered unmanly, they could and probably would be used.

Claus found me in the swimming pool and told me that the Colonel wanted me back upstairs. At least he put the effort into finding me, unlike the night before. My ego was tarnished anyway. The only looks I seemed to get were those quizzical ones wondering how a young boy ended up in their midst. After all, they were enjoying the company of each other so they had no use for whore boys any longer.

Zane and the Colonel sat against the headboard sharing sips from a vodka bottle. If it were at all possible, seeing Zane naked made him look even younger than he actually was. He looked frail as skinny as he was, his rib cage clearly outlined through his skin. Unblemished by even the slightest of pubic down, Zane was certainly a late bloomer.

His longish slender cock was tipped with a bead of foreskin. His balls did hang low I noticed. They were well-pronounced cherry-sized orbs weighted them down in his pink sack that hung between his milky-white thighs. I truly expected that when I entered the room, he would cower with embarrassment; however, he appeared carefree of his lack of development. Either the vodka aided his courage, or he had quickly figured out the Colonel's fetish and was flaunting it. I refused to be upstaged.

The Colonel patted the bed, an invitation for me to join him on his other side. Not bothering to dress poolside, I dropped my clothes and hopped around saying that I had to go down the hall and pee.

The Colonel's shaving kit was on the shelf above his uniforms hanging near the door. Nobody could have possibly seen me snag it. Without a nick and looking like an eleven year old boy, I returned to the room. It wasn't my imagination when I saw the

Colonel's cock twitch and expand. He was looking through his tired squinting eyes which immediately opened wide. His mouth gaped open and then a broad smile appeared. He patted the bed once again indicating for me to join him. I snuggled under his left arm, his eyes never leaving my groin.

Claus had undressed and joined Frank and Franz in the adjacent beds that were still merged together as one. Frank was holding Franz tight against his chest and running his fingers through his hair and kissing him on the lips lovingly once in a while. They needed their privacy. I admired Frank's unselfish distribution of the rooms; he could easily have taken one for himself and his boyfriend.

I good naturedly hauled Claus over by his arm and cuddled him under mine. He didn't resist, he needed some love and attention as well and soon relaxed with his head on my chest.

The Colonel took his arm from around me in order to fondle my hairless tribute to him. He was a little rough not only with me but also with Zane who yelped once he endured the same painful grope. The man's cockhead hovered over his naval twitching with his usual flow of juice in a thin string that I watched as it slowly expanded and slopped on his belly.

I placed my hand behind Zane's head and guided it down the Colonel's chest and belly. He was a little resistant but I led by example with my own face mere inches from the tip of the lava flowing mini-volcano. His contorted face made me wonder if he hadn't gone down on the Colonel yet or if he had only been fucked by the long thick manly appendage.

I directed his head until his pursed lips were sodden and glistening in slime. I licked and mouthed the shaft to give him some encouragement. Claus got impatient. He leaned in and slapped Zane on the head telling him to go down on it. It wasn't really necessary. Zane would have complied in due course. I was angry. I had never laid a hand on anyone before, but right then I saw red and backhanded Claus. He was about to attack me when Frank leaned over and held him back.

The Colonel looked on in amusement. He gave Claus a leer, then held the back of Zane's head and told him to open his mouth. He had no choice but to comply. He did. Ever so slowly the Colonel fed him more and more of his long thick cock which stretched his lips and filled his virgin mouth. I was concentrating on watching the making of a new cocksucker so I don't know how many fingers the Colonel had shoved up Zane's ass. However many it was, it caused the boy to give a muffled scream.

The man had inserted two digits into my rectum and wasn't being very gentle about it. I didn't mind. Most likely, he was aware of why the ease of entry was so smooth and slick. He tickled that special spot driving me wild. I had to assume Zane had succumbed to the same delight because he began fellating the Colonel with a hint of effort. I became suddenly jealous and pushed his forehead back and before the man's cock could sense the room temperature, I swallowed it deep into my throat. I was determined to see how much I could take. When my nose became embedded in the bristly hair of his crotch, I was pleased with myself.

Zane wasn't getting off that easy. I forced his head into the Colonel's balls. He didn't have to be told what to do. I saw his pink tongue lapping and his lips surround a hairy nut and then move to the other. I had to breathe and pulled off enough that I

could at least breathe through my nose. Hands free of his cock; I sucked and bobbed like a madman while his fingers inside me concentrated on that miraculous zone. I swung my leg accidentally hitting him on the head. I planted my knee on his chest with heavenly bliss and, suddenly my cock twitched without manual stimulation and began emptying itself with strong jerks onto the Colonel's abdomen.

Spent of all energy I couldn't suck his cock any longer. I reached over and directed Zane to take over while I tried to catch my breath. I was expecting the amateur, inexperienced cock-sucker to flounder and not give the Colonel the pleasure he deserved.

I needn't have worried. Knowing exactly what to do, Zane's performance had me gaga. Could it be a natural instinctive trait in males to just know how to please another male? Besides myself, Peter, Boris, Franz, and the three nameless novices caught on to it without any direct guidance. Guys simply knew subconsciously how to please other guys.

When the Colonel reached his climax Zane was none too pleased with the load of cum he had to deal with in his mouth. He frowned and made yucky faces looking around for somewhere to spit out the Colonel's seed. I saved him the effort by bringing his face down to mine. My tongue easily forced its way into his mouth before he knew it.

Zane was only too anxious to expel it when he realized that I wasn't trying to intimately kiss him. The oyster-like texture channelled down my tongue and pooled at the rear of it. His saliva added to the Colonels well-known heavy ejaculates. I strained my eyes to the left to assure myself that the man was watching the exchange of his fluid, another bonus point scored.

Frank was covering Franz and lovingly fucking him. He kissed his face, sucked his neck and nibbled his ears. The passion was real. Franz clung to Frank's neck, his hips slowly gyrating to enhance the pleasure inside him.

Once again, Claus was the odd man out. Zane and I continued to share the Colonel's favour tucked under his muscular arms, Frank and Franz certainly didn't want his company. Claus lay between us sulking and was soon asleep. The Colonel was soon snoring as well.

Once Frank had poured his essence up Franz's butt, we all decided to go for a swim. Naked, we made our way down the stairs through the lobby. The Colonel's embargo on security staff within the Inn was still honoured even coming close to sunrise. No soldiers lingered drinking coffee on their break. Only the perpetual sound of dishes clanging in the kitchen could be heard.

Men were sleeping on loungers, or passed out on the grass. A group of four fully dressed men were awake sitting around a table sharing two bottles of vodka among them, obviously very drunk.

Seeing the four of us enter the pool area naked, they whistled and hooted. We ignored them, absorbed in playing a very active game of water-polo. They carried on calling us whore-boys and that we were 'shit out of luck' because all the homos were already sequestered fucking each other. Obviously older, they assumed correctly that Frank was a soldier. They called him a queer, fudge packer, part of the Colonel's 'pansy' brigade and threatened that once they reached the front, errant bullets would exterminate the homosexuals one by one.

Ignored, they began to throw beer bottles at us with one hitting Franz on the head and knocking him senseless I sprang quickly to his aid. I grabbed hold of him, held him above the water and struggled to lift his body onto the deck. Frank became furious, hauled himself out of the pool and attacked the man responsible sending him backward on his chair. The other two retaliated. Frank fought them off with his feet and fists. Zane and I rushed to his aid but were easily shoved aside by these battle hardened men as the two of them beat and kicked the helpless Frank.

I ran. Doors crashed behind me, shattering glass was heard in my wake. Four steps at a time, I ran up the flights to our room. Exhausted, out of breath, all I could do was jump on the Colonel blabbering like an idiot before his eyes opened. Claus woke and must have understood my German gibberish and ran to the window.

With horror on his face he turned and screamed at the Colonel that Frank and Zane were being beaten up by four men. I swear the Colonel's feet never touched the ground before he was at the window. I don't know what urged me, but I ran and grabbed his gun belt and handed it to him. He withdrew his luger and fired off two shots in the air.

Everyone poolside froze looking around not sure where the shots originated. Sleeping men awoke startled trying to grasp the situation. The Colonel screamed down at them to cease and desist. They might not have recognized the Colonel in the dark, but the pistol was enough to mean someone meant business.

Handing the gun to Claus to keep aim, the Colonel tore from the room. Even I, a third of his age could not keep up to the naked man leaping stairs onto landings, the ground level fire door so severely shoved, it hung precariously from one hinge.

I think that it was me who shattered the glass door that the Colonel ran through causing the remaining glass to shatter before him. A crashing noise behind me swivelled my head to see soldiers storming the front doors of the Inn, the gunshots had alerted the alarm.

If the Colonel was not already etched in my mind as a hero, it was reinforced. The four men stood no chance as the madman sending tables and chairs to crash aside in his urgency to protect his boys. It all happened so fast, bodies were thrown knocking over more tables and chairs. Two of the men backed off with their arms and hands stretched before them, fearful, scared shitless making a peace gesture in final recognition of the man.

No time for pleasantries, the Colonel reached down for a separated chair leg and beat the two men already on their knees, arms protecting heads against the onslaught of a very unforgiving man, their supreme leader.

Seeing the Colonel, the security men raged forth in a useless effort to subdue what the Colonel had already managed to single handedly bring to order. Well not really, Zane was like a little mad pit bull. He clung to a man's back who was attempting to rise to his feet while the Colonel was 'chair legging' his buddy. We later joked of it and Zane was so proud of himself. We all agreed that he had every right to be!

Military police soon arrived along with medics. I was very impressed with the response time. The duty sergeant had wasted no time in calling in a disturbance at the Inn. The same Inn that their Colonel resided in explained the overkill of twenty police officers with more arriving by the minute. Many had been summoned from their beds.

He was an important man and even I knew that, however when all hell had apparently broken loose where the Colonel was concerned, all the stops were pulled and a code-red was called in to the base.

Frank was tended to by the medics His broken ribs were evident and he had possible internal injuries that required him to be immediately transported to the base hospital. Franz was treated for the gash to his forehead from the bottle. The four men were arrested for assault of an officer even though they had no idea he was one. Franz, Zane and I all swore to the police that Frank had clearly identified himself before the altercation. We felt that sometimes lies are necessary.

Nonetheless, once again I hated myself, though. Four more men might very well be executed. Four men who obviously opposed the goings on and must have kept a very low profile away from the party. I hadn't noticed them at any time earlier because they were probably seated on the dimly lit outdoor dining terrace.

The abusive soldiers were about to be led away in handcuffs when the main instigator was heard in a loud voice trying to convince the MPs that military rules of conduct had been severely jeopardized by way of blatant homosexual activity and that they should round up everyone, including the Colonel, and arrest them. He sealed his own fate, I thought. An additional charge of slandering a Nazi superior officer would be brought against him. His three cohorts remained silent, smart enough to realize that they were in enough shit already.

He would die a quicker death than the others. The colonel asked an MP for his luger and in a split second, placed the barrel at the man's temple and shot him dead. A gory mess of brains and blood splattered his handler and anyone else within proximity. The Colonel then pointed the gun at the other three arrestees and asked if they wanted to add anything in their defence as to what provoked their beating of a fellow comrade. The fear in their eyes was very real. As the blood drained from their faces, one man collapsed from weakened knees and held in place by his two handlers.

By then, men were fleeing the large tent like rats scurrying in all directions from under the canvas, all naked and looking scared hearing gunshots. The sight of two dozen military police and numerous other Inn security milling about, they feared another raid was in progress. Having nowhere to hide, most lay frozen on the ground while others scurried into the garden. In reality all they had to logically do was feign sleep as many probably were innocently wrapped in the supplied blankets that had been stacked at the entrance. Their guilt overrode their logic; paranoia had taken over.

If the MP Major noticed the abnormal behaviour from within the tent or the fact that everyone else around was naked, including the Colonel, along with the piles of strewn uniforms, all probable evidence of the dead man's rantings, he never said a word. He began ushering his troops to the carriers. The infantry Duty Sergeant sent his men back to their posts. The Major, organised a stretcher to remove the body of the dead antagonistic soldier. He then ordered the cleaning up of the body parts spattered around.

As if nothing happened, the Colonel found an open bottle of vodka and took a few long swigs before he jumped in the pool, bottle in hand. Jovial, he called out to his men to join him; in twos and threes they came out of hiding and massed together with their supreme leader. There was standing room only in the cool water. The water crested and flowed over the cement deck as men made room and piled in. I swear that

not another person could be accommodated; the late arrivals stood poolside shoulder to shoulder.

The relief shown by all was one of exuberance, more vodka was ordered by the gracious host. Zane, Claus and I raided the bar and handed off bottles of any type of alcohol in stock. The Colonel chatted to the captive audience around him. If they had have been in the barracks rather than the pool, you would not have heard a pin drop. Whatever he was saying caused quips of laughter. He was putting his men at ease again, forgoing his stature and becoming one of them. Standing naked shoulder to shoulder, the man didn't seek his deserved personal space. The Colonel was what my father would call a "man's man," leading by example, not by virtue of title.

When he did pull rank, if one could call it that, it was when in a loud voice he announced that all present would be his guests for another day,. He promised them that he would make the necessary arrangements back at base to excuse them of duties. A roar louder than an airplane erupted. He excused himself, gathered us boys and headed back to our room where exhausted, we slept.

Chapter XVI: More Than I Bargained For

When I awoke after a much needed deep sleep, the Colonel was missing. I gathered he had gone to the base. Claus was lying on Franz and giving it to him which might have been the reason I'd stirred. I thought it very callous of him taking advantage of Frank's boyfriend in his absence while he was recuperating at the base hospital. But what the fuck.

Zane slept soundly beside me. I had a rock hard cock and with him lying on his tummy, his ass was much too inviting. I lubricated my cock and crawled over him. He awoke, squealed and squirmed but I easily held down his small bony frame as I entered him. I met Claus's eye, we exchanged a devious smile and commenced to fuck our sobbing bottoms without care or concern for their well-being.

I was changing, not in a good way, and I knew it! Ashamed of myself, I faked orgasm to complete the charade in front of Claus and rolled off Zane. I laid there and watched as Claus took excessive liberties upon Franz, as if he had something to prove. Frank would beat the snot out of him if he found out. It was a chance Claus was willing to take having the protection of the Colonel who would vouch for the unselfish sharing of each other's bodies, as well as, anyone we brought home to play with.

I wondered how many times Claus was physically abused by men in his years of being a whore boy in a clandestine brothel before his becoming an agent of the Colonel's quest for dirt on powerful men. According to all accounts, Claus excelled at his assignment and had become an asset the Colonel could never sever ties with.

Zane certainly wasn't pleased with me. I offered him my ass although he was rather small. He surprised me when he countered the offer for a blowjob instead. Without a doubt, the Colonel would have sucked him off the night before and given him a taste for it. When he rolled over onto his back he was erect and ready for it. Approximately three slender pink inches stood not much longer or thicker than a man's index finger. The foreskin had been completely stretched exposing his purple-red knob giving the appearance that he was circumcised.

Cute, was the only way to describe the fifteen year-olds immature display. His balls were decently arrayed and were like velvet to the touch, both fit in my mouth with plenty of room to roll them with my tongue. His boner was exactly that, lean and solid, fragile looking as if one wasn't careful, it would snap in half. Upon close

inspection, a few blond pubes were barely surfacing from pores along the base of his cock. Easily taken to the base, it had a hint of a metallic taste.

I had to wonder what the Colonel found so exciting about premature boys. There was no fatty tissue to sink your lips into, and certainly no length to masturbate. Also absent was the musty manly smell that I enjoyed so much, as well as, the pubic hair that tickled my nose especially those loose pesky ones that stuck to the tongue or roof of my mouth.

Regardless, I did my best to please Zane who was very eager to be pleased. He rocked his hips, held my head in both hands, sometimes grasped my hair and purred like a contented kitten. Claus let out a barrage of obscenities while cumming. He must have taken a final plunge that caused Franz to yelp in pain. With concern I looked over to see Franz's head and neck contorted at an angle against the headboard that must have been awfully painful. At some point, he must have tried to scurry ahead which Claus used to his advantage by pinning the teen in a position that prevented him from escaping.

Zane, whom I was servicing, might have been under developed genitally but he surprised me by releasing a hefty, sweet as honey tasting, helping of jism as thick and creamy as any mans. With not much casing surrounding the interior duct, I felt his bony shaft spasm violently several times forcing the ejaculate the short distance from his balls to his crown and splatter my mouth with its warmth. I found a new respect for Zane and mentally made a note that I would suck him off anytime he wanted.

It was noon hour by the time Claus and I had finished playing with the younger boys. I could smell a barbecue from below. The aroma was intoxicating and I was starving as were the three other teens. Pulling on our trousers we made our way poolside to find a chef cooking hamburgers and an assortment of cold salads on a buffet table. It appeared that we weren't the only ones to sleep in. There were only a couple of dozen men who feasted on lunch all of whom were modestly covered in trousers or underpants. The few in the swimming pool doing laps were naked and their bare white asses glimmered in the overhead sun.

Even though the bar was open, only three young soldiers made the sickly looking bartender work. It was easily established that almost everyone present was suffering a hangover and the missing souls were still sleeping it off. One by one, as they would wake up, they would leave the tent naked as the day they were born, take a piss or vomit in a nearby bush. Once relieved, they would then search through the mounds of clothing for their own. After a few minutes most would give up the futile effort and succumb to a quick dip in the inviting pool to refresh themselves. But as with all hungry young men, the heavenly odour of food soon overwhelmed them and all modesty was forgotten.

I couldn't help but again admire the German men in all their splendor. While some might not have nice facial features, their bodies were well-toned and proportioned. I was horny because of not having my usual morning release and any one of them would have sufficed having their cocks in my mouth or my bum, preferably both.

I couldn't believe my eyes when I saw Damon leave the tent. I had to squint to be sure it was him pissing in the bush and when he turned around to watch the luncheon crowd for a few seconds, my heart raced calling his name and running around the pool to greet him. Damon was just as excited to see me. He wrapped me in a bear hug

in his powerful arms draining the breath out of me. He was even better looking in daylight than I recalled from that night in the gazebo.

Taller than I remembered him, I felt his thick cock pressing against my sternum as we embraced. His body was slick in sweat that smelled so powerfully masculine. Suddenly, he scooped me up, threw me over his shoulder like a caveman and headed to the tent. Hanging over his shoulder and staring down his back, I had an aerial view of his half moon cheeks that rippled in muscle like the rest of his body. I couldn't resist reaching down and taking one in each hand. Stretching even further I worked my hand between his legs and cupped his hefty scrotum. Damon giggled, reached up to pull my waistband down to partially expose my butt cheeks, leaned his head and painfully bit my ass splayed on his left shoulder.

The darkish interior of the tent stank of body odour and a hint of shit. I could just barely make out sleeping bodies, as well as, several occupants having sex. Slipping me off his shoulder, he lay me down gently and removed my trousers. I found myself face to face with Michel who was equally happy to see me again. My wish had come true. The heat of the moment lent no time for idle chit-chat as Damon rolled me onto my belly and was working his meat into me while I sucked Michel's flaccid cock to life.

My eyes adjusted just in time to see Hans squatted beside us between some guy's legs finishing off a blowjob. He was squeezing and pulling on the deflating cock savoring the last few drops. When he recognized me he was instantly in my face kissing my cheek and licking the side of my full mouth and Michel's shaft. The smell of fresh cum on his breath drove me wild.

Damon had bottomed out in my ass and began long slow strides picking up the pace gradually. He was a gentle lover although, personally, I would have preferred if he had been a little rougher and fucked me silly like a crazed animal right then. However, a small crowd was gathering above us, all stroking their cocks watching the young pretty boy that had been carried in like a sack of potatoes. I was the boy who, the night before, no one seemed to take interest in but now everyone was waiting their turn to fuck me.

Michel shot his seed deep inside me and, the moment he pulled out, Hans took his place in my mouth. The void in my rectum was quickly replaced after Damon was finally satisfied. While not as large as Damon, the new man showed no mercy. He gave me exactly what I wanted which was to be used like a slut as rough as any man wanted to be with me front or back.

My three friends had long gone to have lunch leaving me still being fucked or fellating the awakening soldiers who were far greater in numbers than I bargained for. Many were doing each other but not that I could see or care beyond any given crotch in my face. The sounds of sex resonated around the tent both verbally and physically. My ass was raw and toward the end of my ordeal, I barely felt the cocks inside me until one extremely thick cock caused me excruciating pain.

It felt strange, not normal at all. Not only did it stretch my rectum to the point where I thought it would tear me, it scraped the walls of my passage. With shock and horror, I realized that it was a man shoving his fist inside me. I spat out the cock in my mouth and screamed bloody murder begging him to stop. He didn't nor did anyone come to my aid. As far as they were concerned, the whore boy had merely met his match getting fucked by someone of very large endowment. Even the man I

was sucking off tried to force his cock back into my mouth. I let the head slide between my teeth and then, without warning, bit down on it. He screamed, cursed me, and where I expected a punch to the head, he simply rose and moved out of sight.

The man behind me was intent on shoving his arm up my ass, his fist had since penetrated my sphincter, his other arm looped around my waist and held my squirming body in place. I was being raped in plain sight of oblivious people preoccupied with their own desires. I deserved it. I had gone too far in the midst of strangers.

Bawling, I craned my neck to look behind me and pleaded for mercy. He only grinned at me and his arm forged ahead, I swear he was as elbow deep and began to fuck me. I puked up cum, I could taste it in my bile. Another sad reminder of what a slut I had been ingesting countess gobs of semen from so many men to remember. Thankfully, I passed out.

I awoke to a soldier cock fucking me in my comatose state. The only indication without feeling him inside me was his thrusts that registered and brought me to reality. I didn't have the energy to resist him or the other two soldiers who took advantage of me after him. I was a rag doll, unfeeling and uncaring.

Daylight was seen from under the canvas. Freedom was but three feet away. After the last cock laced my intestines, sheer adrenaline enabled me to roll me five times to slip out of the tent and into the harshness of daylight. I lay there a long time in severe pain from my waist down. When I finally found an ounce of energy to stand, my bowel ceded to gravity and released a flood of feces and cum down my legs. I collapsed.

A stranger helped me up, asking if I was okay. I smiled, trying to assure him. The pain in my lower insides was intense and I fell again, his strong arms reacted to prevent me from sprawling back on the ground. My filth soiling his trousers did not deter him from carrying me quickly to the pool area and screaming for a medic.

Two men ran over, both advising that they were medics and had the man lay me on a lounger where I immediately doubled up in pain and began to vomit blood, hovering on the verge of consciousness.

One bystander noticed blood seeping from my bum, the medics then stretched me out on my back prodded my tummy causing me to scream in pain. The last person I saw before I passed out was Claus hovering over me, a look of concerned terror on his face. My last thought was that he did love me in his own strange way.

A bright light shone in my face when I opened my eyes. I had no idea where I was but was comforted by the Colonels presence. He hovered above me with a wide smile as he wiped a cool cloth over my forehead. Claus stood on the other side of my bed, he laughed, moved his frame with a wave of his hand for me to see Frank in the next bed waving at me.

I was a patient in the base hospital, hooked up to tiny tubes, one of which I soon realized was irritably planted inside my cock. The Colonel became serious and informed me that I had sustained a ruptured bowel and intestinal tearing that could have cost me my life. He demanded to know what happened to me, already concluding that I had been inside the tent and endured my injuries there. He asked who hurt me in such a vile way. I was ashamed that he knew exactly how the internal

damage had been done to me. Upon examination, the doctors would have easily concluded what had happened to me from the telltale evidence.

When I closed my eyes in shame I could see the man's face clearly. I could detail every minute detail of the single, brief glance I gave him. I could not be responsible for another man's death. The whole incident was my own fault for the inane urge to be a slut.

I looked him in the eye and lied. I told him that I didn't know who shoved an arm up into me. The Colonel was aghast, at a loss for words and stuttering in confusion. It dawned on me that everyone thought someone had impaled me with an object. The Colonel became furious discovering the truth but I was resolute in my silence to not give the man away.

We had plenty of visitors over the next few days, but most of all I enjoyed Frank's company the most. Privacy was an issue, having other sick men close by. When I was well enough to walk around, the Colonel brought me my chess set and I taught Frank the basics of the game. He was still convalescing having two broken ribs and a ruptured spleen.

The game board balanced on his belly, his legs bent at the knees and me sitting at his side, nobody would have been the wiser when my hand was under the covers jerking him off at least twice a day. If the orderly tending to him noticed the dried mess on Frank's sheets, he never said a word, although most of it I had licked off my hand.

On the fourth day I was released by the doctor into the Colonel's care. Like old times, it was just the Colonel, me and Claus sharing a bed back at the Inn. The two pampered me The doctor's strict orders were for me to rest and take my penicillin to ward off the poisons of my intestines from infecting my blood. I still had occasional pain, and when Claus once jokingly asked if perhaps the man had lost his wrist watch inside of me, I couldn't restrain my belly laugh which caused me to double over in agony.

He had taken it upon himself to be my caregiver. He went for my meals and my medicine was given punctually. To my surprise, Claus added handjobs and blowjobs just because. Claus even shaved the stubble growing back on my crotch to keep my sex appeal in the Colonel's eye. It was a soft side of him that I hadn't seen in a while. He loved me as much as he loved the Colonel and he was finally willing to share the man without animosity. I was no longer a threat to him and he was no longer a threat to me.

My ass was off limits for some time, but I did enjoy our regular three-way oral sex interludes every night without outside involvement. The Colonel had his private moments with Zane in the room behind his office on base. Claus and I both knew about it and we respected that. Frank had returned to the Inn on light duties He had his Franz back; the Colonel had graciously assigned him a room to himself. The man rewarded loyalty.

I learned from Frank that the Colonel had the large tent set up on base. It was named the 'One-hundred-forty-ninth Division Social Club.' A sign outside humorously read:

NO <u>ON-DUTY</u> MP'S OR OFFICER'S ALLOWED!

Unofficially endorsed by the Colonel himself, no one dared to ask questions. According to Frank, membership in the club was increasing in leaps and bounds, although there was no official 'membership' required ... or dress code!

––––––––––––––

The inevitable day arrived. The Colonel had received his top secret orders to advance his troops and secure the medium size city of Pranski, my home town! When you sleep with a Colonel, you learn secrets.

The Colonel moved Claus and I back to the base. I could literally feel the aura of tension in the air. Men scurried about in preparation of folding up camp; the Colonel barked orders to the many that filtered in and out of his office. A large map hung on the wall that he drew across with colored pencils. This was the city that I knew inside out and could easily have provided him and his intelligence officer with information on the many landmarks that they were trying to identify the significance of.

My final dilemma, a crossroad of uncertainty that I never thought about before; where did my allegiance stand, with my country or my Colonel!

Chapter XVII: Moving to New Quarters

I sat listening in amusement. The Intelligence officer erred one time too many naming innocent public facilities as armories. City hall, he pointed out, was actually a museum, and our beautiful zoo he identified as a Polish army base. I had to wonder if he somehow had the wrong city, and that he knew it, and was bullshitting the Colonel to save his ass.

When he implied that my father's large textile factory situated near the airport was an aircraft assembling plant, the humour of it all was suddenly lost on me. I had been in that factory several times a week, and there was certainly no evidence of airplanes in any shape or form. The building consisted of only huge looms and weavers as far as the eye could see with hundreds of innocent employees toiling to make a living. Their lives, as well as, my father's life were at stake.

The Colonel was in one of his 'children should be seen, but not heard' moods. I knew that mood and always respected it when in his office and he was meeting with people. I jumped to my feet and ran over to the two men. The Colonel, with a quizzical look, read the panic on my face knowing that I wasn't being disobedient. I was screaming that they had made a grave mistake. In my fluster, I spoke more Polish than German.

Immediately, I summoned Claus to come to my aid and interpret. I knew I couldn't possibly trust my limited lingo to be clear and concise enough to explain the misinformation about my father's plant. In order to emphasize my knowledge of the city, I pointed out the intelligence officer's other misguided logistical information. I prayed to God that the Colonel would believe my rantings. Never had he asked where I originated from, nor had I the need to tell him It was something that just never came up in our many conversations.

On the large topographical map, I pointed out and named my street, my school, the park where I played rugby, the butcher shop my mother shopped at, going on until he silenced me with a hand gesture. I got a discerning glare when a moment later I broke the ordered silence and felt the need to point out my grandparent's street. Once again he raised his hand close enough to feel it on my nose, shook his head as if I was daft, and turned to the intelligence officer. I got the message and shut myself up. He already believed me.

The intelligence office glared at me before he turned his head to meet the Colonel with a worried wavering smile. He refused to look his superior in the eye for more

than a second at a time as he busied himself flipping through the paperwork in his file folder nervously searching for what he guessed was his oversight. At a loss for an explanation, the haggard officer looked at the Colonel and threw his hands up in defeat.

The Colonel's strategic map that he was detailing was a farce as far as minor components were concerned. It had become obvious to the Colonel that a tourist brochure of the city would have been more useful than what the Nazi warmongers in Berlin had supplied their front lines with.

The intelligence officer stood me on a chair to face the map and asked me to look over the scribbles that he and the Colonel had previously pencilled on the map. Not able to read German, Claus was positioned beside me and ordered to read the descriptions for me. I detected two more errors. What they identified as a synagogue to the east was actually a large Benedictine monastery where my mother and father sometimes attended Mass and bought gifts of cheese and wine for the monks. Its star shaped design was coincidentally a grainy, blurred aerial image of the housing wings which had been added to the main central structure over the years to accommodate its growth.

The most valuable piece of information I gave them that made the Colonel furious was my noticing a bridge with red arrows drawn through it. The Vladimir drawbridge was one of four access routes into the city. It had been struck by a river barge and been closed for repairs for at least the past three months. I knew that because my father bellyached about the detour he had to make going to and from work almost every day at supper time. In his opinion, the architects who designed the bridge in the first place were nothing but buffoons for not building it higher. Over the years, a few small ships had lost their con-bridges in the dead of night and mechanical failures plagued the efficiency of it since the day it opened.

With that invaluable piece of information now in his possession, the Colonel ordered the sentry at the door to summon a communications officer to his office on the double. He wanted to personally dictate a communique to the High Command making them privy to the latest intel in order to drastically change their strategic bombing plans, as well as, the 121st division's planned access route into the city. The Colonel commented, to no one in particular, that a fourteen year old Polish boy was more useful than all of Nazi intelligence services combined.

I was proud of myself. I preferred to think that the man showed his gratitude by taking me, and only me, to his bed for an afternoon nap before which he made love to me the way I liked him to. My rectum burned, but he was conscious of my injuries and was gentle.

I had betrayed my city and my country in some small way; however, I convinced myself that I may have prevented thousands of unnecessary deaths. In my simple minded knowledge of war games, the small City of Pranski would be no more of a military threat to the Nazi's planned invasion than the docile village up the highway would be. Little did I know then how wrong I was.

The military base camp was placed in lock down for security reasons. Perimeter security had been doubled and extended to a five mile radius. No vehicle traffic was

permitted to use the only highway linking neighbouring villages that by passed the base.

The Colonel feared potential spies witnessing the dismantling of the base and the implications that military movement was imminent. The forested surroundings were crawling with Nazi soldiers with orders to shoot anyone on sight. I heard that many villagers were killed for simply trying to make their way home, caught in the sudden 'no-go-zone.'

He had ordered in another cot. Shoved together, the beds allowed the three of us only minor, cramped comfort and one of us would end up in the empty bed of his second in command who was only too pleased to see the pretty-boy back; his morning blow job - jerk off sessions resumed every morning after shift change.

Claus and I did, however, have free run of the base after the colonel got tired of us moping around his office. We ate our meals in the enlisted men's mess, a silent movie reel usually followed dinner, preceded by a redundant clip of a speech by the Fuhrer.

We would stop by the "social club" tent and peak under the rear canvas discovering that it was quite active at all times of day and night. Sadly, the "social club" was put off limits by the Colonel after we lost track of time one night and were late getting home. However, it didn't seem to matter to him that we'd spent many evenings just sitting around in his office patiently awaiting Zane's departure from the bedroom before we could go to bed.

I saw Frank often. Still on light duties, he was the Colonel's aide running errands or delivering orders on the man's behalf. He was always sullen, not his usual good natured self. He missed Franz terribly and I was pretty sure that was the reason for his melancholy demeanour. On Frank's behalf I tried to talk to the Colonel about it. While he clearly understood the situation as I explained it to him, I was relieved that he didn't get angry at my interference. However, he informed me that he could never take the chance on having the enemy on the base, or allow furlough to a soldier during quarantine. I understood and respected the man's position and his honest response to me. I truly think he was impressed by my candour in expressing my concern for Frank.

———————

One night the Colonel didn't come to bed. I awoke to the sounds of voices in the office. Vehicles roared to life in the still of the night. The squealing of metal on metal could only be heavy artillery moving. The stench of diesel exhaust penetrated the tent thick and nauseous. The Nazi's were moving out, the full scale invasion of Poland was underway.

Claus had also woken just before Frank entered the room and told us to dress and gather up our things. We joined the Colonel at the wheel of his jeep and led a mile-long noisy parade down the dark highway the two-hundred or so miles toward my home. I took a final look back and noticed that much of the base remained intact. I really didn't know anything about military matters so I was unaware at the time but it was to be the future home of reinforcement troops who would be stationed there to await orders.

I felt helpless as I worried about my family. The markings on the Colonel's map clearly indicated that another two battalions would converge on the city; one from the

east and the other from the west. The Colonel would lead his forces into the city from the south. For a long way, the highway followed the railroad tracks on which steam engines pulling boxcars and livestock cars seemed to go on forever were slowly travelling in our direction. Little did I know the significant purpose of all this rolling stock quite then.

As we neared the city just before dawn, the Colonel pulled to the left and slowed allowing several gunnery jeeps to move ahead and lead the convoy. For the first time I felt in danger. Two civilian boys in a jeep with a high ranking Nazi officer would be no deterrent for Polish troops to bazooka the vehicle, nor would hidden snipers care who they picked off under the metal helmets provided us.

Throughout the night, the convoy had encountered only a few on-coming vehicles that were stopped, searched and left disabled. The occupants could do nothing but stand on the roadside, watch and being thankful for their lives being spared. However, closer to the city, the early morning hour brought with it heavier traffic consisting of mostly livery trucks going about their business. Two tanks had by then taken the lead of the oncoming convoy. The trucks were all considered potentially hostile. They were obviated without any concern being given for their civilian drivers and then pushed off the highway by a bulldozer that had earlier been unloaded from its transport.

The carnage was extremely difficult to watch. Where the Colonel saw the enemy, I saw innocent men simply plying a living being slaughtered. The odd car out and about was shown no less mercy, the gunnery jeeps took care of those. My father making his way to work could have easily been a victim. All the while, never for a second did the convoy slow its steady pace and not one bullet had yet been fired in returned enemy aggression.

I was more than relieved when the Colonel pulled off the highway into the Palac Kroleski; the Royal Palace Hotel along with a few troop carriers. I had dined there many times with my family on special occasions, of course, as the hotel was very expensive. My Uncle Bruno held his wedding reception in one of the hotel's elegant ballrooms. The Royal Palace was, in fact, once a castle built sometime in the early eighteenth century. It overlooked the city from atop a bluff.

Nazi intelligence had at least got something right. The hotel made a perfect vantage point for a command centre. Troops stormed the front and back doors gathering staff and patrons into one of the ballrooms as Claus and I sat in the jeep. Claus was oblivious to my anxiety of being so close to home and yet still so far away. I had the odd feeling like that of being a stranger. He asked me if there was a swimming pool. I laughed at his boyishly innocent inquiry, made as if we were vacationing, and assured him there was indeed a large pool.

I wondered what it was like for him to be without a family and I appreciated the fact that he wouldn't understand my emotional state of melancholy that I fought not to display. The only family he knew was the Colonel and he had recently adopted me as his brother. As far as he was concerned, he WAS at home!

Momentarily, the silence was broken by the faraway sound of gunfire and explosions. It was evident that the Nazi convoy that had continued without us had finally met resistance from Polish forces. As if that wasn't enough to jolt me back to reality, the hotel doors burst open and soldiers were herding twenty or more people at

gunpoint down the stairs and into a troop carrier. Many of the men and women were still in their bed clothes, a few were naked, evidently taken from their beds. "Jews," I heard Claus say more to himself than for my benefit.

Frank suddenly appeared out of nowhere, told us to grab the Colonel's and our gear and follow him. Claus jokingly reminded him of who the bellboy was, referring to Frank's previous military duty back at the Inn. This caused us all to double over in laughter. Frank grimaced in pain, his ribs still very tender and gave Claus the finger using both hands.

The lobby was chaotic and noisy. More civilians were being manhandled by screaming soldiers as they were being led from the hotel. These folks were fully dressed and carrying luggage but they looked just as frightened and confused as the last group. One very irate and vocal man complained to a sergeant of his treatment. In Polish, he was trying to relay that he was a man of great importance and demanded to see someone in charge. The sergeant had had enough of the man's belligerence and rifle-butted his face with such blunt force that the pompous man's nose and mouth exploded spewing blood everywhere.

Frank commandeered someone's cart and dumped their belongings onto the floor. Claus and I relieved ourselves of our burden onto the cart and we rushed to a lift. I was thankful to leave the helter-skelter taking place in the lobby behind as the caged-lift slowly groaned upwards. It slowly rose past floors to the welcome sounds of mechanical grinding and squeals emanating from the shaft. It was music to my ears.

The Colonel's befitting presidential suite of rooms took up almost the entire top tenth-floor. It had a magnificent floor-to-ceiling window view of the city. Many men scurried about. Already, in such a short time, the living-room walls were plastered with maps. Radio and telegraph equipment was being set up by technicians, communication officers were already seated at a long table wearing headsets. A huge antenna had been erected outside on the terrace where most of the existing furniture had been stored to convert the room into a command centre.

The only semblance of normality, depending on how one looked at it, was the huge bedroom with a bed large enough to comfortably sleep eight people. An en-suite bathroom with a shower and an oversized bathtub was a welcome luxury. The porcelain fixture beside the toilet, however, confused me. When Claus laughed and pulled the handle, a flood of water surged upward. A very strange drinking fountain, I mentioned. Claus could not control his hysterics. He was practically rolling on the floor in laughter. Thankfully, Frank was kind enough to explain the feminine practical use of the bidet. I felt like an idiot.

The Colonel wanted us out of the suite for good reason. It was a beehive of activity and we would only be in the way. I was happy to learn that he appointed Frank to be our officer in charge. It was the first time I had ever seen him wearing his sidearm. Where other young men his age and stature proudly displayed their arms like jewellery, it occurred to me that Frank was anything but egotistical, although he was always smartly dressed and handsome in his uniform.

At that same moment, I noticed corporal stripes pinned to his shoulder. The Colonel had recently promoted him. There was no fanfare, bragging or gloating. I made a mental note to find needle and thread in the hotel to properly stitch his unsung honour badge to his shirt.

We had a late breakfast in the dining room where, not surprisingly, no one else dined. The stiff maitre'd was reluctant to seat us. Claus didn't hesitate and told him to fuck off as we seated ourselves. Perhaps, given the fact that one of us boys was armed, he dispatched a waiter to serve us. When the staunch man delivered the bill, Frank signed the Colonel's suite. Word must have travelled fast about who now occupied the Presidential Suite because the maitre'd looked at the bill and looked back at Frank with fear. As the handsome uniformed teen stood to leave, the man was astute in his cordial duties and pulled Frank's chair out from under him.

Claus, deciding to have a bit of fun, remained seated, cleared his throat when the man seemed to ignore him and cocked his head expectantly when he got his attention. The maitre'd was none too pleased, however he complied begrudgingly. Swiping the linen napkin from Claus' lap, the man jumped back and almost toppled over. The teen's cock and balls lay exposed from his trousers in all their glory. His antic was certainly a gut breaking laugh for some of us.

Claus was in rare form that day. Many of the hotel guests were German citizens. The lobby was still abuzz with activity as civilian men and women idled about waiting to be accommodated in alternate rooms as the military had taken over several floors. Many of them had witnessed and, those who didn't, heard about the incident involving the pompous man so everyone was the model of patience as the hotel staff made every effort to accommodate them.

A life size statue of Michelangelo's 'David' stood on a four-foot pedestal dead centre of the lobby. Claus, with his lack of ethics and morals, climbed on the pedestal and knelt before the statue mimicking fellatio on David for all to see. He even tilted his head to the side once and feigned a choke and cough before he resumed his self-demeaning performance. Women shrieked, men laughed, and when he was finished with his shenanigans, he turned, wiped his mouth with his forearm for added comical value, and leapt down.

People stared agape and in shock at the "filthy" lad, as one woman described him. Unfettered, Claus beamed at his audience and took a bow. Frank hauled him away by his shirt before any other officers recovered their wits enough to apprehend him. It was all very humorous indeed, even Frank as angry as he was couldn't suppress his amusement after reminding Claus that he was ultimately responsible for the boy's reckless behaviour.

However, it didn't stop there. When Claus saw the marble swimming pool his clothes were off and left in a trail behind him despite the several women enjoying a cup of tea under a tiki-hut. Daring me to follow, I looked at Frank who shrugged his hapless permission and I raced after Claus with my own clothes scattered in my wake.

I believe we would have gotten away swimming nude unscathed had it not been for claus' antics. The genteel lady folk snickered in amusement but really paid us no attention. We were seen simply as innocent allurement of young boys taking advantage of a swim and modestly hidden for all intent and purpose. That is until Claus decided he liked the diving-board and got a kick out of watching his growing cock flop up and down as he jumped on the springboard. And to make matters worse, Claus felt the need to bring it to my and Frank's attention and, of course, anyone else within earshot.

146

The prissy, weasel-like waiter might have only tolerated events because the ladies never complained. It could also have been perhaps because he was being intimidated by the young, good looking Nazi officer who escorted us. He had had enough and ran over to Claus with a towel pleading with him to cover up. Claus kept jumping on the board as he turned to face the waiter with no intention of obeying the beckoning man with the outstretched towel. Instead, he did an amazing back-flip dive. The result was Frank ordered us both out of the pool much to the waiter's relief.

Claus had no idea how to behave in public. How could he? He had very little exposure to life skills beyond the Colonel's world, a man's world chalked full of masculinity, sexual abuse and lack of discipline. I didn't think that he'd gone to school beyond learning to read and write, yet Claus spoke fluent German and Polish, and the Polish he spoke was impeccable, without a hint of an accent or flaw. His doubted story that his father was once a prestigious Polish ambassador may very well have been true, but his young life drastically changed forever at the loss of his parents.

Like Claus, I had become a survivor. However, unlike him, I had a home and my parents were not too far away. Perhaps it was that realization which churned my homesickness. I resolved that somehow I was going home where I belonged. I didn't wish to live the empty, loveless life Claus lived any longer.

CHAPTER XVIII: CHANGING DESTINIES

I had a love-hate relationship with Claus, nothing could be truer. One moment he was the enemy, the next, my ally. I swear that he sensed my sadness of being so close to home and was trying to humour me with his silly antics. I caught him looking at me several times, not a stare, just fleeting glances that his eyes seemed to show concern, a slight, warm smile formed whenever I caught his gaze.

Security inside the hotel had been established in short order after the pandemonium settled. Teams of armed soldiers were stationed at every entrance and fire exit stairway as others roamed about the ground floor. We were challenged when we entered from the terrace, and again several times afterward as we made our way to the lift.

Claus knew most of the guards and we passed through the security gauntlet easily until we got to the lift where, normally, only senior officers had secured access. After a long interrogation, Claus finally convinced the obstinate master sergeant to verify our permission with the top floor security to allow us access to the command post. Upon radio verification, I overheard the man relay to his men with a snicker that Claus and I were whore boys for the top brass and ordered the guards inside the lift to take us to the top floor. As hard as it was, even Claus kept his mouth shut at the insult.

The suite of rooms was still buzzing with activity. The parlour had been all but stripped of its eloquent furnishings, men sat at a long table in front of large radio and wire transmitters. Maps of the city covered most of the ornate artworks hanging on the walls and were spread over a large table where men gathered around discussing strategies while moving tiny armament replicas that reminded me of children's toys.

It was as if we were invisible. Nobody paid any attention to the odd presence of two boys mingling about. The Colonel was nowhere to be seen, however the guard standing outside our bedroom spoke volumes. Zane was in there getting his brains fucked out.

I walked out onto the patio to view the city and fear struck me bone-dead. Repetitive gunshots echoed, explosions gave way to additional fires burning giving off an eerie glow to the dusk of nightfall's horizon. My home city was under siege.

I couldn't imagine the peaceful inhabitants taking up arms in retaliation. I assumed that surely the Polish military had more important political stakes in other, larger cities to protect. Perhaps, I thought, they had left only a small squadron behind in the

unlikelihood that the Nazi would have any interest in the small city of less than three-hundred-thousand.

I peered to the north-west outskirts where my parents resided elated to see a calmness. There were no fires burning in that area. The focus of the Nazi attack appeared to be centered in the city's core. However, I feared that the carnage would branch out eventually, placing my mother and father in danger. Fearing for their lives, I started to cry. Claus made his sudden presence known. He stood behind me and wrapped his arms in a strong embrace around my tummy. He rested his chin on my left shoulder peering in the same direction that I was. Not a word was said between us as I sobbed.

Claus' warmth soon went cold when he advised me that the other two battalion colonels had joined the command post and we were to sleep with them, Colonel's orders. I had noticed the two men immediately when we entered the suite, one obese with a jovial face, the other slender, almost skeletal reminding me of my uncle.

The day had finally come when I was expected to earn my keep as a spy for the colonel. Claus briefed me on what to do and what to say and not say. As far as the man was concerned, I was a simple Polish whore-boy with no ties to the Colonel. Claus gave me a choice, I chose the weasel-like commander, not that my would-be-abuser was the least bit attractive, but I found the fat man repulsive.

Frank introduced Claus and me to our respective playmates. The weasel seemed pleased with my looks, running a hand through my long blond hair. He scanned my body with a lurid grin, his baggy trousers bulging in anticipation of having me. The fat man appeared equally enthused scoring Claus posing as a Polish peasant boy.

The men took us to the dining room for dinner and all but ignored us as they conversed about war matters and the foothold they had gained in such a short time. The two men conversed freely, neither knowing that we understood German. They talked about their families; both men were married and had children about our age. The weasel boasted of a son enrolled in first year officer school. I had to wonder if the boy wasn't being taught the things that his father was planning on doing to me.

Both men occupied smaller suites on the top floor as well. No sooner were we behind closed doors than the man was stripping me naked with his trembling hands muttering something about a life-long fantasy come true. The son-of-a-bitch was literally drooling from the mouth and panting like a dog. He was on his knees when he pulled my pants down and instantly took my flaccid cock in his mouth. He'd obviously never sucked cock before because he was biting it and held my balls painfully clamped in his hand. All the while, the other slowly roamed my lower back before he sought out my butt-hole. He wasn't using any lubricant when he forced the first dry finger inside me. His secret was divulged. Whether the man had ever given way to his inner urgings before, he was definitely a homosexual paedophile in every definition of the word. The Colonel would be pleased.

The sex fiend tossed me onto the bed and undressed himself. He was even scrawnier in his nakedness. He was all skin and bones His ribcage was so prominent that if I desired, I could count them. His cock head was saturated. In his excitement he had cum in his pants but had remained hard. His thin cock, when erect, had an unusual curve near the crown that pointed downward.

The man lay between my legs and resumed sucking me. I closed my eyes and for some odd reason, I thought about my dearly departed Jon's beautiful body. This, in turn, caused me to have an erection for the boy-cock hungry man to excitedly devour with no less pain from his teeth scraping and biting my tender shaft or scooping my testicles into his mouth to chew on. I begged him to fuck me simply to stop the torture upon my genitals. He had other ideas and knelt in a fetal position telling me to fuck him. Oh yes! The Colonel would be pleased indeed.

I gave it to him dry and so rough that I hurt driving into him inch by inch. He screamed but never told me to stop. He had waited a long time to be fucked under the control of a boy, unannounced to him, one that knew what he was doing. I fucked him hard and mercilessly. To increase the pain, I held his long hanging balls gripped tightly in my left hand while I used the other to milk his cock. I loved being in sexual control of a man for the first time. I made him beg me not to stop, pausing a few times to hear him grovel and beg like the slut that he was, mentioning that derisive remark several times.

When he came, I cupped my hand to let it gather in my palm and fed it to him. Like a hungry dog, he lapped it up. I was ready to cum as well and scurried over his back forcing his head upright to take my feces speckled cock and unloaded in his meat-grinder mouth.

The man rolled over and was fast asleep. I took the advantage and left, no one insinuated that I had to spend the night. I had done my duty and couldn't wait to tell the Colonel that whatever his motives were, he had another influential man by the balls!

I was detained outside the Colonel's suite and control centre by two young guard officers. They knew full well who I was. They had seen me leave the room of another colonel. They negotiated entry with me on my knees. I was sick and tired of being a boy-whore by then however, because both of the young officers were really cute, I obliged both men.

The Colonel was busy in the beehive reading incoming wires, talking on a radio and giving orders to men around him. Claus was nowhere to be seen. I assumed that he was still with the fat man. Zane was present and ran over in his drooping uniform and proudly informed me that he was officially one of the Colonel's aides. Frank was standing at the door and rolled his eyes. We both knew that Zane, like us, was merely one of the Colonel's boy-toys to keep close by.

The odd nearby explosions shook the hotel as Frank and I played chess in a quiet corner of the busy room. I had to force my eyes away from the floor-to-ceiling window because the night sky shone a crimson red that was often blotted out by grey-black smoke. Even the room began to take on the acrid smell of burning wood and sulphur.

It was Frank who casually interrogated me on the events with the scrawny colonel. I was eagerly anticipating divulging all first-hand accounts to the Colonel himself and, hopefully, winning his gratitude for a mission well done. All I got was a wink from across the room when Frank pulled the busy man aside and relayed my information. Claus returned about then and instantly had the Colonel's ear. I was jealous.

Whatever advantage the Colonel held over his counterparts was a mystery to me. Perhaps he threatened to expose them to the absentee General-in-Command. He was

probably a man who sat in an office of the Oberkommando der Wehrmacht (also known as the OKW or, in English, Supreme High Command of the German Armed Forces) safe and out of harm's way. Clear as day, it would later be seen that our Colonel had assumed command over all three battalions; the other two colonels would become mere puppets on a string. Power and its many uses. That's what motivated the Colonel and, through the use of blackmail and by coercion, he had achieved his goals thus far. A promotion to the rank of General Major was very obtainable in the near future if he played his cards right.

Frank took the liberty of explaining the Colonel's complexities to me. I knew he was a close confidant to the man, just as Jon had been. Even though it defied all military protocol of rank, the man confided his utmost trust in his young subordinates and valued their opinions over the seasoned war mongers at his disposal. His ranks consisted of mostly young men, his choosing, who learned to respect and admire him. Mind you, being able to get on one's knees from time to time to service the beloved Colonel's scepter certainly helped. He had achieved his goal of a peaceful and harmonious environment for the mass troops under his command. Young men who would look out for one another as brothers would. The Teutonic Knights philosophy had been successfully implemented.

Taking the city and subduing its people with minimum German casualties and destruction of newly acquired Polish assets was the key. Almost immediately upon his self-appointed leadership, the bombings and gunfire ceased. All that remained was only sniper fire from the enemy and the necessary retaliation necessary to combat that. The silence was suddenly surreal, although fires still burned.

Over the course of the next few days, the Colonel held several social parties at the hotel inviting off duty soldiers from the other two battalions to mingle with his own troops. Rooms were abundant in the large hotel, many got to practise what they were taught at their respective military schools without need of discretion or fear. The Colonel's reputation as a fair, non-judgemental leader spread like wildfire. He was soon known to be strict about military protocol and performance of duty, however lenient with time spent off duty.

Rest assured that there were many men of high-ranking status who opposed the Colonel's outrageous tolerance of conduct unbecoming soldiers in his unofficial command of more than sixteen-hundred troops. The outspoken ones were discredited by loss of rank imposed for frivolous reasons, or eccentric officers became victims of unfortunate wartime casualties, executed by stray bullets from their own platoons.

I could not swear in court to overhearing proof of the anarchistic ways and means, or who gave the directives. I could only assume that the other two colonels were under pressure to keep their respective rank and file in line. Oppressors of the Colonel's new and improved military ideals of comradeship would obviously voice their concerns up the lines of command. Those at the highest level who didn't turn a blind-eye and became persistent adversaries were harshly dealt with if they couldn't be reasoned with. Without a doubt, my Colonel oversaw and controlled matters when they reached that level. I firmly believe today that the Colonel formed a personal 'hit'

squad. Frank along with Peter and Horst, were suddenly assigned the colonel's personal protection team; again, the Colonel's faith in the younger soldiers prevailed and may have well been instruments of conveying the Colonel's orders to others.

What was truly amazing was the fact that a man's need for sex in any shape or form superseded all logical behaviour; men were willing to kill for the freedom of it. The Colonel's vision of a unified army could only have far exceeded his expectations.

That first night in the hotel, Frank ushered Claus, me and Zane into the Colonel's bedroom. We joined the two beds together as we had done at the inn. No instructions were necessary, bedtime protocol warranted nudity. Except for Zane, the three of us stood by in our nudity, unencumbered by our clothes or uniforms.

The huge ensuite bathtub was much too alluring when I suggested it. Zane finally gave in and stripped out of his ill-fitting uniform to join us after much prodding. I could understand his embarrassment of being fifteen and a late bloomer. It was an amusing sight, but never had any one of us commented on his immaturity. Zane covered his shame until he was seated deep in the tub.

Somehow, we ended up snuggled at the head of the bathtub. Faces in chests, chins resting on heads and wandering hands randomly exploring each other's genitals where hands moved from one to the other, rubbing and sensually masturbating each other. There was no sense of urgency to get off. It was simply a case of four boys quietly enjoying the harmonic pleasures of giving pleasure to each other. There was hardly even a ripple on the surface of the water. We just lay there neck deep peacefully and contentedly with the constant exchange of hands in an endless cycle of groping and light mutual hand jobs. Zane was nervous and telling silly jokes, but I could tell that he was somewhat smitten with Frank. I was quite surprised when Frank told the boy to join us in the bedroom. I guessed that the Colonel had grown bored with him and he was no longer his personal fuck-boy, instead, just another one of us to be shared around.

I suppose that we were all feeling frisky soon after fooling around in the tub. Surprisingly, Zane had no reservations about sucking Frank's beautiful cock as we fell into an oral four-way. I was pleased having Claus' fat German-sausage stuffed in my mouth with his heavy balls in my palm as Frank graciously sucked me. Claus never even insulted Zane's shortfall in genitalia as he went down on the boy soldier.

I had forgotten my homesick feelings and concentrated on my part in completing the erotic circle of friendship. Frank and Claus were like brothers, I decided. My family away from family, even Zane was suddenly growing on me once I sensed he'd lost his arrogant persona. The Colonel had successfully broken the boy's spirit, not that there was ever a doubt that he would.

Frank fucked the apprehensive Zane first. Claus and I held his legs to his chest as Frank smeared petroleum-jelly over his cock. I was envious that it wasn't going inside me instead as I took the lurid liberty of guiding the slickened stealth beauty to its mark. I watched as Frank's heavily loaded foreskin was forced halfway down his shaft. Zane screamed, although he had been well-broken in by the Colonel, Frank never paused. I was fascinated as his cock disappeared inch by inch into the upturned ass while Zane's small erection shrivelled to a caterpillar-like cocoon. I heard Claus

snicker, but thankfully he reserved comment. I had never used the anatomical term of penis, casually referenced perhaps to little boys; however it suited the description of the fifteen-year old's goods. He would never be a woman pleaser, even less, a man pleaser. He was destined to be used as a bottom, in my humble opinion, and he'd best get used to that reality.

Frank was gentle, in keeping with his nature. I wondered if he and Zane would become boyfriends, perhaps Frank was getting over Franz and moving on. I wished that I could make him my boyfriend. I was jealous when he leaned over Zane and tried to kiss the shocked boy intimately. Zane soon obliged the handsome teen's tongue and let it enter his mouth. A wet, sloshing sounded, accompanied by muffled grunts and groans as they made love oblivious to the rest of us. Frank, picking up the pace, never lost mouth contact with the spasming boy that decided to let himself be taken to oblivion.

No need for us to secure Zane any longer, he planted both his large feet on the bed with wide spread knees, one arm around Frank's neck and the other stretched with his hand grasping Frank's ass. Zane was enjoying his fuck, but probably more so, Frank's loving attention that went along with it. Yes. Again, I was envious.

What surprised me was Frank rolling off Zane and Claus quick to fill the void as Frank watched looked on. Claus was not so gentle and loving as he fucked Zane. I was next and was certainly no less merciful but, at least his rectum had been spread and the previous two loads of cum eased the way for me so my smaller cock literally floundered inside his chasm, barely scraping the sides. I didn't cum and simply gave up pretending that I had. But! At least I could say I had indeed fucked him, if that was any consolation to my ego in keeping up images.

It was now official, he was definitely public property and no longer the Colonel's private stock. Frank later took him to the adjacent room. A bedroom with an adjoining door supplied by the Colonel for his trusted assistant, Frank, and his handpicked personal security detail, Peter, Boris and several other overzealous young infantry soldiers pleased to be assigned the prestigious post and kept out of harms-way of the front. It was all part of the Colonel's reward scheme for loyalty. Zane would be well-received in his new military role as bum-boy for the revolving two shifts.

———————

It was well into the night by the time the Colonel was able to retire after his long, stressful day of coordinating the initial phases of the invasion of Pranski. He looked haggard and tired as he undressed, a thin smile directed at the naked Claus and I lying on the floor playing chess was his only acknowledgement, saying not a word.

Without being told, Claus was on his feet in an instant to run a hot bath for his master. I felt the need to contribute and pulled off his boots and damp, sweaty socks as he sat on the bed. Removing his tie and unbuttoning his shirt, he stood and shed his uniform at his feet that I quickly gathered in order to hang in the closet. I placed his gun belt on the nightstand, sensing that that was the proximity he would want it. I earned a ruffle of my hair, and a broad smile for my efforts.

The Colonel relaxed in the tub with his head against the wall. Claus was soon to join in the tub. He squatted on the man's lap and with shaving-brush, soap and

straight razor. The Colonel relaxed as Claus began to gingerly shave his face as I rinsed out his socks in the basin and hung them on a towel-rack to dry.

The pampering only ended when he finally lay in the bed as Claus and I each straddled a muscular leg and worshiped the genitals of the most powerful man to ever enter Pranski since the Polish Royals had occupied the very same stone and vine covered structure they once ruled from.

CHAPTER XIX: SAD BUT HAPPY HOMECOMING

It was during the wee hours, Claus and I were asleep on either side of the Colonel when a huge deafening explosion went off somewhere outside the hotel jolting the three of us awake. We were suddenly very alert. The flash lit up the room brighter than day, followed by subsequent blasts near and far. I was so frightened that I peed the bed.

The Colonel scrambled from the bed snatching his gunbelt and bolted naked through the door shoving aside panic stricken soldiers entering from the parlour-converted command centre to rouse and advise their commander and chief officer. My hysterical needs at the time were to never lose sight of the man in charge who would somehow make things right and protect me. Claus was on my heels looking just as scared. I don't think for a moment that the thirty-odd men in the room even noticed or cared we were nude as many more modesty-unencumbered people filtered into the room.

The Colonel barked orders at harried radio communications officers who appeared as scared as anyone else in the room. Although they were screaming out intel findings to each other, the seasoned officer calmly digested every single piece of logistics relayed and shouted to each what I could only assume were coded counter offences to the three battalions. The other two colonels clad in only their underwear stood by like whipped puppies, seemingly having had no time to confer with the late arrivals. Our Colonel assumed the leadership over the other two, he was in charge.

I stood at the large window overlooking the city. After a few moments, I even ventured outside onto the patio to watch the travesty unfold over the city once again. My eyes were focussed on the quadrant where my family resided. Where there hadn't been a glow of fires earlier, I could only fear the worst had happened. Tears poured from my eyes, then sobs, then followed by a complete breakdown. Not knowing he was behind me, Claus prevented me from collapsing by securing my underarms and dragging me back inside to the bedroom where he lifted me onto the bed and lay beside me holding me tight. We just lay there listening. No more bombs exploded near the hotel; however the mortar fire over the city continued to be unnerving until I relented and fell into to a deep sleep.

I thought it was a dream, or maybe just a continuation of the nightmare of events I'd endured when suddenly someone was shaking and slapping my face. At first, I thought I saw a reincarnation of Jon staring down at me. His eyes, his smile. Then I

realized it was Frank, how similar they looked. Claus came into focus leaning over to face me while my foggy brain began adjusting to the surroundings of where I was. I had no idea why I was in such an hallucinogenic state.

Their expressions turned from happy to serious, my clothes were being pulled onto me as if I were a baby. And then, there was the sensation of Frank carrying me. I detected a sense of urgency. My dry mouth and the desire for water brought back a vague memory of a doctor telling me to drink. Had I had been given a sedative? I saw Claus toss my duffel bag over his shoulder. I immediately knew we were moving out, but where?

It was almost daybreak, I noticed. Birds were chirping when I was loaded into the back of a jeep with Claus supporting my body holding me tight. Frank was at the wheel grinding gears and soon had us mobile and speeding from the hotel parking lot. With a sharp right turn the city came into view from above the mountain. Fires burned everywhere; however, if gunfire was commencing or ongoing, its sound was drowned out over the drone of the jeep's engine, at least no bombing could be heard.

I tried to talk to Claus who either didn't hear me or was ignoring me. There was a very frightened look about him; his eyes darting every which way. He held me so tight it hurt, as if he were afraid I was going to bounce out of the jeep which was really not out of the realm of possibilities considering the lack of suspension supporting the old jeep.

We came up to a heavily manned checkpoint a mile or so before the city. Frank shoved papers in front of the guard. His arrogance was very unbecoming of his nature, but I'd learned that most Germans appeared rude at the best of times. The guard scrutinized the document and made a bored, lame attempt to salute Frank before ordering the barricade opened for us to pass down the winding highway as the visibility deteriorated and the stench of smoke became more prevalent. My eyes burned and I choked. Claus held an oily rag to my face as he did to his own. Frank had pulled his uniform shirt above his nose.

I was relentless in asking where we were going and scared shitless at the guns pointed at us from everywhere. The four Nazi flags attached to each corner of the jeep did give us some comfort that we wouldn't be shot at immediately.

Close gunfire still rang out and I shuddered at every shot. Claus buried my head in his crotch and cowered over me. We were in dangerous territory. Frank sped only to be stopped at another checkpoint for another interrogation and then we sped on to the next city block. Frank must have shown at least twenty soldiers the mysterious documents in his possession justifying the transportation of two civilians. The Germans had certainly seized the city in very short order.

We came to another stop, however there was no conversation. Still afraid, I trusted Claus when he lifted my head from his crotch. The moment was surreal. I rubbed my sore eyes and then rubbed them again. I must have been hallucinating. Everything was very familiar. The butcher shop, the bakery, the shoemaker store, ice cream parlour, Danski's Tailors, Jaffi's book store … I was home again! This was the street I grew up on and I knew every inch even if I was blind folded.

I swivelled my head so hard to the right that I felt a sharp pain in my neck. Eyes wide, there stood my brownstone home. Mom had kept her flower garden as

beautiful as ever, dad must have slaved to cut the lawn on his own without having me to argue with to get it done.

The symbolic friendship wreath my mother made to welcome guests hung on the door. I was positive that the welcome mat, also lovingly weaved by her, would lie sprawled at the front door stoop. We didn't hide a key under it; there was no need back then. I would walk through the door, kick off my shoes in every which direction and shed my school bag off my shoulders wherever it happened to land and scream out that I was home. I would always ask my favourite question 'what's for supper' as I peeled off my school uniform before I even reached my bedroom leaving a trail of discarded clothing along the way. I was forever getting shit from my mother. Suddenly, I could smell the cookies and cakes she baked for me despite the acrid scent of burning rubber and wood.

My escorts who both brought me home stared at me in happiness, yet I read a conflicting hint of sadness in their eyes. There was no time to waste, Claus jumped out of the jeep and hauled my duffle-bag onto his shoulder and dragged me by the hand in a trot to my doorstep. He hugged me and wept. I felt his tears streaming down my neck. Mine own were soaking his hair.

Honestly? I wasn't sure where I wanted to be anymore. I was in a total dilemma. I was torn between two families. It was either I run back to the jeep or I open my door to go back to a life I grew out of and doubted I could ever fit into again.

The decision, my decision, was made when the jeep exploded in a fiery ball. Claus and I both stood in shock and horror as we helplessly watched Frank perish in the flames. Together we made a slight advancement towards the burning jeep and then realized it was futile, Claus stopped us in our tracks.

Emotions overwhelmed me and I broke free of Claus and ran to the street looking from building to building. I was screaming and cursing at the phantom sniper that he'd made a huge, terrible mistake. Not caring if I was blown away, I cried and ranted at the top of my lungs that Frank was a good boy until I fell to my knees, my fists slamming the ground in utter devastation. I was still muttering he was a good boy when someone strong picked me up under his arm and ran.

I saw the bench placed over the blue ceramic tile where I rarely used to sit and take my shoes off and deposit them on the shoe-rack in the cloak vestibule. None of that mattered now as I was whisked deeper into known territory. Pictures, mostly of me, hung in the hallway. A large decorative ceramic vase from India accented the middle of an oak table with a mirror that hung above.

It was the reflection in the mirror that I recognized my dad as the one who frantically carried me in his arms into the safety of our home. My mother came into view in a frenzy, her hands smothering my face, her lips on mine until dad gently placed me on the settee.

Another adult appeared, it was my mother's youngest brother, Seth. He looked exactly like my mother. Claus would later note that Seth was the spitting image of what I would look like at age twenty-seven -handsomely cute. I recalled my parents talking of him coming to Pranski from Sweden to learn my Father's business and I had met him several times before.

Claus spared me explaining the details as to how I came to be back home from where I was supposed to be stowed away safely. He told them that I was abducted by

a Colonel to become one of his man-servants, as he, was himself, many years before. He confirmed for my mother's sake that we had been looked after well by the man. Of course he left out the gory details that he had fucked Mother's and Seth's sister, almost fucked their young niece, and got a blowjob from my aunt's husband. He mentioned no part of even knowing them. Nor did he mention how I had been sleeping with half the German army!

What he said next I didn't even know. The Colonel knew I lived in the city he was about to invade right down to my address. I believe in order to qualify his story, Claus pointed out the fact, and my sudden realization was, that our tiny section of the city had been spared the bombings being endured by the rest of Pranski, somehow, even the electricity remained.

Sadly, he relayed that Frank, a trusted assistant to the Colonel and good friend of Claus and I, had been assigned to transport me home to my family. The man had drawn up documents to allow Frank and his entourage free access to the city's checkpoints. I broke down crying again because Frank had died taking me home. My mother held me in her bosom like she did so many times before. If only she knew how many other men died because of me. I then sobbed all the more thinking about them.

When Claus announced that he was leaving, I came to my full senses. Where would he go? How would he get back to the hotel? My father advised that it was well past curfew hour, if he wasn't shot by the Germans, then the Polish snipers would do the deed. I begged him to stay the night. My mother insisted upon it telling him that we would figure things out in the morning. Besides, she told us she had just baked a fresh batch of *ciasteczka orzeszki*. These were absolutely scrumptious polish cookies with a cream filling that made my mouth drool at the very thought of biting into one. Uncle Seth bellyached good naturedly that he wasn't prepared to share his cookies with a couple of vagabonds. All of us had a good laugh which was so very much needed.

Sleeping arrangements were established. We only had two bedrooms so there was no luxury of other accommodation. Since Seth was settled into my room, all of us guys could sleep in my large feather bed. I rebutted Seth's cookie joke and hem-and-hawed about sharing my bed and suggested banishing him to the settee. Frankly, I was quite used to sharing a bed with many occupants.

I was happy to be home again. The love in the air had been sadly missed. Although I loved the Colonel and my friends, nothing could ever replace the warmth of a family at home. Claus fitted in like a glove. Mother doted on him as if he was another long-lost son come home. Father talked business to him, now if that wasn't dad's way of expressing warmth, nothing was. Claus was also on his best behaviour, the perfect young gentleman, I was immensely proud of him for that. Maybe there was some couth in his blood after all.

Father had to have been stressed about the future of his factory. He lived for it and his loyal employees. Somehow Claus must have detected the man's angst and humorously relayed the story of Nazi intelligence believing the warehouse to be an airplane-assembly plant and my convincing them otherwise. Perhaps the Colonel had spared that entity belonging to my family as well. Dad brightened on learning that it earned me the rarity of a hug and a kiss on the cheek.

Seth played chess with the master himself, my father, as Claus and I enjoyed a game of cards. I knew that look in Claus' eye, the random exchange of looks and smiles between him and Seth. When I went to the bathroom to pee, he was right on my heels with his cock out and stood there pissing beside me. He dropped the bombshell that he was certain my uncle was a queer and the man had the hots for him.

Claus had spent almost a lifetime seducing men. He could read them like a book after all; that's how he managed to survive. He took my cock in his hand, shook off the dribbles and stroked it telling me that he was going to make a move on Seth in bed and if I wanted, a three-way was almost certainly guaranteed.

It had been a stressful day, Frank's demise was still very much on my mind and I felt guilty as hell getting an erection at the thought of having sex with Seth, my own uncle, my mother's brother. Yet the idea was appealing, doing so under my parents roof was downright wrong. I would have to change my ways and forget the past. However, Claus' devilish look and my hard cock in his hand swayed my self-control. I wanted a man and that particular man appealed to me. Seth wasn't muscular, a little chubby even, but he was very attractive nonetheless. I definitely wanted to see him naked.

When we returned to the parlour and our card game, I began playing the eye game with Seth. An amateur at best, I was unable to keep from blushing. A short while later, I sensed what Claus had so solemnly sworn to have some kind of connection. Mental-telepathy, today called 'gaydar.' I was sure of it when from the corner of my eye, I saw him discreetly adjust whatever he had hidden in his trousers. I was nervous and suffered through the agony of a bent woody in fear of him seeing me do the same. There remained a shadow of doubt that we had misconstrued the man's sexual interest. Perhaps he was simply trying to be friendly, amused at our gawking, innocently confused by our attraction to him? I suddenly felt silly.

Our cuckoo-clock announced twelve in obnoxiously loud cuckoo bird chirps. I hated that clock from the day my mother proudly hung it on the wall. In all the years it adorned the hallway, it never failed to startle and annoy me, especially in the later hours of the evening when it seemed to go on forever. I used to bend my elbows with my thumbs tucked under my pits and sarcastically mimic the bloody thing in scorn. I would lie in bed fantasizing about standing on a chair anxiously waiting for the little doors to open and choke the life out of the obnoxious little wee bird.

I was never nervous about going to bed with men or boys. I learned quickly to fully expect that sex was an inevitable expectation. However, the uncertainty about Uncle Seth's true sentiments kept me ill at ease. Claus, on the other hand, had nothing to lose exposing himself should Seth rebuke the sexual advances that Claus was intent on undertaking. He was a professional whore-boy who I was convinced enjoyed the challenge of bedding men while working for the Colonel or not. What his motivation was for seducing Seth was, I could only sum up, the exploiting of the situation just because he could.

CHAPTER XX: AFTER THE HOMECOMING

I hold it true, whate'er befall;
I feel it, when I sorrow most;
'Tis better to have loved and lost
Than never to have loved at all.'
Alfred Lord Tennyson, 1850

My bedroom was just the way I left it. Model airplanes hung from the ceiling as others sat on shelves among classic children's books that hadn't been opened in years. Miniature tin-soldiers were still battling in suspended animation on my chest-of-drawers and poster-size cartoon characters plastered the walls. A little boys room, I thought, somewhat embarrassed in front of Claus who was looking around in amusement as he shed his clothing, Seth had not yet joined us because he was making a stop at the bathroom.

Claus was nonchalantly walking around my room, as naked as the day he was born, picking up my paraphernalia to look at, or to study the wall posters and finally gaze up at the numerous flying machines in a giant perpetual dogfight that I spent hours on a ladder using fishing-line and tacks to arrange just perfectly. For the first time knowing him, I saw the young boy in him jumping on the bed and stretching to make the dozen or so models sway in imaginative battle with a brimming smile and delightful giggles as he stared up at his handiwork.

Seth entered the bedroom closing the door behind him just in time to see the naked boy clapping his hands and bouncing up and down on the bed in glee. His erection was definitely in plain sight bouncing around haphazardly as he enjoyed the toys. I was brave enough to have only removed my shirt before Seth arrived despite Claus urging me to fully undress.

Seth beamed ear to ear as he watched Claus and began to undress in a frenzy. Once naked, he joined the childish antics on the bed being as immodest as Claus about his excited circumcised state of arousal. Seth wasn't large, but neither was he small. He was average in my experienced outlook. His plump testicles were worn tight to his groin. A tuft of blond hair centered his chest and trailed down into a flourish at his groin.

I needed no more assurance that Uncle Seth was into a little fun. Claus was dead-on nailing the man's vulnerability of being had. I dropped my trousers and with my cock proudly leading the way, hopped onto the bed to join in the play with my airplanes that immediately resulted in a circle jerk with the planes and their invisible pilots left to guide themselves out of spins and preventing their flying into each other. We fell onto the bed uncaring of the aerial dogfight taking place above us or the reality of the ongoing fighting outside our home.

I was the first to suck my uncle's cock. Claus was preoccupied sitting on the man's chest and fucking his mouth. I loved his strong manly aroma. His modest manhood was easily consumed so I was able to enjoy shoving my nose into the creases where his balls met his uppermost thigh. He blasted all too soon most probably because he was sexually overwhelmed but I was relentless in my letting him know that I was willing to take him to the end. When he shot off, it was thick and voluminous but quite bitter.

I heard Seth choke only to assume that Claus had fed my uncle an unsuspecting assault of rapid-fire shots to his throat. I could have warned him of the boy's considerable capability to produce an abundance of semen had I been given the chance. Shaking my head to rid myself of the unthinkable possibility of him getting my aunt pregnant, the sister of the man from whom I was now coercing the last few reluctant driblets of his own 'baby-makers'. I was struggling with both realizing and reminding myself that he was a blood relative, not paternal where we would share the same genes, but maternal, nonetheless, blood kin.

Everyone was spent and satisfied except me, as usual. I wouldn't even say that I was unsatisfied; I received great satisfaction pleasing others. The pleasure was when their hips gyrated in their selfish desire to force their cock deeper whether it was oral or anal sex knowing that I was the instrument of their sexual gratification to be used however they wanted it. That was my own satisfaction.

The three of us lay down with Seth in the middle. An awkward silence ensued, quite ironic I thought, in that this awkwardness should have preceded the sex with the uncertainty factor of who was or wasn't interested in doing what to whom. Claus managed to eliminate the grey area giving Seth the green light by means of his nudity and silly antics. Seth could simply have laughed off the whole charade, undressed and climbed into bed. I contributed to the easing of the tension by exposing my own erection and whoever made the first play on the others genitals was a blur. It just happened in a permissible convergence of mutual desire.

Claus broke the silence as I knew he would eventually. He blatantly asked Seth if he was a queer and where he learned to suck cock so well. Coming from tactless Claus, it was meant as a compliment and Seth didn't seem offended in the least. Actually, he chuckled.

Seth claimed that he preferred guys since he was twelve. He looked directly at me and confided that my father was one of many older teens he had sex with. According to his story, my father, at nineteen, was courting my mother and slept in Seth's bed when he frequently visited. He admitted to feeling-up my sleeping dad one night. However, my father was not asleep and encouraged the thirteen-year old brother of his fiancé. Seth attested that it was mutual sex and strictly oral at first, my father later being the one to take his virginity when he was fourteen.

What was even more shocking and disturbingly unbelievable was the knowledge that the two men were still getting it on together as recent as the previous night in my bed when mom was at her ladies auxiliary meeting. I was dumbfounded; Claus laughed emphatically saying he knew my father had that look about him and could be had. He was talking about my dad for God's sake, so I tried really hard to ignore him.

Why Seth chose to reveal that dark secret to me, I haven't a clue. It may have been to ease my conscience about my own sexuality after Claus had spilled the beans as to exactly what my role was with the colonel and others. It was abstruse to realize that I had sucked the same cock that my father had been sucking in the same bed only last night. Nonetheless, I also felt a certain charge discovering my staunch father was a closeted cock sucker and sodomite. Absurd as it was, I thought that possibly my father and I could find a common ground and that he could show me the same level of intimacy as he had shown for many years with Seth.

I remembered not so long ago having wondered what my old man's cock would look like and my giving him a blow job. I felt as deranged and disgustingly dirty as I did back then. I was so deep in thought that I was only vaguely aware of movement. Seth's ass was pointed due north while Claus' cock pointed to the west. Seth howled, sputtered and spat as Claus drilled deep into him.

My thoughts had aroused me, and when Seth grabbed my arm and guided me to the head of the bed in order to give me a blow job, I was sexually primed to enjoy the offer from my father's secret lover. Uncle Seth was a very deliberate, adept master of fellatio. He knew how to use his fingers and tongue to tantalize and tease those many erogenous folds and crevices that male genitalia secrets away knowing full well that only another male can relate to and appreciate the added value of male-male sex once he's experienced it.

Spreading my legs wide, I thought I would cum the next time his brazen tongue worked its way around my crown, inside my slit, down my shaft, and over my balls ending the distance of sensation by toying at my rectum before returning by the same sensuous route back to engulf my cock and make love to it with his mouth. He repeated the process over and over. I had experienced some great blow jobs since my being introduced to homo-sex but, by far, Seth's ministrations exceeded all others and had me wild with pleasure.

The bedroom resonated from a chorus of oohs-and-aahhs, slurping wetness, and skin slapping skin with Claus banging away. I wasn't the least bit concerned that my parents could hear us. The thin wall separating our rooms gave a false sense of privacy through which I had often heard them in passionate coupling. Mother might not comprehend the sounds but, assuredly, my father would know what was going on. I envisioned him all-ears lying beside my mom discretely stroking himself fully cognisant of the happenings just meters away wishing that his wife's presence wasn't a deterrent in his being a part of our erotic orgy. It was that fantasy that brought me to a violent orgasm I pulled Seth's hair and screamed out obscenities that my mother would definitely understand.

Seth became no less quiet after spitting out my spent cock and rearing his head back in heated passion crying out for Claus to fuck him harder. The bed springs protested and if it wasn't for the cushioning of my stomach, Seth's head would have been repeatedly driven into the wall behind me from the force in which Claus had

honoured the man's request to show no mercy. The German boy was no longer kneeling behind my uncle; he was on his haunches using his full body mass in order to pile drive into my mother's masochist-minded brother and my father's long time secreted fuck-buddy.

Mother had made a fine hearty breakfast of waffles, bacon and eggs. Little did we know and appreciate then that it would be one of the last, that in only a matter of days, food would become scarce and rationed with whatever was left after feeding the German army. Our families above average standard of living would be reduced to that of common paupers.

Casual dress for breakfast, Claus found a pair of my long forgotten swim-shorts that no longer fitted me and were worn on him like a sausage casing. His privates left nothing to the imagination, accentuated by the bulge in the thin white material. Mother had prepared the feast and thankfully had to leave to her early morning volunteer work at the parish, otherwise, Claus' choice of skimpy attire would have been inappropriate in the presence of a lady, however, somewhat tolerable in the company of males.

Seth had risen moments earlier and was sitting at the table with my father in his robe drinking coffee. Dad, as usual, was absorbed in business documents and lifted his eyes to acknowledge us, giving Claus a second, and then a third longer appraisal staring at the youth's prominently displayed crotch. It was probably the first time I could ever remember my old man break his morning routine and ignore his paperwork to socialize with anyone over breakfast, let alone being all smiles and cordial to invite Claus to help himself to the food warmers on the stove.

If I had not learned of his extracurricular sexual interests, I would have found his sudden sociability odd, joking and laughing with Claus. The night before he had been strangely friendly to his young guest as well; not realizing then that Claus had already begun to seduce the handsome man in subtle ways that only Claus was manipulatively competent at. He read men like a book, estimating their level of sexual weakness and exploited it. The Colonel had taught him that most males had vulnerable libidos and could be coerced into almost any offer of sexual gratification.

My father mentioned that he was going to shower and since there were now four of us, we would have to take turns and wait for the limited hot water to replenish. Claus was quick to suggest doubling up and didn't wait to hear anyone else's opinion telling my father that he could join him first, then Seth and I could follow when water temperature made it convenient to do so. Problem solved, my father was all for the idea. I almost laughed out loud at his ulterior motives of getting Claus out of his sexy shorts and letting fate take its course. He may have just as easily taken Claus directly to bed for all anyone cared. Most boys would be shamed by their father's behaviour, I had slept with enough men to know that my dad's desire for young cock was not unique, nor did I associate it with screwing around on my mother. As a matter of fact, I considered the alternative and preferred it that way.

Alone, Seth and I smirked at each other knowing what was going on in the bathroom. When asked, Seth claimed that if my father heard or suspected anything, he never mentioned it. No doubt, after his carnal rendezvous with the very eager to please boy, he would assume that Claus and I had been sexual with each other. Therefore I wasn't worried when Seth and I went back to bed for some oral fun, our

prolonged absence behind the closed bedroom door should have been obvious, like father, like son!

Seth told me that he would show me a park and a public bathroom where men hooked up for sex. However I knew that German men were plentiful around the city for giving back-alley blow jobs and I had developed I had a fondness for German cock. I would also meet up with my cousin Henri and his best friend Joseph and show them what I had learned while away. I never did have sex with my father, he never took the bait and I respect him for that today.

Of course Seth and I would become regular fuck-buddies, my father having no choice but to turn a blind eye and share Seth as blatantly as them going to my father's bedroom for sex whenever they could, or, if mom was home, Claus' idea of water conservation, that unwittingly, she thought was a great idea to get the two men on their way to work quicker. Never in her wildest imagination was there anything wrong with two men showering together, even the odd time when I showered with Seth, it was perfectly normal back then.

Claus left us later that day confident that he would make it back to the hotel safely by dropping names and eventually finding an ally to take him home to the Colonel. It was very emotional for me to watch him walk up the street and out of sight. I still miss the best friend I ever had and never fully appreciated it. I miss Jon and Frank, also my good friends, who watched over me like big brothers.

I miss the Colonel who also kept me safe, and in some strange way, I know in my heart that he kept my family from harm's way during the siege of the city. Even my father's textile plant was left standing fully intact around bombed out ruins. My family would never understand their good fortune. Although we endured hardships and worry, it was minor compared to the atrocities others went through. My mother went to her grave praying to God in thanks of providing us a guardian angel in our time of need. That guardian angel was a very handsome German man, who in the end, as I always knew, had loved his NAZI BOY and set him free.

The End

I would like to thank the overwhelming thousands of fans who inspired me with their loyalty to keep writing the story. To the sites that allowed me the privilege of posting even when understandably sceptical of the sensitive content. A dear and special thanks to editors Len Homber & James Fitzhugh for sharing their individual expertise and support. Taken under their wing, I can only hope they will stick by me in aide of future endeavours by this amateur writer.

Auf Wiedersehen Freunde, until we meet again!

ROBERT COLT

If you liked this book, please leave a favorable review. Those reviews are what generate new readers, which helps the book. And thanks for the support. I appreciate it!